The Eight-Year Lie

J.M. Hewitt is the author of five crime fiction novels. Her work has also been published in three short story anthologies. Her books usually incorporate twentieth and twenty-first century events and far-flung locations, and her novels explore the darker side of human behaviour. In contrast to the sometimes dark content of her books, she lives a very nice life in a seaside town in Suffolk with her dog, Marley.

Also by J.M. Hewitt

The Life She Wants

THE EIGHT YEAR LIE

J.M. HEWITT

CANELO

First published in the United Kingdom in 2022 by

Canelo
Unit 9, 5th Floor
Cargo Works, 1–2 Hatfields
London, SE1 9PG
United Kingdom

A CIP catalogue record for this book is available from the British Library.

Print ISBN 978 1 80032 458 9
Ebook ISBN 978 1 80032 457 2

Look for more great books at www.canelo.co

Printed and bound in Great Britain by Clays Ltd, Elcograf S.p.A.

1

For Sandra

And in memory of Tony

Prologue

Tape recording of Louise's original police statement

Commissariat de Police, Avenue de Grasse, Cannes, France

8 years ago

LOUISE: The streets were dark as we drove up into the hills. The house where the party was being held was also in darkness. The entire road was. Jessica asked if we had the wrong night, the wrong house. I got the flyer out of my bag and switched the light on in the car.

I remember suggesting that the party was in the back, like, in a gazebo or something. Jessica didn't answer me, but I got out of the car and went to the boot to get my camera equipment. Jessica followed.

I asked if she thought it might be a power cut, but when she didn't answer and I turned around, she'd gone.

OFFICER MARON: Gone?

LOUISE: Yes.

OFFICER MARON: What did you do next?

LOUISE: I put a bag on each shoulder. I was a bit annoyed at having to carry everything because Jessica had vanished. I hung my camera around my neck and walked towards the house. When I reached it, I saw a gate to the side. It was open, so I went through it to see if my original thought about the party being in a tent out back was right. It was really dark. The pathway twisted and turned through all these vines and hedges. I walked for a long time. I kept tripping when I walked off the paving and my heels sank into the soil. I didn't want to spoil my shoes – they're expensive, you know – so I got a couple of film bags out and put them on as overshoes.

OFFICER MARON: Film bags? Overshoes?

LOUISE: Yeah, they're bags made of muslin, really cheap, and I've got hundreds of them; they're what photographers keep their film in. I put them on over my shoes because I didn't want to spoil them. As protection, you know?

OFFICER MARON: Protection. I see. What happened next?

LOUISE: I felt like I was in a maze, and I'd turned in so many directions I no longer knew where the house or the road was, or even where I was at all. It was dark. It was too dark.

OFFICER MARON: How did you feel at this point?

LOUISE: I was scared, and angry…

OFFICER MARON: Angry?

LOUISE: Yeah, angry. I thought I was being… I thought they were… it was just scary, you know?

OFFICER MARON: Why were you scared?

LOUISE: Because it was dark, I felt like I was lost. All that time, I was thinking about me… [Audible sobbing] I'm sorry, this is… difficult. Okay, so I decided to try and get back to the car, go home, forget all about the party and the job.

OFFICER MARON: And then what happened, Louise?

LOUISE: The lights came on, one by one, all the way down the street, and I realised I was right next to the back of the villa. I could see the French doors in front of me, and then the lights came on inside, and... and...

OFFICER MARON: Yes?

LOUISE: [Audible crying] And I looked through and saw Alexis and Jessica. They were... there was blood...

OFFICER MARON: Take your time.

LOUISE: The lights dimmed again. I thought the power had gone out again, but maybe it was a surge or something. Anyway, I screamed, then the police were there and... that's all.

OFFICER MARON: What were they doing? Were they... fighting?

LOUISE: [Silence]

OFFICER MARON: What were they doing?

LOUISE: [Inaudible]

OFFICER MARON: I'm going to have to ask you to speak up for the tape.

LOUISE: They were both on the floor. It looked like they'd both been attacked.

Tape recording of Jessica's original police statement

Commissariat de Police, Avenue de Grasse, Cannes, France

8 years ago

JESSICA: When we got there, the street was deserted, like, really dark. I thought we might have had the wrong night, but Louise checked the invitation. She told me to wait in the car while she got her camera stuff out of the boot.

OFFICER MARON: What did you do?

JESSICA: I waited for a minute, then when I looked out of the back window I saw Louise heading towards the house.

OFFICER MARON: Could you still see her when you got out?

JESSICA: No, but the front door was open so I presumed someone had opened it and let her into the house. So I went in, and it was all dark inside, just like the street, no light at all. I used the torch on my mobile phone and saw a light switch, but it didn't work.

OFFICER MARON: What did you do next, Jessica?

JESSICA: I was standing in the hallway, and I could see through to another room, a lounge or something, through an archway opposite me. That's when I saw her.

OFFICER MARON: Saw who, Jessica?

JESSICA: Her, Alexis, lying on the floor by the fireplace.

OFFICER MARON: And what did you do?

JESSICA: I found her like that – someone had attacked her. I tried to help her, to save her. There was someone else in that house tonight who hurt her. I went over to her, I thought maybe she was drunk, like, passed out, you know? She was on her front, and I turned her over, tried to wake her, right? Then I saw it.

OFFICER MARON: What? What did you see?

JESSICA: [Inaudible]

OFFICER MARON: I'm going to have to ask you to speak up a little, for the ta—

JESSICA: The blood! I saw the blood! I called for help, I shouted, and then… then…

OFFICER MARON: And then?

JESSICA: I could smell the blood. It all happened at once. I felt funny, someone was there, someone hit me. I was attacked and I couldn't see because it was so dark. I think I lost consciousness for a minute. When I woke up, I panicked, I grabbed the poker.

OFFICER MARON: You had a panic attack?

4

JESSICA: I was attacked! Someone hit me – look, look at my head! Someone attacked me, I didn't have a panic attack. Jesus, like, can you get a translator in here?

OFFICER MARON: Pardonnez-moi, an attack on you, not a panic attack, oui. Please, continue. Tell me more about this weapon that was used to attack Alexis.

JESSICA: I was attacked too! They hit me with it too!

OFFICER MARON: Oui. Please, go on.

JESSICA: I'm not saying anything else.

OFFICER MARON: We are very nearly finished with the interv—

JESSICA: [Shouting] I'M NOT SAYING ANYTHING ELSE!

Constable Nina Hart held a finger over the tape recorder. She waited. Having already listened to the tape, she knew what was coming. On the recording came a pause, shuffling and the chink of handcuffs while the interviewee was led out of the room. A crackle of static, then Maron's voice.

'One of them is lying,' she said to an unseen, unheard person, eight years ago and nine hundred miles away.

Nina flicked off the tape and shot a triumphant glance at her colleague, Detective Sergeant Richard Robinson.

'What do you reckon?'

Richard shrugged. Nina watched as he chewed thoughtfully on the end of his pen. 'But she was released, right? This was eight years ago, and the case never even got to court.'

'And this Jessica ended up marrying the lawyer who got her off the murder charge, and moved here to our fair country. It's like a fairy tale.' Nina grinned at Richard. 'Or a soap opera.'

He smiled, shook his head in gentle chastisement of her sarcasm.

'And now Jessica's husband, the lawyer, is dead too.' Nina jumped up, straightened her shirt and swept her hands through her hair. 'Come on, we'll see what story Blondie comes up with for us.'

Richard drained his coffee, but remained in his seat. 'Take it easy, Nina. Sometimes they are actually innocent.'

Nina snorted, heading for the door. 'I can tell you one thing, Richard,' she said. 'She won't pull the wool over our eyes as easily as she did with the French authorities.'

Finally, Richard stood up. He walked over to her and placed a hand on her shoulder, a fatherly gesture. 'Nina, innocent until proven guilty.' He swept past her, through the door that she held open for him, then paused, turned and almost as an afterthought added, 'I'll lead the interview.'

'Yeah, right,' she muttered under her breath as she followed him to the interview suite.

Chapter 1

Louise

Then

I'd been in France the longest, but still – *always* – I felt like the new girl. More so than ever in front of these men.

It had been over. I was finished. Just over a year I'd managed to struggle along here, alone and out of my depth. At nineteen, I'd been too young. I'd also been penniless, broke, and more often than not unemployed. My case had been packed. I had accepted – albeit bitterly – that I was going home to the north of England. Back to my parents' house. Back to the land of beige.

Then I had been hired as the photographer for the opening night of a hotel. It had been sudden and unexpected. It was a reprieve. And no matter how brief it might be, I took it.

Marco Cooper sat beside me now, one half of the partnership that had set up Cannes' newest hotel and adjoining casino, Jenson Coast. *French Country* magazine had requested the use of the hotel grounds for an interview and photo shoot with Ben Albin, the other guy on our table, a British nature and wildlife expert who was spending the summer in France. The use of the hotel guaranteed publicity for Jenson Coast, and a room had been made available for the man of the hour at a heavily discounted price.

The night was over. The opening had been a triumph. My own success hung in the balance, dependent on the quality of the shots I'd taken. I itched to get back to my tiny apartment and start the developing process.

But with a man like this beside me, I also didn't want to leave.

Not that he would ever look twice at me. Not here, with wall-to-wall slender young French women his for the picking. With my larger-than-average build, flame-red hair cut in an unstylish, no-nonsense bob, whiter-than-white skin and nervous disposition, it was rare that anyone gave me a first glance, let alone a second.

I itched at the tender, cracking skin between my thumb and first finger. The heat of the place that I'd tried to make my home disagreed with the eczema I'd suffered from since childhood.

Absently I noticed the flaky skin that settled on my trousers. Remembering where I was, who I was with, I brushed it away and glanced around to check nobody had seen.

Was it my imagination, or did Marco throw me a look that seemed very much like disgust? I opened my mouth, unsure if I should explain my condition or pretend nothing had happened.

But he was up, restless Marco, always on the move, constantly looking for opportunities. His eyes followed a gaggle of nubile young women, all legs and bare tanned flesh. 'Excuse me,' he muttered, and downing his drink, he was off.

I watched him go, envy settling in my stomach like a stone, only half listening to Ben, the wildlife guy, as he described his work and his life. I nodded along, knowing just by looking at him that he usually had women falling at his feet – he was certainly good-looking enough – but even as he talked attentively to me I found my gaze wandering back to Marco.

He had reached the group of girls now, had them gathered around him, his arms draped across their shoulders.

'Business booming?' Ben asked as Marco eventually wound his way back to us. He gestured with his glass to the women, who were now filing out of the hotel into the night, on to the next party.

'Yep, supply and demand,' laughed Marco.

Suddenly I understood. It wasn't the girls Marco was chasing, it was their money.

When I looked at Marco, I saw that he knew I knew. I saw that my knowledge would cause this night to slip away from me, my wage along with it if I upset the owner of this place. Suddenly, desperately, I needed to make it all right. I needed Marco to know that I didn't care about his business sideline, that I was so pleased to have been included in their after-hours drinks I wouldn't tell a soul. That if anything, I was jealous of him and the notes stuffed in his pocket and the easy way he mingled with the girls.

'Have you got any of that going spare, then, for a hard-working girl who's been on her feet all night?' My words were deliberately casual, as though it was the sort of thing I did all the time, even though I couldn't afford three meals a day, let alone an expensive drug habit.

Marco smiled, wide and full. It was like the sun coming out. 'Sure, in exchange for, say, a discount on your work tonight?'

9

I joined him in his laughter, hoping mine didn't sound forced. 'No chance.' I shook my head with mock regret. 'I've got bills to pay, you know.'

I didn't get any of his cocaine, not then, not that night, which was good as I wouldn't have known what to do with it. But the banter continued, and later, so much later that the sun was coming up, I returned home hungry but happy, no longer caring that I had no food in the house. That night, I'd found something far more important.

Acceptance.

I didn't care about the drugs, or dodgy dealings or even dodgier people.

With hindsight, I really should have.

But my rent was still due and the promise of the life I'd sought was within reach. The potential blinded me. I needed to keep up the momentum.

I wasn't like them, any of them. But I was good at what I did.

Mindful that I needed to stay in the picture, the day after the opening I made my next move. I got up extra early to organise the photos I had taken. While they were being processed, I pulled off my standard-issue comfortable jeans and baggy shirt and replaced them with a long olive-green summer dress that skimmed my ankles. I scraped my jaw-length hair back off my face into a low ponytail and fished around in my bag for my dark shades.

Finally, I appraised my reflection.

A small smile twitched the corners of my mouth as I dared to admire myself.

I would think of that moment later. I would reflect that pride comes before a fall.

'Hello, can I help?' Andrew Jenson, Marco's business partner, asked politely as I stood like a spare part in the cavernous reception area.

I smothered a smile. Despite several previous meetings, Andrew never remembered me. This time I wasn't offended. I had taken care over my appearance. I barely recognised myself. 'Louise Wilshire,' I said, transferring my bag to my other shoulder and holding out my hand for him to shake. 'I'm the photographer from the opening night. I brought some proofs along for you to have a look at.'

His eyes, sea-green emeralds, widened slightly, and with a few words of instruction in French to the maintenance man, he led me to a chair in the lobby.

'A drink, perhaps?' he asked as I took the envelope containing my shots out of my bag and spread them on the table. 'Tea, coffee, champagne?'

It was too hot for tea or coffee, and I wondered if my new guise could make me seem like someone I wasn't but desperately wanted to be. I took a deep breath. 'Champagne would be lovely,' I said.

While we waited, I passed him my magnifying glass and sat back as he flicked his gaze over the negatives. I caught sight of my hands, red raw and ugly. They didn't go with my new look. Disgusted with myself, I tucked them in my lap and hoped Andrew didn't notice.

The champagne arrived. I tried to sip at it while he perused the photos, even though I wanted to drink it all down at once to steady my nerves.

'Nice,' he said. 'You've done a great job, Louise.'

I preened internally, trying desperately to remain cool on the outside. 'I can leave them with you – maybe we can arrange another meeting in a week or so, give Marco a chance to look over them too?'

'Sounds ideal. Next weekend, perhaps? I'll check with Marco and we'll arrange a time, a dinner.'

–

I floated through the week, anticipation mixing with my scared rabbit persona, but like the opening and the photographs I'd taken, the meal was another success.

'All right, I'll leave you two kids to it,' said Andrew after we'd finished eating. 'Put it on the tab, Marco. Louise, I'll see you soon.' With that, he was gone.

Without the three-way conversation, I felt suddenly adrift. During dinner the chat had been easy, but with just the two of us, I stalled.

'Andrew's stressed about Jessica's arrival,' Marco told me.

I looked at him blankly. 'Jessica?'

He took a long swallow of wine, grimaced and beckoned for the waiter. 'Whisky,' he said, and turned to me expectantly.

'I'm fine with the wine,' I said. It wasn't my first choice of alcohol, but there was still a good half-bottle left. If I let it go to waste, I'd lie awake thinking of it during the long, lonely nights when I had nothing but tap water to drink.

'Jessica is Andrew's daughter. She's been in Germany. She was supposed to be coming for the opening night, but she's arriving in a couple of days.'

I sat back, thinking hard. Andrew had a daughter. What was she like? What did she do in Germany? Was she with her mother? I didn't even know if there was a Mrs Jenson.

'Is her mother coming too? I mean, has Andrew got a wife?'

'No, she died a long time ago now. It's just him and Jessica.' Marco smiled, nudged me in the ribs. 'Why, you got designs on old Andrew?'

'No, God, no,' I said, aghast, then forced a laugh when I saw he was joking.

'Good,' he said, as the waiter arrived and set his whisky down in front of him.

I looked at the tabletop. *Good*, he'd said. Good that I didn't want Andrew? Did that mean Marco was interested in me? I felt my face grow hot. Or, God forbid, was he simply saying it because the drink he had ordered had arrived?

'Terrace?' He scooped up his pack of cigarettes and inclined his head.

I nodded eagerly. I didn't smoke, couldn't afford to, but I'd happily sit outside with Marco. Anything for this night not to end yet.

'What's Jessica like?' I asked shyly. Female friends – any friends, come to think of it – were tricky for me.

'She's cool,' replied Marco with an indifferent shrug. 'She's, what, twenty-five, so around your age.'

I stared at him. 'I'm nineteen,' I replied quietly.

'Get away! All that photography talent and you're still a kid!' He leaned over, shoved an elbow in my ribs again. I rubbed my side discreetly. Marco had no idea of his own strength, but I liked the feel of him. Though it hurt, I'd never tell him.

'Andrew's putting on a dinner for Jessica's arrival. You should come.'

My breath caught in my throat. 'When is this meal?'

'Um, Friday, next Friday I think, at Jenson Coast.'

'What time?' I asked, striving for casual.

'Not sure. Hey, do you want to go on to Baoli?'

I nodded, letting the issue of the time of the meal go. I had Andrew and Marco's final selection of prints to get to them, I could easily arrange to take them over Friday afternoon, and I was certain that upon delivery, an invitation to join them and the mysterious Jessica for dinner would be forthcoming.

On the walk to Baoli, Ben fell into step beside us. I didn't mind him joining us, but I worried about the payment to gain access to the nightclub. My concern was unwarranted, as when the bouncers saw Ben and Marco, they ushered all three of us through the red cordon. Inside, Marco stationed us at the bar and left. I watched him as I sipped a Bellini, bought by Ben. Marco moved easily, identifying people he obviously knew. Across the floor, different kinds of men stood. They were not smart-looking like Marco. They wore their hair long, tied back, smoothed and slicked with grease. With narrowed eyes they muttered to each other and watched him too.

I kept my eyes on Marco as he wound his way through the room, greeting people, free with hugs and handshakes and fist bumps, transactions made easily, little bags passed from palm to palm until he completed the circuit and came back to us.

Gathering us in a huddle, he produced a tiny envelope from his wallet and held it out invitingly. Ben declined as he bopped along to the music. When Marco offered it to me, I hesitated only for a second before taking one of the blue pills and swallowing it down.

Marco grinned at me, grabbed my hand and twirled me in an insane dance. I forced myself at first, my feet moving stiffly as I put on my act, trying to fit in. Eventually, thirty minutes or more later, I realised I was no longer pretending. The drug took over, and I joined him in his laughter.

–

On the Wednesday before the Friday meal, before 'Jessica's night', as I had begun to refer to it in my head, I woke up to find an extra €1,000 in my bank account. I scrolled through the transactions, finding that the payment had come from Andrew Jenson. I hadn't yet invoiced him for the photographs I'd taken on the opening night, and my fee was nowhere near the amount he had paid me. I pushed open the fanlight window and fell back against my pillow, staring at my laptop screen until it timed out and logged me off.

Should I spend it? Should I mention it to him – what if it was a mistake? After all, the sum was double what I would have charged him. What if he realised he had made an error with the payment and requested it back? If I'd spent it, I wouldn't be able to repay him, and God knows how long it would take until I had four figures in my bank account again. Before I could change my mind I hopped out of bed, dressed in a turquoise maxi dress and, grabbing my keys, headed towards Jenson Coast. My wardrobe flashed through my mind as I hurried through the winding streets, and I hoped fervently that Andrew wouldn't want the money back. At their invitation I had joined Marco and Ben twice for drinks since our dinner. I had just managed to scrape together a different outfit each evening, but if I were to keep up my new persona, I desperately needed to hit the shops.

Andrew was just pulling into the parking zone of the hotel as I climbed the steep driveway to the reception. I turned my face away, not wanting him to see me red and panting with the exertion of the hill, but for the first time, I wasn't invisible.

'Louise!' He called out a greeting, slamming the door of his Bugatti.

Slowly, trying to get my breath back, I made my way towards him. 'Hi, Andrew, sorry to disturb you.' I cringed inwardly. Why was I always apologising to him?

'You're not disturbing me. Come in, have a cool drink inside. It's a scorcher today.'

Obediently I followed him towards the bar. 'It's just I received a payment from you today, and I wanted to… I wasn't sure if it was the…' I stopped, cleared my throat and tried again. 'I think you overpaid me.'

'Not at all. Think of it as a bonus. You've done a great job, Louise. We'll certainly use your services again, and recommend you too.'

The breath left my body and I grinned like a simpleton. It wasn't just that the money was mine to spend as I wanted, Andrew thought I had done a good job – no, scratch that, a *great* job. And that bite of envy: how much money did these guys have that they could think nothing of giving it away? 'Thank you,' I whispered, my voice suddenly and unexpectedly hoarse.

'And you're coming to dinner on Friday evening, yes?' Andrew slid behind the bar and poured two lemonades – home-made, I knew from the opening night; no store-bought stuff in here. 'Marco said he'd invited you.'

I nodded politely, even though I wanted to punch the air and jump around the room. Marco hadn't forgotten his casual invitation, he had mentioned it to Andrew, and Andrew clearly wanted me there too. I accepted the glass of lemonade, sipped through the straw.

'It's good stuff, isn't it? Made with lemons from the grove behind the hotel.'

'Yes,' I whispered, 'it's very good.' I summoned a smile from somewhere, and hoped Andrew thought that the pungent fizzy drink was responsible for the tears in my eyes.

Chapter 2

Louise

Then

I arrived embarrassingly early for Jessica's welcome dinner. After struggling up the hill, I darted around the side of the whitewashed wall, pulled a bottle of water out of my bag and sat down on the grassy verge. I pretended to read a text message on my phone in case anyone came around the corner and asked what I was doing.

As I gulped the water, I became aware of a couple arguing not too far off. At first it was just a girl's voice, high-pitched and nasal. After a moment, a man joined in and I sat bolt upright.

Marco. Could it be Jessica that he was quarrelling with?

Clambering to my feet, I edged to the corner with my back to the wall. Here, at the rear of Jenson Coast, the view was of immaculately maintained gardens with a backdrop of La Bocca beyond.

It was Marco, I saw, but it wasn't Jessica he was arguing with. I looked the woman up and down: the glossy dark brown hair, flawless ivory skin, the legs that went on for miles encased in skinny jeans and ending in her trademark scarlet Jimmy Choos. If she removed her oversized shades, I knew her eyes would be the brightest, deepest blue. I knew; I'd looked into those eyes. I'd drowned in those eyes.

Alexis Dubois.

I pulled my head back and flattened myself against the wall. Their French was batted between them too fast for me to follow, but as Alexis's voice got higher and higher, I heard the word *drogues* clearly.

They were arguing about drugs.

And then I heard another word, a name this time; a name I knew and that chilled me.

Nathan Saint.

As I worried at the skin around my fingernails, I realised Marco and Alexis had fallen silent. I risked another peep around the wall and heaved a sigh of relief at the sight of Alexis stalking away through the overflow car park on the opposite side of the hotel. Picking up my bag, I hurried to catch up with Marco.

'What did Alexis say to you?' I asked breathlessly as he turned at the sound of my heavy footfall.

'Hi, Lou,' he said. 'She was just giving me a "warning".' He grinned, apostrophised the word with his fingers and snorted a laugh.

'About selling drugs? Marco, you need to listen to her. I know the guy she's in with, that Nathan Saint. He's dangerous.'

'*You* know Nathan Saint?' His voice was incredulous, mocking even.

I felt my face flame. Of course I didn't *know* him. I could never be part of that circle. 'I know *of* him,' I said.

The grin on his face didn't waver and I knew he was laughing at me. I didn't blame him. What did I know about how those people lived? If I'd heard me, I'd laugh too.

But I *did* know about those guys. One of the benefits of being invisible was being able to listen, watch and learn.

'So you're giving me advice about what I do, where I do it?' Marco's eyes were small and hard like pebbles. 'You sound like that idiot who's always on my back.'

I gave him a questioning look.

'That fool Patrick King, shoving his nose in where it's not wanted, not needed.'

Patrick King.

I knew the name, knew he was Andrew's friend and lawyer. I knew he and Marco often locked horns and that his interference drove Marco wild with barely concealed rage.

I had never met the man, but I didn't want to be compared to him. My concern was justified. I *cared*. I had no other agenda.

Although that was a lie. I did care, but the smooth running of this place was essential to seal the deal of my new-found life.

'Hey, I just don't want you to be in any danger.' I bit my lip as I heard my words. They sounded foolish and dramatic.

'What do you know about Alexis Dubois and her little boy bitch?' he asked, giving me a sideways glance as we fell in step together.

I shrugged. I knew she ruled the town. I knew her father was the richest man in Cannes. I knew you didn't mess with her, her family or those who associated with her – people like Nathan Saint. I knew without a shadow of a doubt that though I had worshipped her from afar since I had arrived here, she didn't even know my name. As I struggled to put my concerns into words without making myself sound ridiculous, Marco laughed and slung his arm around my shoulder.

'C'mon, let's go inside and meet Jessica.'

Just like that, thoughts of Nathan, Alexis, the mysterious Patrick King and all the trouble they could bring melted away. I let Marco lead me into the sectioned-off portion of the restaurant and slid around the drapes to see a table laid for five. I shivered, anticipating the intimate meal I was included in. Andrew and Ben sat with their heads bent together, and they both looked up when Marco and I came in.

'Ah, hi, you two,' said Andrew. 'I thought you might be Jessica.'

'She's not here yet?' asked Marco, grabbing a bread roll and stuffing it in his mouth.

I looked at the basket of bread, my mouth watering. I'd not eaten all day. Marco, catching my gaze, picked it up and passed it to me. I declined. He might be at home enough here to begin eating before we'd even sat down, but I had to remember my manners.

'Jessica is coming from Berlin,' Andrew told me.

'What was she doing there?' I asked politely, wedging myself into a seat beside Marco and opposite Ben.

Andrew shrugged. 'I don't know, whatever it is you youngsters do when you're travelling.'

His response held the hint of a question, and I blushed. I didn't know what people like that did, I'd never had the chance to live a life like that. Cannes was the one and only place I'd been to outside England, and I constantly thanked my lucky stars that I was still here. Albeit by the skin of my teeth.

A waiter arrived with two bottles of wine, one red, one white.

'We'll open them,' Andrew told him; then, 'In fact, we might as well start eating.' He nodded to the waiter, who bowed his head and withdrew.

'Are you not going to wait for Jessica to arrive?' I asked.

'She could be hours,' retorted Marco. 'Or days, knowing her.'

I narrowed my eyes at him. Did he know her? And if so, how well?

It doesn't matter, Louise, I reminded myself. Don't worry about impossible scenarios such as Marco being interested in you. Just being here is enough for now.

–

Jessica arrived as dessert was being served.

I was watching the crèmes brûlées as they were passed around, my mouth watering at the thought of cracking into the hard caramel topping. Suddenly the drapes were pushed aside and a blonde head appeared, and I knew in an instant that this was Jessica Jenson.

'I'm here!' she squealed, and I watched, dessert forgotten, as she sprang through the entrance. 'Daddy!'

Andrew threw his napkin on the table and stood up. With her feet barely touching the floor, she launched herself into his arms. As though they were the only ones there, they twirled around, gripping each other tightly. The sound of carefree laughter flowed over the table and I hunkered down in my chair. How were there people like this in the world? I'd never acted that way around my father, my mother neither. The Jensons were from my country, but they could have been from a different planet.

They separated. Andrew fell back into his seat, arms folded, smiling, as Jessica moved around the table, enveloping Marco in a hug, shaking Ben's hand politely and lingering over his touch. Then she turned to me.

As I looked at her, I felt my cheeks grow hot. I'd thought Alexis Dubois was beautiful, but Jessica Jenson took it to a whole new level. Her hair was the whitest of blondes, contrasting with the deep tan that one only got by spending who knows how many summers in hot climates. She didn't wear as much make-up as Alexis did, but Jessica had no need for layers of slap. I felt my eyes travel down her body. She was skinny – if it were anyone else I might have said too thin – but her energy seemed to counteract her fragile frame.

'Who's this, then?' she asked, hands on hips.

I shifted uncomfortably on my chair under her green-eyed gaze. Ben had been immediately introduced, but I had been overlooked as usual.

'This is Louise Wilshire, she's doing the PR for Jenson Coast,' said Andrew. 'Louise, this is my daughter, Jessica.'

I stared at Andrew. *Public relations?* I was a photographer. I knew I was forgettable, but still…

Realising that Jessica was still standing in front of me, I rose from my chair. I had to take charge of the situation, of the mistake that Andrew had made. 'Hi, it's good to meet you. I took the photos of the opening night and these guys have made me feel very welcome since then.'

'Cool,' said Jessica, and plonked herself in the chair next to me. 'Did I miss dinner?'

'You're in time for dessert,' I replied helpfully, and my smile matched Jessica's own as she giggled at me.

'That's the best bit!' Taking two crèmes brûlées, she passed one to me. 'Dig in.'

As I observed Jessica, I realised two things about her. She was all about herself, like Alexis, but somehow had the charm to pull it off in an inoffensive manner. And she clearly had her sights set on Ben.

As the evening wore on, she edged her chair further away from mine and around the table towards Ben. I didn't mind; in the part of my mind where I kept my fantasies, that meant Marco was still available. But as the wine flowed and the laughter followed and it grew later and later, I found it was *her* I couldn't stop looking at, not Marco.

–

The four of us – Andrew having departed to his suite hours ago – staggered out of the main entrance just as the sun was emerging into the sky. I rubbed at my face, knowing I had a job over in Tanneron in a few hours. Word had spread since the opening night, and my phone had rung more with potential clients in the last couple of weeks than the whole time I had been here.

'Breakfast?' suggested Marco.

I groaned. I really didn't want to leave them – the longer I stayed on this first night, the more likely Jessica would be to remember me – but I was desperately tired. If I went to bed now, though, I'd never wake up to travel the hour to Tanneron. I hadn't even checked out the bus timetable yet.

'I have to work,' I moaned. 'You guys are a really bad influence.'

'You ain't seen nothing yet, baby,' said Jessica with a nudge. 'Hey, where's your job?'

'Tanneron, I don't even know how I'm going to get there yet.'

'Ben will drive you, won't you, Ben?' she called, batting away my protests.

He looked back over his shoulder and gave a thumbs-up.

That was her power, I realised then. She had known Ben for just one night and was already calling in favours from him. She hadn't even asked him – that he would do as she requested was an assumption, I noted as I followed them towards his car.

I had known him for weeks, but still wouldn't have dared ask him for a lift. Jessica, on the other hand, had no qualms about handing out requests. She had a way about her, a certain something. And despite only knowing her since last night, I recognised that people were more than happy to do anything she asked.

Me included. Even though she'd not asked me for anything yet, I knew that when she did, I would jump.

She smiled winningly at me as she held open the car door. At that look, aimed just at me, I glowed inside.

'What's the job in Tanneron, then?' she asked as Ben drove up into the hills.

I glanced over at her in the front. She'd changed into cut-off shorts and her long, tanned legs were propped on the dash. Marco had returned to Jenson Coast, for 'forty winks' before the day started, as he put it.

'Photos for a leaflet and a website they're having made up for the vineyard,' I replied.

Twisting in her seat, she looked at me. 'You've got such a cool job, Louise.'

I blushed, mumbled something unintelligible.

'The photos she took on the opening night were really good,' Ben commented, throwing me a grin over his shoulder.

'What were you doing in Germany?' I asked her, moving the conversation away from me.

Jessica shrugged, pulled a crumpled pack of cigarettes from her back pocket and shook one out. She didn't offer one to me or Ben.

'Clubbing, drinking, partying.'

Not working, I noticed. I wondered if she had ever worked. It was unlikely. Andrew, her father, was loaded.

'I came here for a break,' Jessica went on. 'When I woke up in my friend's guest house in a pool of vomit, I knew it was time to move on.'

She spoke airily, like it was no big deal to exist that way.

'It was a bad bunch of gear, I think.' She let out a laugh and spread her hands wide. 'I don't even know if it was my vomit!'

I made myself join in her laughter, but inside I was filled with disbelief. In the rear-view mirror I saw that Ben's face was expressionless. I wondered if Jessica's stories of extreme drug and alcohol use would put him off her. From what I'd seen, he was pretty clean-living, never drinking as much as Marco or me, and never accepting any of Marco's 'gifts' that he carried around in little plastic bags and handed out like sweets. Jessica didn't seem bothered by what Ben thought of her, though. I wondered what that was like, to be totally yourself, never having to put on an act or a show or a false exterior.

'You should give the drugs a rest,' he said mildly. 'There are so many natural highs to experience, but if you're already out of your head on other shit, you miss out on them.'

A heavy silence fell inside the car as Jessica and I digested his words. I looked from him to her. For a moment she appeared deep in thought, then she hooted a laugh and slapped his leg.

'Who are you, my dad?'

He smiled, but as she sat back in her seat and looked out of the window, I saw a new expression on her face, as though she was wondering if what he'd said was true.

Before long, we reached the vineyard. A wizened old man came out to greet us. I studied him as he told me in halting English about the website he was planning to build to draw more visitors. He looked ancient, his face heavily lined, his skin that of someone who had spent decades working outside. I wondered where or who he had got the idea of twenty-first-century advertising from.

'We'll wait here,' called Jessica, leaning against the car. She didn't look at me as she spoke; instead she kept her eyes on Ben, who was sitting on the crumbling stone wall that bordered the vineyard.

Disappointed that my new friends wouldn't see me doing the one thing I was good at, I trudged away, a camera bag on each shoulder, following the man, who walked at a surprisingly fast pace.

He left me in one of his fields, pointing out scenes that he thought showed his property in a good light before withdrawing to a little wooden shack a few hundred yards away. There he lowered himself into a chair, placed his hat over his eyes and tipped his head back.

Wanting to get back to Jessica, I worked fast, changing film, taking shots in black and white and colour of the panoramic view. My client had set up a table of his wine, and I took some shots of the labels, arranging bunches of grapes in the forefront. As I clicked, I wondered about a locally sourced house wine for Jenson Coast. Did they have one already? I couldn't recall; when us 'youngsters', as Andrew referred to us, were together, we moved pretty quickly on to spirits. But I thought it might be a good idea for the hotel to adopt a particular vineyard. Maybe it would be a way for Jenson Coast to get on side with the locals.

With my job done, and a promise to return in four days with the proofs, I hurried back to the car, eager to try out my local house wine idea on Jessica.

But when I reached the car, neither Ben nor Jessica was anywhere to be seen. I imagined they had gone for a walk, and caught my breath, sure that the owner – my customer – wouldn't appreciate strangers roaming around his property. Slinging my camera round my neck, I hurried across the road towards the wall Ben had been sitting on when I left him.

The view stopped me in my tracks. Miles and miles of blooming mimosa trees, yellow and gold as far as I could see, interspersed with vines. The grapes looked like blood blotted on the landscape. It was strangely beautiful.

Clambering over the wall, I walked down the rows, forgetting why I was here, forgetting who I was looking for. A strange feeling came over me, a lightening of my whole body.

I lived here.

I turned a full circle, realising that I'd become so accustomed to my little life in Cannes in my crappy rented flat, I'd not noticed the beauty that enveloped me outside. All I'd had was worry about where my next rent cheque was coming from. But now, as though I'd been touched by the mimosa and the vine's vibrant colours, I felt that I could be beautiful too.

I snorted to myself. Life even *looked* different on the other side.

Two brightly coloured birds emerged from a tree to my right, their squawks joined by human laughter, alternately high-pitched and low and throaty.

Jessica and Ben.

Dragging my eyes away from the view, I pushed my way through the gnarled branches, batting bunches of grapes away from my face. As I stepped over a low fence and rounded a bend, I stopped.

I should have left, I should have backed up, returned to the car and waited there. But my feet, soundless in their sensible sneakers, wouldn't move. Rooted to the spot as though I too were one of the ancient vines, I let myself see it all.

Jessica up against the wall, her hands gripping the sturdy trunks of two vines. Her shorts discarded a few feet away, all she wore was her tiny vest. Ben's shorts were round his ankles, and he was bare-chested. The sun glinted off his short hair and his eyes darkened as he spun Jessica around so her back was towards him. He moved up to join with her, and I covered my mouth as she uttered a little cry.

'Is this one of your natural highs, then?' Her voice carried to me on the breeze, hoarse and husky.

Ben leaned forward, his body covering hers, and whispered a reply in her ear that I couldn't hear but that elicited a delicate gasp from her.

Just then, she turned her face in my direction. Now my feet moved, and I shuffled a couple of inches backwards. But she had seen me, and as Ben moved hard against her, she smiled at me. A wicked, delicious grin.

Chapter 3

Louise

Then

The breath was knocked out of me as I caught my foot on a twisted root and went down hard. Was that a giggle I heard behind me? Not pausing to look over my shoulder, I pushed myself up and ran the rest of the way back to the car.

My face burned at what I had seen, Jessica and Ben, locked together in the most intimate way. And Jessica had seen me watching them.

I put my head in my hands. What would she think of me? I imagined her laughing about me, about the girl who would never be found in a position like that. Even *I* couldn't imagine myself doing something like that, in a vineyard, with a boy.

Marco.

His name flashed through my mind before I could stop it. Angrily I dashed the thought away. Why would Marco be interested in me when there were dozens of girls like Jessica and Alexis Dubois in Cannes?

Back at the car, I sat down in the road, pulled my camera from around my neck and loaded up the shots I'd taken. At least when Jessica and Ben came back, I'd be engrossed in my work and wouldn't have to look at them.

But my camera lay uselessly in my hands. I didn't look at the photos I'd taken in the vineyard. My mind's eye was fixated on the snapshot in my head of Jessica and Ben. If I had thought quicker, I could have taken a photo of them.

The idea, unbidden but not unwanted, set my body on fire.

It wasn't long before they traipsed through the vines and up the hill towards me. I stood up awkwardly, leaned against the car and scrolled through the frames on the camera.

'Hey, Louise,' Jessica called. 'Hope you didn't take any pictures of us back there.'

I reddened. Had she sensed my depraved thought? 'Of course I didn't.'

'Well, if you did, I want to see them. I need to make sure you got my good side, right, Ben?' She threw a wink his way, and as she passed me, she reached out a hand and tickled my ribs. He didn't answer, but he rolled his eyes at me.

I watched agog as she climbed into the passenger seat. She didn't care that I'd seen her making love to Ben. She wasn't offended or horrified. Neither of them was.

During the journey home, I sat in the back and looked at her profile. My feeling of shame melted away and something else replaced it, something that stirred low down in my belly. Something I couldn't even begin to explain.

As we neared Jenson Coast, Jessica turned to me. 'Coming in, Lou?'

I nodded. Really I should go home and start developing the prints for the vineyard, having promised to deliver the proofs in just four days. But an invitation from Jessica wasn't something I was going to pass up.

'Cool. We'll get some food, maybe hit the casino.' Jessica stroked Ben's leg, including him in our plans. 'Right, babe?'

He nodded, pushed his shades up onto his head. 'Sounds good to me.' As he made the turn to drive up the long road that led to the hotel, he braked sharply. 'Shit.'

'What?' Jessica looked out through the windscreen. Her hand moved from Ben's leg and she folded her arms over her chest. 'What's *she* doing here?'

I craned to see who they were talking about.

Alexis Dubois.

Remembering Alexis's row with Marco, I touched Jessica's shoulder. 'Do you know her?'

'I knew her around the Italian scene,' she said, her words clipped and short.

'Italian scene?' Ben asked.

'Clubbing,' said Jessica by way of explanation; then, at Ben's confused expression, 'We used to go to the same clubs.'

'In Italy?' I chimed in, disbelieving.

'Yeah, the clubs are the best there.'

'So if you know her, that's good, you can clear the air between her and Marco,' I said.

Jessica turned in her seat to face me. 'What do you mean, "clear the air"?'

I told myself I'd forgotten that she didn't know about the argument between Alexis and Marco the night she had arrived. I admitted to myself that some part of me wanted Jessica to know that I was here already, before her, part of the gang alongside Marco and Ben. I said to her, 'I heard them arguing; Alexis was angry because Marco was attracting a younger crowd to Jenson Coast and taking business away from Nathan Saint.' I paused, and in case I hadn't made it clear, added, 'With Marco selling drugs, you see?'

Jessica snorted and turned back to face the front. 'Who does she think she is?' she muttered darkly.

We drifted slowly past Alexis, and Jessica's hand shot out again to clasp Ben's leg.

'Stop the car!'

Ben groaned, pulled his shades down to cover his eyes and let the vehicle roll to a stop.

Jessica hit the switch to open the passenger-side window. 'Hey, what's up?' she called to Alexis.

I watched as Alexis strolled over. Placing her elbows on the window frame, she bent over, giving us an eyeful of her cleavage.

'I thought it was you, Ben,' she drawled in her clipped, crisp English, ignoring both Jessica and me and looking past us to the driver's seat. 'Long time no see.'

Ben faced forward, not even glancing at her.

A long, slow smile lit up her face. 'I see you lowered your standards since we were together.' She was looking at Jessica, but her words were meant for Ben. And even though it was nothing to do with me, I leaned forward in my seat.

'Hey, shut up, Alexis.' My northern accent, which I normally tried to smooth out, was heavy and brash in the midst of the flare of anger that caused me to speak.

Three pairs of eyes turned to stare at me. I put my hands to my face immediately, feeling the burn in my cheeks. Never before had I told anyone to shut up, and definitely not someone of Alexis's calibre.

Jessica broke the silence by shrieking out a laugh. Twisting in her seat again, she held up a hand. Weakly, already back to meek again, I high-fived her.

'Drive,' she instructed Ben, and pressing the button for the electric window, she sent Alexis stumbling backwards as we pulled away.

As we exited the car outside the hotel, I couldn't help but feel a burst of pride that it was Ben tagging along behind Jessica and me. Usually I was the one bringing up the rear. In the reception area, Marco was talking to the porter. I slowed my step when he turned to smile at me. Ben paused. Jessica grabbed my arm.

'Come on,' she hissed. 'Come with me.'

I didn't need asking twice.

I would do anything Jessica told me.

I hurried along, trying to keep up with her long strides as together we raced to her room.

'That shit, sleeping with her!' She slammed the door and leaned against it.

For a long moment I forgot her, and looked around at the breathtaking suite. On the huge vanity table, pots and bottles of creams, perfumes and potions sat in a haphazard fashion. I peered at a moisturiser. As if in response, the skin between my fingers itched suddenly, longing to be soothed by one of the expensive products. They were mostly organic, which I found funny, considering all the bad stuff Jessica enjoyed putting into her system.

She cleared her throat, clearly expecting my undivided attention. I turned back to her and shoved my scaly hands in my pockets.

'You mean Ben? But he didn't sleep with her while he was with you, did he?' It was doubtful, seeing as they'd only cemented their relationship that very afternoon.

'But I thought I was special!' Jessica's lower lip trembled and she wrapped her arms around herself. 'I didn't realise he was sleeping with everyone in Cannes.'

I wanted to point out that Alexis was hardly everyone, but I didn't dare. It was clear that Jessica needed reassurance.

'He isn't, he hasn't been.' That was true. Whenever I'd been out with Ben, he hadn't expressed an interest in any other women. I told her as much.

'Really?' She brightened, pushed herself off the door and walked over to the bed, flinging herself onto it. 'Still, let him stew for a while, hey?'

I laughed as I edged over to the bed and sat down, wondering if I was being too forward in our new friendship. 'Treat 'em mean, right?'

'Exactly.' Pulling her cigarettes out of her bag, Jessica lit one up. 'You're a good friend, Louise,' she said, blowing smoke rings up towards the ceiling.

I blushed with delight. But without warning, thoughts of her and Ben entwined like the vines in the fields rushed at me. I felt my face get even hotter. Should I mention it? Or act like it never happened? Jessica seemed to have forgotten all about it, so I decided to take my lead from her.

'Tell me more about Alexis and her beef with Marco,' Jessica demanded.

Obediently I told her what I'd witnessed, word for word as best I could remember. When I was finished, Jessica angrily crushed her cigarette out in the ashtray.

'That bitch, acting like she owns this town.'

But she did, or rather her father did, but I didn't say that.

'Maybe I'll take her precious Nathan's customers away and point them in Marco's direction.' Jessica tossed her hair and her eyes narrowed to green slits. 'See how she likes that. There's a new girl in town now, and little Miss Dubois will just have to get used to it. Right, Louise?'

I found myself nodding. 'Right, Jessica.'

Our summer moved on in much the same vein, and for the first time since I arrived in Cannes, I was truly happy. Once Jessica forgave Ben for his alleged love affair with Alexis, the two of them were inseparable. Jessica even scaled back on her drug use, I noticed, though Marco was still pushing and selling every night.

'Does your dad know about Marco dealing in the hotel?' I asked her one night as we sat out in the lemon grove at the back of Jenson Coast.

'My dad knows everything,' said Jessica. With an air of mystery she added, 'Yet he says nothing.'

'What do you mean?'

'He treats me like I'm a child,' she burst out. 'He thinks I'm still a little girl, he never talks to me.' She rolled over, twirling a long blonde lock around her finger. 'He doesn't even talk about my mother.'

'Can I ask... what happened to her?'

'She drowned. I was tiny, I don't really remember anything about it. Just afterwards, Dad... he became so protective of me. He hated me going in the sea, or even a swimming pool.' Her gaze drifted towards the window, to the sea that glittered beyond the lush green gardens. Wistfully, she said, 'I'd like to hear him talk about her, I know so little about her.'

'Maybe it's too painful for him.'

She whipped her head round to face me, green eyes flashing as they bored into mine. 'Don't defend him, Louise. You don't know anything.' She threw herself face down on the ground, and I stared, taken aback by the childlike action.

Unsure of what to say or do, I watched her as she breathed heavily. One eye peeped out at me, full of tears that fell freely and easily.

'I'm sorry,' I whispered.

My chest tightened painfully as she looked moodily away from me. Was this it? Had I messed up so royally that I was to be discarded? Friendless, penniless. Cast out.

No.

Frightened now, I moved closer to her. 'I'm sorry, Jessica, please don't…' Don't what? Be angry with me? Ditch me? Leave me?

She sighed, long and loud. 'Oh, shut up, Louise.'

I did. For a long while we remained like that, silent, motionless. I kept my breathing short and shallow.

'Why do you think I checked into La Villa Mauresque spa before I came here?'

I jumped when she spoke after what seemed like an eternity.

'What… why?' I asked.

She rolled her eyes. 'My father knows about Marco's dealing and turns a blind eye, but I'm a different story. And he'd have taken one look at me and known exactly how hard I'd been using.'

'But he doesn't mind Marco selling drugs here?'

Jessica shrugged and rubbed her fingers together in the international sign for money.

'I think we need to be careful of Alexis, though,' I said. 'She and that Nathan seem to have it in for Jenson Coast.' I spoke cautiously, nervous of making her angry again, of giving an opinion when it wasn't wanted.

Jessica flicked the ash off her cigarette and looked over at me. 'You're so sweet, Lou, worrying about us.'

Her tone, her whole manner was so different to that of just moments ago that I didn't know what to say. Embarrassed, I looked down. 'I just don't want any of you to get in trouble. I'm… I'm having such a great time with you all, I'd hate for anything to end it.'

Jessica grinned, stubbed her fag out on the bark of a lemon tree and lay back with her hands behind her head. 'This is it, sweetie, this is our life – your life now. Enjoy it.'

And I would enjoy it. But in order to do so, I knew I'd have to be very careful to stay on the right side of Jessica.

–

Whenever Marco was free, we became a foursome. I was comfortable around him now, and able to admit to myself that his appeal to me had been scaled back somewhat by Jessica's arrival. It was her I wanted to look at, to daydream about. In turn, she revelled in my obvious fandom. She loaned me clothes that were too big for her; she styled my hair, and the frizzy, errant mop that I couldn't do anything with suddenly became slicked-back and fashionable. She loaned me her body creams, the vegan ones, the good stuff, and I almost moaned in delight as the skin on my hands was soothed. I wanted to smell like her too; that scent she gave off was like nothing I'd ever smelled. A mixture of coconut and expensive perfume. I reached for it once, but her hand closed over mine.

'Not that one,' she said.

Under her touch, I soon forgot the rebuff.

I no longer worried about money. When I was with Ben, Marco or Jessica, their almost-celebrity status meant we got into the best clubs for free, and restaurants pandered to us. Everything went on the Jenson Coast account. It was an incredible summer, marred only by the quiet threat of Alexis and her sidekick Nathan Saint. Though they didn't approach us, I was sure I saw her everywhere. It seemed like she was in every restaurant, every beachside bar. I swore I saw her cruising past Jenson Coast in her snappy little Mercedes convertible. I felt her eyes on us, but the other three didn't seem to notice anything out of the ordinary.

Then, as summer moved towards autumn, everything changed.

'Ben is leaving for Italy next week,' Jessica announced one evening when it was just the two of us. 'He's going to ask me to go with him.'

My heart lurched and then sank to the bottom of my shoes. 'Are you going to go?' And my unspoken question: where would it leave me if she did?

She raised her shoulders to her ears. 'Probably.' Flipping onto her front on the queen-size bed in her suite, she grabbed my hand. 'I have to go, Lou, I can't imagine being without him.'

I tried to smile, but failed.

'Oh, Lou, be happy for me, sweetie.' She dropped my hand and grabbed me in a bear hug. 'We'll still see you; Italy isn't far away.' Lowering her voice, she whispered in my ear, 'And you'll be bridesmaid at my wedding.'

I pulled back. 'Ben asked you to marry him?'

She laughed. 'Not yet, but we're heading that way. Oh God, Lou, can you imagine how happy we'll be?'

I couldn't, not really. Ben was lovely, a calming influence in our group of four. Even though he was only in his late twenties, he always kept an eye on Marco and Jessica on our sometimes insane nights out. But – and I'd never say it to Jessica – he seemed more into his career than he did her. I knew he liked her, but I'd spoken to him; we'd talked a lot when he and I were the only sober ones left. I knew that his plan was to bring nature and wildlife to the forefront and make it cool and hip for the next generation. He wanted to become the Justin Timberlake of the environmental world – his words, not mine. He was a little geeky like that. Timberlake was so last-decade.

I tuned out as Jessica talked on about the life they would lead. Selfishly, I hoped that her premonitions about her future with Ben were wrong.

–

Jessica's suite was one of the most expensive ones in the hotel. She'd claimed it on her arrival, even though it had been booked out and the guest had to be refunded to downgrade. There it was, that power again. Would I ever be so special as to be able to demand and expect like that? I doubted it.

But I was glad she'd got the suite. I spent more time in it than I did in my flat.

Jessica's best quality was her generosity, and only a couple of days after meeting me, she had given me my own key card. I had access to her suite and permission to borrow any of her items, except for the special scent. At first I was reluctant, but soon I realised how much it annoyed her when I asked if I could use this or that, when she had already told me that nothing was out of bounds. Eventually I treated her suite and everything in it as my own.

That night – the night that the first fracture appeared in our summer family, as I had begun to think of it – I was in her bathroom doing my hair when I heard the door to the suite open.

I carried on straightening my hair, trying to get it exactly as Jessica did it. Making me beautiful seemed to come naturally to her. I thought she knew I was in the bathroom. I was wrong.

'I have to leave soon,' I heard Ben say. 'Everything's booked in Italy.'

Carefully, silently, I switched the straighteners off and padded on the soft carpet to the door, which stood ajar.

'How soon?' Jessica asked. I peeped round the door, saw her reflection in the large vanity mirror. She was sitting cross-legged on the bed.

Ben walked over to the bar, waited until his back was to her before he replied. 'Tomorrow. My flight's at midday.'

Jessica stretched her legs out in front of her and rubbed at a tiny patch of dry skin. Pulling her bag onto the bed, she reached into it for her moisturiser. She didn't say anything. The only sound was the clink of the ice as Ben made cocktails.

I knew she was waiting for the invitation to join him in Italy, but the silence stretched on, only broken by a 'cheers' as Ben handed her a glass.

The atmosphere in the suite changed as suddenly as if the air conditioning had been switched on.

My right eye pulsed with a sudden tic.

The new, repaired skin on my hands began to itch.

There was going to be no invitation.

Long, long minutes of silence stretched out, excruciating to bear witness to. They drank their cocktails quietly. I sat on the raised step in the bathroom. I couldn't leave now; they'd know I'd been there, listening, all the time. I hoped they would finish their drinks and go for dinner or something. But then I heard a rustling noise, a tiny groan, and I crept on my hands and knees back to the doorway.

He took her on the window seat and Jessica wrapped her legs around him. She looked over his shoulder and I jumped back behind the door. But she wasn't looking at me, not this time; she was gazing at their bodies in the mirror that hung on the opposite wall. Daring now, I moved back to the door and watched. This time, the second time I had watched them having sex, they were both entirely naked. Jessica's skin was bronzed, her hair bleached even blonder than when she'd first arrived. She was glowing with health and vitality, beautiful on a summer diet of good food and great sex. How could Ben not want her to go with him? If I were with her, I'd want her by my side at all times.

I closed my eyes, listened to the rhythm that their bodies made as their skin slapped together. It formed a drumbeat in my mind: *stay with me, Jessica, stay with me...*

Later, much later, after they fell asleep, a tangle of limbs and hair and skin, I crept from Jessica's suite and, for the first night in ages, went home.

My flat was dull and claustrophobic in comparison to Jenson Coast, but I couldn't stay at the hotel tonight. I had to be alone to process not only what I'd seen and heard, but how I felt about it.

Ben was leaving.

Jessica was staying.

I wondered if I was a bad person, for I was happy, ecstatic in fact, that Jessica – my new friend, my best friend, my *only* friend – would remain with me. She was clearly upset at the turn of events; after all, she'd thought that she and Ben were destined to be together.

I would look after her, I decided. I'd be the most loyal friend she could ever want or need, and in no time at all she would forget about him.

–

I didn't sleep that night, not really, and the morning after Ben's non-invitation, I couldn't wait to go to Jenson Coast and start my new role as Jessica's protector. But first I had to drop off a price list and portfolio to a new beachside bar. I'd been getting more requests for quotes lately, and I knew it was down to my friends. They had clout, Marco, Andrew and Jessica, even Ben, and I knew they recommended my photographic services any chance they could.

I dressed carefully, as I usually did these days, and headed to Bocca Beach, clutching my folder of work. Before I went inside, I assessed the immediate area, taking notes of shots that would work, ones that captured the ocean in the background, scrawling a reminder to cut out the slightly shabby corner store that spoiled the view.

'Louise, mate.' I spun around at the sound of my name and saw Ben behind me, holding out a piece of paper. 'Will you pass this on to Jessica?'

She didn't have a phone yet; it had been lost in Germany or somewhere. But this summer, everyone was right there at Jenson Coast. We didn't need phones while we were all in one place. At the reminder, I felt a little surge of panic at the thought of her getting a new mobile, of her widening her net of communication to the other European cool girls who thought nothing of crossing country borders just to party.

I took the note from him reluctantly. 'Why don't you give it to her yourself?' I asked.

'She went off this morning before I even woke up. I have to get my flight; I'm cutting it fine as it is,' he said.

Unfolding the paper, I read the message he'd written, inviting her to join him in Italy. My heart sank. I wanted to ask him why he hadn't mentioned it last night, when she'd so obviously been expecting him to, or before then even. He'd known about the job in Italy long enough. But deep down I knew why: he was only now realising just how special she was. I smiled to myself smugly. *I'd* known since the second I met her.

Too bad, I thought. Too late, Ben.

I let him pull me in for a friendly hug, then watched him jog back to his car. I waited until he had disappeared from view before I walked over to one of the fire pits and dropped his note into it. I didn't consider it, or overthink it, or worry about it – I just did it.

When nothing but curled blackened edges of their love remained, I dropped my portfolio off at the bar and glanced at my watch. I should get back to Jenson Coast, Jessica would need me when she returned.

Only as I said my goodbyes to the owner did I see Alexis. She was watching me with narrowed eyes. She'd overheard our conversation.

She had seen exactly what I'd done.

Chapter 4

Jessica

I knew my husband was dead as soon as I walked into our bedroom. Before I'd even registered that his chest was no longer moving. Before I clocked his eyes, open, cloudy, his stare fixed on something not in this room, not in this world. Maybe it was the scent, because death carries an aroma, you know? Musty, a tang of sweetness that catches in your throat and leaves a bitter taste. And I've been unfortunate enough to smell it before.

Something moved in my chest, shifting deep within me as I looked at him. He was on our bed, on his back, his hands at his sides, dressed smartly as always in his suit trousers. His shirt was white and crisp, the sleeves rolled up to the elbows, the tie loosened, everything suggesting that he had simply fallen asleep. But this sleep was forever. He looked peaceful. I'd never seen him look that peaceful before.

Practically since I had known him, he'd believed he had a cancer. It had assaulted him periodically over the years, striking like a depression, sometimes with breaks of years in between and then returning, no rhyme or reason, like a bolt of random lightning or a sudden April downpour.

45

My husband, Patrick, was very much in control. In his work and his personal life he would not accept anything that he couldn't manage. Somewhere in a deep, dark recess of my mind, I knew that one day this illness, be it real or imagined, would threaten to claim him. But he would never allow that to happen. He would deal with it in his own way first, so he still held the power. It looked like that day had arrived. But there were no self-inflicted marks on his body. No pills missing from the medicine cabinet. No way to tell how he'd done it.

This was what I told the police. I directed my words to Detective Sergeant Richard Robinson, who sat opposite me in the small grey room. His colleague, Constable Nina Hart, sat beside him. Richard's face was open, he made all the right listening noises and I definitely felt more comfortable with him. I glanced at Hart. She was a different story to Richard with his soft-shell exterior. She was all hard angles and edges, cheekbones that could cut glass, dark eyes behind fashionable, thick glasses, and neat white-blonde hair that touched her shoulders. I watched her carefully, saw how her pupils grew huge when I said something that interested her. Her eyes narrowed to mean slits at certain points – when she thought I was lying? I got no sympathetic vibes from her. In fact, apart from her expressive eyes, I got nothing from her at all. She just sat, not questioning, not speaking, occasionally jotting something in her notebook, her only apparent reaction in those big dark eyes.

'So this cancer,' Richard said, making a little inverted comma motion with his hand around the word, 'did he go to the doctor, the hospital?'

'I think so, I don't know.' I shifted on the uncomfortable chair. 'He was a very private man.'

I saw the look that Nina shot Richard, a 'who's she kidding?' kind of expression. I felt my hands closing into fists. Deliberately I straightened out my fingers, told myself not to react.

'But he was your husband – did he not share his diagnosis with you?'

I was surprised that he didn't make speech marks with his fingers around that word too. I knew how ludicrous it sounded: a husband who believed he had a terminal illness but did not involve his wife of eight years. But Patrick was different, an enigma. I told Richard Robinson as much, added a helpless shrug and lowered my eyes.

'Do you have a list of the medications he was on?' Robinson asked.

'No,' I whispered. 'Do you know when his… affairs will be sorted out, his bank stuff, financial matters?' I swallowed and looked down at my lap. It was a crass question to ask, but I had no way to access any of the money that was rightfully mine.

Picking up my shoulder bag, I pulled out the papers I had been able to find at home, bank accounts, savings, debit cards but no PIN numbers; all the financial affairs, none of which were in my name. In my haste, bundles of paperwork along with the contents of my bag fell to the floor. I placed the rest carefully on the table, breathed deeply and rubbed at my forehead, trying to ease the ever-present tension headache that simmered there. As I massaged my scalp, I felt the scar, knew it glowed shiny and white; the scar from that night. Sitting up straight, I pulled my hair forward to conceal it.

'All these things… my home, it was my father's home, yet my name is nowhere on any paperwork.'

Nina exchanged a glance with Richard. He cleared his throat as he flipped a page in his notebook. 'That's not really our department. Do you want us to call anyone?'

I met his gaze. 'Like who?'

'A friend, family, Patrick's parents maybe,' he replied, his tone gentle.

But I didn't have anyone. Neither of us did. It had just been the two of us. No friends, no family, not any more. Patrick had a mother somewhere, but I didn't know how to reach her. 'I don't have his mother's number.'

Richard nodded, scribbled something down. I listened to the scratch of the pen on the page, tried to see what he had written, but failed.

'Okay, Jessica. Let's talk some more about your earlier life with your husband,' he said, with an almost-smile.

Up until now, I'd remained calm. I understood why they were questioning me; the unexplained sudden death of an apparently healthy middle-aged man, they had to look into that. But our past was unnecessary; it was just that, the past. I wanted to shout, *He's dead, what does our past matter?*

But I said nothing, because really it wasn't his past they were interested in. It was mine. A sigh escaped me as I shoved the financial paperwork back in my bag.

'When did you first meet your husband?' pressed Richard.

He knew this already, but he wanted me to say it. I squared my shoulders and looked him straight in the eye. 'I first met him eight years ago, in France. He was my lawyer and he was hired to defend me…' I paused, fixed my eyes defiantly on Hart, 'when I was arrested.'

Did I see a flicker of a smile from her? A small sound emerged from Richard and I turned back to him. He nodded his head, leaned back in his chair. Then *she* spoke for the first time. Her voice had an accent – American, perhaps, or Canadian. 'Why don't you start there: what were you arrested for?'

And taking a deep breath, I looked her square in the eye. 'Suspicion of murder.'

Chapter 5

Jessica

Now

As I stood outside the police station, I gulped in fresh air. I wished I had a cigarette, but the few I had were at home, concealed in a box where I kept all my secrets. I felt something close to hunger at my need for nicotine. Cigarettes and alcohol were the only things I felt ravenous for these days, I couldn't recall the last time I'd had a proper appetite or energy that was brought about by exercise or exertion or a joy for life. A fact betrayed by my tired skin and too-thin frame.

The inner door of the police station clanged and I looked over my shoulder. Constable Hart was making her way across the lobby. Pulling my scarf high so it covered the lower half of my face, I hurried down the steps into the car park.

Where the hell did I leave the car? Shading my eyes from the low sun, I scanned left and right, finally seeing Patrick's saloon in the far corner. I heard the external door behind me swish to a close and speed-walked to the car, where I fumbled with the lock and sank low into the driver's seat.

I didn't want to leave yet. After having exhausted myself with stories of my own past, I just wanted to sit with my eyes closed. But as a blonde head bobbed along the rows of cars, I started the engine and pulled out onto the dual carriageway.

The police station, everything it represented, scared me. I thumped my hands on the steering wheel in frustration. I never used to be frightened of anything, but in the last eight years, my life had been fuelled by fear almost every day. Could it really be just eight years ago that I had not a single care in the world, when I had been a spoilt brat travelling Europe on my daddy's money? How times had changed, how *I* had changed, and not only in appearance.

But it was over now, I reminded myself. The lost years were gone. I was my own woman again; I could do whatever I used to do.

Except go back, a little voice whispered in my head. *You can never go back.*

Tears pricked at my eyes, blurring my vision, and I scrubbed angrily at my face. I couldn't go back to France, the place where it had all begun, and yet despite everything that had happened in Cannes, it was the last place I'd been truly happy. But there was no point going there anyway. Louise and Marco had abandoned me, Ben had left for pastures new, and my father was dead.

A cry emerged from my throat, strangled and raw, the way it always did when I thought of my father. I missed him.

At the same time, I blamed him. On really bad days, I hated him.

In spite of the pain-fuelled wail that I let out, no tears came. I was a dry well, my tears used up long ago.

On autopilot I drove the twenty minutes from the police station to my Suffolk village home. At the wheel of Patrick's Mercedes, I looked in the rear-view mirror more than I watched the road in front of me. Were there unmarked cars following me? Were they going to sit outside my cottage and watch my movements? Did they blame me for Patrick's death?

I was uncomfortable with the questions that Robinson and Hart had asked me. I replayed my answers in my head, satisfied that I'd said nothing to warrant them contacting me with further queries. I hadn't been arrested or cautioned, and this would have reassured me if it hadn't reminded me of another time when I thought I had been helping the police with their inquiries, only to be locked up myself. But there was nothing in Patrick's untimely death that pointed to me; why would there be?

There wasn't back then either, a voice taunted in my head. *And you still got blamed.*

I pulled off on the penultimate exit before the sea. I counted the vehicles behind me, one, two, three, four, and watched as the fifth one turned off too. I squinted in the mirror: was it a woman's silhouette in the driver's seat? But it was too far back for me to see clearly, and I wasn't about to slow down to satisfy my curiosity. My grip tightened on the steering wheel. I kept to a steady speed, forty miles per hour down the carriageway, thirty on the main street, and instead of turning right to go down the road where my home was, I kept on going straight. The car that had pulled off the dual carriageway at the same time as me *did* turn right. I groaned, tired of second-guessing everything, exhausted by always looking over my shoulder. I had been with the police all day, my mouth was dry from talking, and I was shattered. I stopped the car at the first junction, swung round and headed for home.

I felt the familiar jolt as I bumped over the train tracks and carried on at a slower pace as the road narrowed into a country lane. My cottage – or more accurately, my father's cottage that he had bought when I was twenty years old and then gifted to Patrick and me as our wedding present – was the last in a row. On the right-hand side were fields that stretched all the way to the docks and formed part of the nature reserve.

I hadn't ever thought I would settle down, and if I'd had that dream, this sleepy little village wouldn't have figured in it. But the place had grown to be a part of me over the last eight years. More often than not the land matched my mood: bleak and brown. Now, at the beginning of September, the nights were already starting to draw in, and the sun had dipped behind me as I finally pulled into my drive. I looked around for the car I suspected had been tailing me, maybe sent by Robinson or containing Hart, and my gaze alighted on a lone vehicle in the small parking area of the nature reserve. I didn't know if it was the car that had been behind me, but the interior light suddenly flicked on and I drew a quick breath as the figure in the driver's seat turned towards me.

I hadn't seen her for eight years, but I recognised her instantly. In the light of the single lamp that illuminated the car park, she exited the vehicle, closed the door and looked at me over the roof.

She had changed, I saw now. Her hair was longer, lighter; more strawberry blonde than the natural red it once was. Those extra pounds she had carried were gone, as were the ill-fitting, unfashionable clothes.

Bile rose in my throat as she approached me.

My God, she no longer looked like herself.

Chillingly, she looked *just like me*.

I swallowed down the horror and imagined her in our old life in Cannes. Now she would fit in. Then I remembered that it wasn't *her* old life, that she still lived there; no doubt now she *did* fit in. I imagined her waltzing around on a handsome man's arm, attending benefits and parties that only the high rollers got invited to. The ones I used to get invited to. She was the cream of the crop, in charge now that I was no longer around. Now that Alexis was no longer there.

At the thought of our nemesis, my stomach cramped painfully, the brief pain turning to envy. It swirled in my belly and rose up, leaving a bad taste in my mouth. Then she was in front of me, regarding me, dissecting me, taking in my ragged appearance as I stood motionless.

I tried to hold myself straight. Tried to forget that she had never seen me looking like this before. Was that pity in her eyes?

I shoved my hands in my pockets. I didn't want her sympathy.

She broke the silence with a smile. 'Jessica,' she said, 'I came as soon as I heard.' The accent she had unsuccessfully tried to smother, that harsh northern heaviness, was finally gone. Her voice rang out clear as a bell, her tone confident and knowing, her words clipped and precise.

My stomach clenched again. Not only did she now look like me, she sounded like me too.

'How did you know?' I stuttered the words, smoothed my hands through my hair, suddenly aware that it was lank and greasy. I couldn't take my eyes off her. Her own locks were bright and fresh and hung in a curtain of sunshine that rested against her shoulders. I gave up, tucked my own dark blonde hair behind my ears and shoved it into the collar of my coat, hiding as much of it as possible.

'News travels,' she replied. 'He was a high-profile guy. How did he die?'

Her eyes gleamed; her tone was one of gossip rather than empathy. And her question was unexpected. The Louise I knew didn't get straight to the point. She waited until she was asked for her opinion, and then she gave the answer she knew was expected. I was caught off guard.

'I… I don't know, not yet. He was ill, but he might have…' I tailed off, unable to say the words. I shook my head, blinked again as if to prove to my disbelieving eyes that she was really here. She was *here*, and with her were all the memories of that time, of my people. The good times and the bad and the wicked, they crowded in my head.

A strange sensation started in my chest and travelled upwards, getting stuck in my throat before I pushed it down by swallowing. I wouldn't cry; I'd not cried since the day after my wedding. Instead I took my hands from my pockets and lifted my arms, unsure whether I wanted to embrace her or strike her. As if sensing this, she made the decision for me.

She dropped her bag and enveloped me.

'It's okay,' she murmured, 'I'm here now.'

Eventually we shuffled inside, stood awkwardly in the hallway. I remembered how we used to be, totally comfortable in one another's company, sharing everything. Now look at us.

'How's that gorgeous little boy of yours?' Taking the lead the way I used to but had become unaccustomed to, I steered her into the kitchen and pointed to a chair before I went back down the hall to remove my coat.

I wondered if she would comment on the fact that I'd referred to him as gorgeous when I didn't know; I'd never seen her child, not even a photograph of him. I doubted it. Louise didn't correct people. She agreed with them, bowed and scraped to them. A yes girl. Inwardly I sneered at how weak she was, always had been.

'Robbie isn't so little any more – he's almost eight, you know,' she called out in response.

'Wow, eight.' I shook my head as I came back into the kitchen. 'I don't know where the years went.'

Louise narrowed her eyes and our moment of strangeness passed. She moved very close to me, so close that I could smell the scent of cigarettes that clung to her hair. Underneath it, a familiar scent. Coco, my signature perfume, the only one I'd ever worn, simply because my father had once told me it was my mother's favourite.

I hadn't breathed in that scent for years. Because of the personal connection, it was the one thing of mine I'd never let Louise borrow. Now, she smelled like she had bathed in it.

'I know where the years went; they went on that fucking husband of yours. Honestly, Jessica, I'm so sorry that you're a widow, but my God, all this time you've been a stranger, you've not wanted to know me!'

The aroma of my perfume on her body overwhelmed me, taking the edge off the bitter words she spoke. I moved away, across the room, and pulled open the back door. The scent of the fields permeated the kitchen. For the first time I welcomed the odour of manure and damp, cold countryside air.

'You cut me off.' My voice was a whimper, small and hoarse. 'You all abandoned me, even my dad.' This time the lump in my throat was so big I couldn't swallow it. I closed my eyes, waited for it to pass. 'I had to stay here,' I said. 'I had no choice, I couldn't come back.'

My tone was pleading, cajoling, like it was when I used to be able to twist everyone round my finger. I needed her to understand and I expected that she would; after all, that was what she did, side with me. But when I looked at her again, I blanched at her expression. She looked thunderous, livid, fists clenched and lips squeezed tightly together.

'My God, you don't know anything, do you?' She stopped, barked out a harsh, angry laugh and shook her head. 'I thought you were smarter than this, but you've got no idea of what really happened, have you?'

I searched for the words that wouldn't come, but before I could find them, she leaned forward, grasped my wrist and pulled me towards her.

'Patrick didn't get you out of prison, but he took all the credit and removed you from my life. He poisoned you against me, and you let him.' She let my hand go and it fell limply, banging hard on the tabletop.

I rubbed my wrist, regarded her uneasily. 'I don't know what you're talking about.'

She yanked her bag off the back of her chair and pulled out a packet of Marlboro Lights. Without asking if it was okay, she lit one, chucked the pack on the table and walked through to the conservatory to sit in the comfortable chair that overlooked the fields. She crossed one leg over the other, inhaled deeply and spoke through a plume of grey smoke.

'Do you ever think of those days?'

I shrugged, wanting to appear nonchalant, not wanting her to know that it was all I thought of, all the time: those magic months, that memorable summer, the sunshine that was our constant until my world went dark.

Louise told me nothing of importance, nothing I didn't already know as she made herself at home in my house. All she wanted to do was relive that time before it all went wrong. I tuned her out. I imagined her life now. The parties, the glamour, the money that came with the lifestyle that she had fallen into – no, *stolen* – from me. Because that used to be my life.

Eventually she exhausted herself talking about the past. Leaning back in the chair that overlooked the fields beyond my house, she fell asleep. I remained motion-less on the threshold of the kitchen, watching her, her mouth slightly open, a little snore emerging. As she slept, her fingers twitched. Livid red scratches criss-crossed her knuckles. The eczema was back, then. Which meant there was stress in her life.

For some reason, the knowledge gave me a little hot wire of pleasure.

I thought back to *that* summer. It had all fallen apart, but Louise was wrong about one thing. It wasn't Patrick's arrival that had fractured us, it was Ben's leaving. When he went away, I slipped back into my old ways: heavy drug use, drinking until I passed out. Louise had sworn to look after me, but I hadn't needed her. I'd needed him. And in spite of her promise, she didn't take care of me. She encouraged me.

I thought back to the day Ben left, the morning I crept from the bed and drove away before the sun had even risen, hunched over the wheel like a wounded animal. I ended up in Vaucluse, Provence. To me, Provence always spoke of wines and vines. This was a different part, though; this was Jean de Florette country, and as

I wandered around, I dearly wished I'd brought Ben here. I stood at a point overlooking the Fontaine-de-Vaucluse, tilted my head back and let out the hurt of Ben leaving. My pain emerged in a scream, jagged and broken, which caused the idling pigeons to take flight from their perch underneath the bridge. A cluster of Japanese tourists watched me, open-mouthed. I turned and walked back to the car, where I sat motionless while the tears dried on my face.

They thought it was a summer fling, my father, Louise, even Ben himself. What they didn't realise was how much Ben had changed me, had helped me, had saved me. Nobody knew what I'd been like in Germany, with the drugs and the partying and the men. I'd used so heavily that my life was hanging by a thread. Ben made a comment one day as we drove, about the natural highs that we should all experience, rather than the false ones that I was imbibing, like coke and weed and MDMA. I laughed at him, thought he was such a square, but his words got me thinking, and for the rest of the time he was there, I cut back, tried some of his natural highs, like midnight swimming in the ocean with only the moon as our guide, and clifftop walking along trails that had no barriers. The thrill of knowing that one false step could send me plummeting to my death was like no drug I'd ever tried.

Ben was right.

And then he left, and everything fell apart, leading me here, to this prison of a cottage in a place where I didn't belong.

I looked over at Louise. She had woken up, was staring at me through half-closed eyes.

As she smiled sleepily at me, I felt my fists clench. Her life hadn't ended. Hers had only just begun when I was spirited away.

I turned away from her, slid soundlessly upstairs through my bedroom and into the bathroom. From my box of secrets I pulled my mobile phone, and tapped out a quick text before turning it off again. Back downstairs, I watched from the doorway as Louise stirred and stretched.

Chapter 6

Louise

Then

That night, when Jessica returned to her suite from wherever she had been so she wouldn't have to watch Ben walk away from her, I plied her with alcohol to make her forget him.

She drank quietly and quickly, one glass after another, until her minibar was empty. I held her close, my red hair fanned out over her face and neck, breathing in the special scent of her, the Coco perfume she wore every day without fail. Behind her, I looked at the expensive bottle on her dressing table. It was the one thing that was off limits to me, and like a child, I wanted more than anything the thing I couldn't have.

One day, I told myself as I stroked her silky blonde hair, one day she'll let me wear it.

She struggled in my grip. Disappointed, I reluctantly released her. 'I'll get more drink,' I announced.

As I slipped out of the room, I glanced back at her. She had a pendant in her hand, a turquoise one that I knew Ben had given her. She stroked it lightly with her thumb, her gaze far away.

I closed the door quietly behind me. Reminded myself to lose the pendant when she wasn't watching.

Downstairs, I requested a bottle of vodka from the bar.

'Twenty euros,' replied Gustaf as he slid it across to me.

I frowned. I knew him; why didn't he – *anyone* – remember me? 'It's for Jessica's suite,' I replied, plumped up with self-importance. 'Bill it to Andrew.'

With the slightest raise of an eyebrow, he gave a small nod before moving on to the next customer.

I grabbed the bottle and was sweeping back to the room when I stopped short at the sound of Andrew's voice. It wasn't his tone that caught me, it was his words.

'Jessica needs a firm hand. She needs guidance, someone to show her.'

To my left I saw the top of his grey head, his back towards me. Gripping the vodka tightly, I slipped into an empty booth behind him, hunched down low, listened.

'Show her what?'

The voice, when it came in reply, was low, deep, and I knew even without seeing the speaker that this was Patrick King, Marco's adversary, Andrew's friend.

'I'm bailing her out all the time, everywhere. Germany, Spain, Italy. And she's heading the same way here, out all night, sleeping all day.' Andrew broke off and uttered a laugh. 'But she's worth her weight in gold. She's really rather special, you know.'

'I know, I've seen her.' A beat, then, 'Your daughter is beautiful, Andrew.'

I fought the urge to gag, listening to her father and his friend talking about her as though she were a fine piece of art or a valuable antique. It was creepy, sinister.

'She's at an age where she should be settling down, thinking of the future, thinking of giving me grandchildren!'

My mouth twisted. I didn't want to hear any more. Moving along the seat, I made to stand, thinking of Jessica, how mortified she would be if she knew her father was trying to matchmake on her behalf now that Ben was gone. I was embarrassed for her, but something else lurked beneath that emotion. Something like envy. Nobody would ever talk about me that way. I didn't do bad enough things to make someone worry about me. I wasn't beautiful enough to have someone set me up.

Standing, I grabbed the bottle, and had begun to move off when Patrick King spoke again.

'Arrange it, Andrew.' There was a smile in his voice, or was it a leer? 'I'll meet your daughter.'

—

'What do you know of your father's friend Patrick?' I asked Jessica when I returned to her suite.

She eyed the bottle of vodka hungrily and grabbed for it. I handed it over.

'Who?' she asked.

'Patrick King, he's a friend of your dad,' I said again.

'Patrick King, Patrick King... Yes, he's hot.' Unscrewing the cap, she swigged straight from the bottle, then coughed and handed it to me. 'Why?' she demanded. 'You got designs on him?'

I scrunched up my face. How much should I tell her? If she thought Patrick was hot, if her father tried to set them up, she might go for it. Then where would that leave me? Out in the cold again.

She leaned back against the wall. She was still holding the pendant again, and ran it through her fingers before clenching it tightly in her fist.

'Jessica,' I started. But I didn't know how to finish.

With faraway eyes she let the necklace slip from her hand. Unsteadily she stood, zigzagged towards the bed.

'Louise, come sit with me.'

As I stood, I kicked the turquoise pendant, Ben's gift, underneath the heavy drapes.

She grabbed my arm, pulling me to sit beside her. 'I'm so sad, Lou,' she whispered.

I stared at my wrist, sure that the electricity I felt when she touched me would have left a mark. 'You don't need Ben,' I said, my own voice barely more than a whisper.

She sat cross-legged, her face obscured by her hair as she looked down into an empty glass.

'I'll look after you,' I said, plucking the glass from her hand and putting it on the table beside the bed.

There was nothing in her face. It was empty and blank. How long would it be before she couldn't stand to be in this place that held too many memories of her lost love? How long before she upped and left, maybe to Italy, in the hope of coming across Ben? He would thank her for accepting his invitation, she would be confused, she would discover that I had lied, had burned his note.

She glanced to the side of the bed that Ben had slept in all summer. Thoughts of him were coming back to her, I could tell, as she reached across, intending to bury her face in the sheets, maybe hoping to inhale the remaining scent of him. I caught her hand, pulled her back towards me and opened the little bag of powder ketamine I'd snaffled from Marco days ago. With a shaking hand I held her face; with the other I invited her to snort it off my finger. She dipped her head, inhaled greedily. I laid her gently down. I became another person as I led her back to her old familiar life.

–

Jessica expressed no interest in anything except spending time with me. I was elated, happy to be the only one she wanted to be with. We stopped hanging out with Marco in the evenings at trendy bars; instead we took slow walks along the ocean edge or wound our way through the lemon groves at the back of Jenson Coast. Sometimes she would get a faraway look in her eyes and I knew she was thinking of Ben. At those moments I would produce whatever drug I'd manage to lift from Marco's stash when he wasn't looking and feed it to her. As she swallowed and snorted and smoked, I'd watch her come back to me.

As August drew to a close, we began to drive into the hills, away from the sea. She told me this was where she'd come the morning Ben had left. His name again. I didn't want her to think of him, didn't want to encourage talk of him, so I silently gripped her hand across the seats.

Vaucluse was all mountains and hillsides, greenery in which medieval-looking buildings sprouted at random. Through the tiny winding streets we drove until we reached the Verdon Natural Regional Park. We pulled up alongside the motor homes and camper vans and made our way carefully on foot down from the road to the little beaches. After we had walked around a mile, we found a sandy cove, obscured from the view of passers-by or drivers. We stripped naked and lay in the sun. I was totally at ease with myself in her company. From behind my shades I thought of what we must look like, what people would think if they saw us like this.

They would think we were together.

I didn't mind. It only validated my position and status.

As we strolled back to the car, I took her hand. She let me; girlfriends, of both varieties, did this.

Then I saw the four-by-four parked a few spaces down from us. The passenger window rolled slowly down and I blinked as I saw Alexis, her face covered by the huge shades she wore, her smile on view for everyone to see.

–

I stood outside my flat, examining my finger where I'd managed to catch it while I was putting away the fold-up bed in my lounge. Jessica and I had enjoyed a heavy night last night. So heavy, I'd had to come home to grab a couple of hours' kip. With my eyelids still puffy from both sleep and lack of it, I started at the sound of Alexis's voice calling me. A while back, before she knew who I was, my name on her lips was all I longed for. Now, today, it filled me with dread.

'Hey, lady, long time no see,' she breathed as she came to stand beside me. It was her standard form of greeting. She had never directed it at me before.

I looked her up and down, glanced behind her to see who she was with. She shouldn't be here; this wasn't her patch. I was surprised she even knew my road existed.

'Hi, Alexis,' I replied weakly.

'So, you've stepped in as Mister Ben's replacement, yes?' she asked, getting straight to the point while coyly fiddling with a long strand of her perfect auburn hair.

I remained still, silent, looking down. All I could see was Alexis watching as Ben said goodbye at the beach bar and gave me his address in Italy to pass on to Jessica.

Now, standing on the cracked pavement, my face felt as hot as Ben's note had when I burned it.

When I didn't reply, she laughed and leaned against the wall of my building before pushing herself upright and examining her white blouse, as though suddenly realising where she was, that my building was dirty and wasn't washed every day like the white walls of her million-pound home.

'I won't tell. I'd hate to ruin your... whatever it is.' Her voice was stern now, though her smile was still in place. 'I came for a different reason. My man, my Nathan, he's not happy, you know?'

Marco had moved in on Nathan's patch. The memory of Alexis and Marco arguing seemed so long ago. But where did I come in? Why was she here now?

'Your man at your intolerable hotel, he is pushing Nathan out, and this is Nathan's town, *I* call the shots, not your *escroc*.'

Crook, she was referring to Marco as a crook. My face grew hot. It was people like Alexis who owned Cannes, and my friends – Jessica, Andrew and Marco – had made a serious mistake in getting too big for their boots. Alexis Dubois could ruin them. And if they were ruined, so was I.

'I'll speak to him,' I blurted.

This was bigger than us, bigger than Alexis even. This was drug wars, and they were not just dangerous, they were deadly. Suddenly it was as though Alexis had blocked out the sun. My world dimmed, grew darker.

But still, I thought as I moved a few steps away from her, at least my own secret was safe. At least Jessica didn't know I had betrayed her by not passing on Ben's message.

And she could never know.

'When is little Jessica going to Italy to be with Mister Ben?'

I stiffened as Alexis caught up with me, skipping by my side as I walked as fast as I could down the street. I ignored her.

'Because he invited her, right? You took the information from him at the bar, yes?' Feigned confusion on her face, still with that hard, mean smile.

I knew then that she definitely had seen me burn the note. And I knew she would use the information if it suited her. I slowed my walk until I came to a stop. I couldn't ignore it – her – any longer.

'What do you want from me?' I asked softly.

'Tell your man Marco to back off.' She smiled again, showing perfect even white teeth. 'Then maybe your new girlfriend won't find out your secret.'

Something squeezed my chest hard. 'I'll speak to him,' I said.

She nodded, once. Looked me up and down. 'Good.' With eyes that were narrowed to hard slits, she turned on her heel.

–

The email came from her assistant. Yes, she had an assistant. Even though Alexis didn't actually do anything, she was important enough, rich enough, to warrant paid help. I printed it off, read it, screwed it up and threw it across the room. Later, intrigued, ideas forming about how I might put things right, I picked it up, smoothed it out and took it to Jessica.

'It's a birthday party. They want to hire me as the photographer,' I said. 'Will you come with me?' I held my breath as I showed her the information, trying to cover the name of the birthday girl with my thumb. She snatched it out of my hand, read it and shoved the paper back at me.

'Alexis Dubois?' She shook her head, raked her fingers through her blonde hair. 'No way.'

I knew why; I knew Ben had been fucking Alexis before Jessica came along. *But he's gone*, I wanted to shout. *You have me now!*

'She's got that beef with Marco because he's selling on Nathan's patch,' I reminded her, finally getting up the courage to do what Alexis wanted of me. 'Perhaps we could smooth things over before it gets out of hand.'

As Jessica considered it, I wondered if it was the smart thing to do, to take her along with me. God knows she belonged at a party like that, with those girls. What if she looked at them and their lives, then compared them to me? And what if Alexis got to Jessica before I sorted out the Marco and Nathan problem and told her about Ben's note?

My head began to hurt. I backtracked.

'You don't have to go,' I said hurriedly. 'Actually, I don't think I'll take the job.'

Jessica picked up the info sheet and read it again. I wondered if she knew just who Alexis was. If we were in Hollywood, Alexis would be BFFs with Paris Hilton, or one of those Kardashians who were on the television all the time.

'I'll go. I've got nothing better to do,' she sniffed.

I smiled tightly, but my heart was pounding. I'd just have to make sure Jessica stayed with me the entire time, and that Alexis didn't manage to get her on her own.

For the party, I slipped on a maxi dress, summery and cool, with nude heels. The stretchy jeans and comfortable sneakers were gone. I checked out my reflection in the mirror, noticing every bulge. I raised my arms, turned around, craning over my shoulder to check my reflection from behind. When I could stand to look no more, I picked up the mirror and turned it to face the wall.

Jessica, who didn't have to worry about spare inches on her washboard stomach, agonised over what to wear. I sat on the bed, ready to go, trying to ignore her sulky expression.

She's not coming, I thought, unsure if I were relieved or disappointed, but as I picked up my camera and prepared to leave, she darted out of the room, returning moments later in ripped skinny Levi's and a plain red T-shirt.

'I'll say I'm your assistant,' she said airily. 'I'll carry your fucking camera or something.'

Our roles had reversed. I was the one who looked like I belonged now. Jessica, in her casual clothes, looked just like the old me.

We drove to Alexis's place in silence, both of us lost in our thoughts. The streets were dark as we wound our way up into the hills, the only light coming from the head-lamps on the car we had borrowed from Jenson Coast. The house, which I'd scoped out earlier, was also in darkness. The entire road was.

'Did you get the wrong night?' Jessica asked, one hand on the door handle as I slowed to a stop.

Ignoring her accusatory tone, I flicked on the interior light and pulled the info sheet out of my pocket. 'Nope, tonight's the night.'

We sat in silence for a moment, waiting for other headlights to appear out of the darkness.

'Maybe the party is in the back, in a gazebo or something,' I said, and pulled the keys from the ignition.

Jessica shrugged, picked at a nail and didn't answer me. I got out anyway.

'This is freaky,' I said as I heard her door slam. I rummaged in the boot, using the light from my phone as I collected my equipment together. 'What do you reckon, a power cut or something?' I turned to pile my bag of lenses into her arms, but she had vanished.

I caught a glimpse of red flashing through the shrubbery that led to the front door. With a sigh, I stacked my bags on the pavement and turned back to close the boot of the car.

'Jessica! Wait up!'

Struggling under the weight of two shoulder bags, I made to follow her. I wrestled my camera out, hung it around my neck and snapped as I walked, the flash lighting up my vision if only for a moment. As I reached the top of the large circular driveway, I diverted off to the side, through to the rear of the property. It was impossibly dark, the pathway twisting and turning through vines and immaculately groomed hedges. I walked for a long time, stumbling as my heels sank into the soil when I wandered off the paving. I brushed the dirt off, cursing under my breath as I streaked the mud into the satin. Pulling two muslin film bags out of my bag, I slipped them over my shoes. I was hoping desperately to hear the sounds of a party ahead, for outdoor lanterns to appear. Finally, I stopped, lowered my bags to the ground and looked around. The party wasn't out here; nobody, not even the locals, could negotiate this maze of a path with confidence.

It *was* like being in a maze, and I'd turned in so many directions I no longer knew where the house or the road was, or indeed, where I was at all.

'Jessica?' I called, my voice high-pitched with panic. 'Where *are* you?'

Hoisting the bags onto my shoulders, I raised my camera, shot pictures of nothing, just using the split second of flash to light my way back.

Anger simmered inside me that I'd been hired by Alexis, the very girl who had suggested she could blackmail me, and now seemed to have played me.

I stopped. Was that what this was, or was it something more sinister? Had they – Alexis and Nathan – got Jessica somewhere? Were they right now telling her how I'd burned Ben's invitation so I could have her to myself? My body flashed hot and cold at the thought of Jessica discovering my lie, and I broke into an awkward jog. As I moved through the landscaped garden, a bird shrieked out. I jumped, it seemed so close, and as I spun around, I saw the villa looming up a few hundred yards away.

As I pushed onwards, tottering on the balls of my feet, one of the bags slipping off my shoulder, the bird called again. I stopped, almost at the house now, so close that the sliding French doors were within touching distance. I blinked blindly into the darkness as I realised there was something off. There were no birds at this time of night.

It had been a person screaming, and as I swung in the direction of the French doors again, a high-pitched wail replaced the screams.

Discarding my bags, my camera banging painfully against my chest, I ran the last few feet to the house. Cupping my hands on the glass, I peered through. The room was in total darkness.

I opened my mouth to shout, to call her name again. Before I could exhale, I stilled. One by one, the street lights came on. And as the room began to light up, the first thing I saw wasn't the two bodies slumped on the floor, but the blood that pooled around them.

Now I found my voice.

Now I could scream.

Chapter 7

I was never certain how Patrick and I ended up in his bedroom. Suddenly shy – something I'd not felt in years – I stood inside the door. He moved across the room, closed one of the shutters and switched on a bedside lamp. He removed his cufflinks and his shirt, and bare-chested, walked back to me.

'I'll look after you, Jessica. I'll not let anyone blackmail you, or persecute you. And I think I'd like to take care of you for the rest of my life. We can be a good team. You'd make a great wife.' He took hold of my hand, which lay limply by my side, and stroked my ring finger. 'What do you say?'

I blinked at him. What was he actually asking me?

After a beat, he laughed. The sound was rich and deep and he put his arms around me and spoke again.

'Shall I show you how much of a good team we could be?'

'Show me,' I whispered, because that was what I was good at, that was where my power was. Shrugging my shoulders out of the thin straps, I let the dress that Patrick had bought for me fall to the floor.

–

It wasn't bad. It wasn't great, but it wasn't bad. Unlike a lot of women I know, I've never minded the first time with a new lover. The unknown touch and feel and smell and reaction give it an edge.

Pulling the sheets modestly up to cover myself, I turned to Patrick.

'How long have you lived here?' I asked.

'A while,' he replied. 'Why, do you like it?'

I did like it, very much. It was one of the nicest places I'd stayed in, and I told him so.

'It could be yours, you know,' he said.

'H–how?'

He rolled over onto his side, pulled the sheet away from my body and looked at me. I let him; I liked the desire in his eyes. Since my arrest I'd been looked at with disgust, shock, horror and, from a select few, sympathy. Desire was a welcome change.

'If you stay with me, live with me.' He put a hand on my hip and looked into my face. 'Marry me.'

I laughed, more relaxed now. 'I'll think about it.'

He didn't laugh this time, and my smile faded.

Chapter 8

Jessica

Now

Louise began to talk. As she did so, she slipped back into the girl I'd once known. Eager, awestruck by a world she didn't feel was rightfully hers. Her northern accent, the one she tried so hard to quell, came back in full force, like it always did when she was animated or excited.

Her real self didn't lurk too far under the surface, then.

'That summer was just the beginning for me,' she finished, a dreamy half-smile on her face. 'It was the summer I was born.'

Crack.

I looked down at the wine glass I held. It had splintered in my fist.

'Jessica?' She said my name questioningly.

'I don't want to talk about...' I tailed off. What didn't I want to talk about? Her? That summer? Because talk of back then would invariably lead to talk of that night, and I didn't want to go there. It was the biggest thing that had ever happened to us, and yet we'd never spoken of it. We hadn't had the chance. I'd been ripped away, sent away. I knew it was inevitable that we discuss it, just not yet. I wasn't ready for that.

'Do you want a coffee?' I asked, getting up and moving across the room. I didn't wait for her reply; instead I flicked the kettle on. Leaning my elbows on the worktop, I looked unseeingly outside.

'I brought something for you.'

I jumped and spun round. Louise was behind me, holding aloft a carrier bag. She reached in and pulled out a bottle of wine.

'It's Saint-Jeannet,' she said, her voice a breathy whisper.

The shutters came down. I turned my back on her.

'Jessica?'

'Later,' I managed.

When she spoke again, her voice was low and hesitant, like I remembered it.

'Why were you not at your father's funeral?'

I closed my eyes. I didn't want to talk about my father to her but I had to say something. I turned back to face her. 'Do you still see Ben?'

She shrugged, annoyed with me answering her question with a question, no doubt. 'Sometimes. He makes a point of stopping by when he's in town.' A beat, and then, 'When was the last time you saw him?'

'Ages ago,' I replied without hesitation. 'Years.' My kitchen felt like it was closing in on me. Pushing myself off the counter, I moved around her. 'Back in a second,' I said.

In the conservatory, I sat in one of the comfortable wicker chairs that faced the dark fields. This room was lit only by a single lamp; it was my favourite room to sit in, where I could look outside, watch the dog walkers and the cyclists and the birdwatchers as they made their way into the heart of the nature reserve. I liked to imagine their lives. I liked that unbeknown to them, they were being scrutinised carefully by me. It was a chance to become the watcher instead of the watched.

After I first moved here with Patrick, once the dark curtain of my depression had lifted, slightly and briefly, I would sit in this chair and speculate on my life. I resented it: the view, the whole situation. I had swapped the scent of Malibu tanning oil for the smell of mould and manure. I yearned for the searing heat of the Riviera sun instead of the damp mist that hung low over the land here. But there was no going back. And now, after all the time that had passed, I couldn't even summon up the aroma of that happy, balmy summer.

In the distance I could see the cranes that lifted the containers off the ships at the port. HGV lorries waited patiently at all times of day and night, trucks like the ones with which my grandfather had made his fortune, a fortune that now I guess belonged solely to me – if I could ever figure out how to get my hands on it. It had always been mine, but I'd had no access to it; after my father's death, it had ended up not in my bank account, but in Patrick's. Now, though, Patrick had died too, so I guessed that finally it would come to me.

I closed my eyes and thought briefly of my father. It was the only way I could remember him now, in small, regulated slots of only a few minutes at a time. Anything more and I lost control, started thinking of how my entire life's memories were spoiled because of how his life had ended, without me at his side or even at his funeral.

That was the moment, that time around my father's death, when I finally woke up and began to realise that Patrick, who lived happily in the house that my father had provided, had imprisoned me as surely as if I'd been left to rot in that French jail. The rage still came when I thought of it, of how duped and swindled I had been, and how helpless back then I'd been to stop it.

'Jessica?'

Louise's voice startled me and I snapped my head up. 'What?' I said.

'Sure you don't want some of this?'

I only let my gaze rest on the label for a second before I turned away. Saint-Jeannet, in Vence. We had done a wine tour there that summer, all of us, before I was arrested. Saint-Jeannet had become synonymous with those happy days, and we had adopted it as the beverage of choice, not only for us but for Jenson Coast as well.

'No, I don't,' I said. Once again I left her in the room, hurrying past her back into the hall and up the stairs. I hoped she wouldn't follow me. I knew she would.

There wasn't much in the upstairs of my cottage. The stairs opened up into a large open-plan bedroom, a converted loft. There were floor-to-ceiling windows and roof lights on three sides, giving a panoramic view of the nature reserve and the fields and forest beyond. Usually I paused here, taking the time to look outside. Living here, you never knew what you'd see: geese in flight, deer in the fields, happy dogs running through the mud. I knew which season it was by what was happening outside. The arrival of autumn was announced by tractors and combines trundling along the lane. They started early, before the sun came up, and continued their endless journey up and down, up and down all day long. Summertime dawned with the birds. Blackbirds sang their sunrise chorus, beginning at four a.m. and carrying on all day until the darkness of night fell like a blanket over the fields, silencing them for a few short hours. In another time, another life, with a different man, with a *specific* man, I could have loved living here.

I didn't pause or even break my stride tonight, I moved across the natural oak floor to the en suite bathroom and slipped inside. I caught a glimpse of my face in the mirror-fronted cabinet and didn't like what I saw. I was pale – paler than usual – and my skin was shiny with perspiration. I plucked a tissue from the box on the side and wiped it over my face and neck.

Automatically, born out of years of practice, I reached into the cabinet and plucked the Tampax box from the back. Burrowing to the bottom, I pulled out my birth control pills, concealed underneath the tampons, and washed one down with a mouthful of tap water. I replaced the pill sleeve and carefully piled everything back on top, but as I put the box away, tucking it behind another box of feminine products, I paused. I felt myself break out in a sweat again, but this time it was almost euphoric. *I didn't have to hide my birth control pills any more!* Hell, I didn't even have to take the damn things any longer.

I pulled them back out of the box and put them on the side of the sink. They could stay there for now. Later, I might move them, to my night stand or my dressing table. For now, I could store them wherever I damn well wanted to. It was like a victory, and when I closed the cabinet door, I didn't flinch away from my reflection – I smiled at it.

I heard Louise's footsteps and she called my name as she reached the top of the stairs. I stepped out of the en suite to meet her.

'Jessica, I came here because I wanted to talk to you about everything that happened all those years ago. Will you hear me out?'

I nodded. I was reluctant, but I needed to know the extent of Patrick's actions back then. It had never been clear, and I had been floundering, unsure of who to cling to for support. I had been weak and frail, a little girl lost, so far removed from who I had been when I arrived in France. Now I had changed once more. I would never be that same life-loving girl again, I was someone entirely different now. I wanted nothing more than to walk out of this house and go far, far away. But I had to stay, at least for a little while.

Louise sped ahead of me, tripping back down the stairs, light on her feet these days, clouds for shoes. By contrast I was heavy, lumbering along; our personality and visual swap was like a slap in the face to me.

Grudgingly, I nodded for her to open the wine. Eagerly, happily, she passed me a full glass. I couldn't drink it; the aroma alone was almost too much. An assault on my senses that smelled like time gone by.

She had no trouble gulping down her glass. Talk was scattered and fragmented, lucidity draining away with the dregs of the Saint-Jeannet. Eventually she leaned her head back and fell mercifully quiet.

Leaving her asleep in the chair by the window, I crept from the conservatory into the lounge. I would have closed the door behind me, but Patrick had taken the doors off soon after we moved in.

She hadn't mentioned him much, I noted, considering that was why she had come here. Had he not died, I doubted I'd ever have seen her again. But she seemed to remember that summer through rose-tinted glasses, before it all went sour. Patrick had been there all the time, lurking in the office with my father, cooking up their plans and scams, but she hadn't seen him. All Louise saw was what she wanted to. First, Marco, then me; then, when I was out of the picture, she saw my life and the opportunity to step into my shoes and steal it from me.

I heard a creak from the room next door, then footsteps on the stairs. I let out an involuntary shudder. The noises in this house did that to me.

I rubbed at my shoulders, trying to relax. *You don't have to be scared of the sounds now,* I told myself. *He's gone. It's just Louise.*

Still I jumped when she came through the doorway into the lounge. I blinked at her.

'I borrowed a pair of your pyjamas,' she announced. 'Fleece isn't my usual style, but they'll do. It's bloody cold here, how do you stand it?'

Horror trickled through my veins. She was intending to stay. But what could I do, kick her out after she'd travelled hundreds of miles to see me?

'Jessica?'

She was waiting for a response, but I couldn't remember what her question was.

'What?' I asked dully.

'I said it's really cold.' She wrapped her arms around herself. 'I'm not used to it, the seasons, any more.'

'It's not too bad. Patrick doesn't usually put the heating on until at least November.' I stopped, looked out of the dark windows. There I went again, Patrick's rules still pinned to the noticeboard in my head, his instructions embedded so deeply that it would be a long time before I realised I could do what I wanted to now.

I stood up, walked past Louise into the kitchen and peered at the thermostat on the wall. It made no sense to me. As I straightened up, I realised that in the eight years I had lived here, I had not once been in control of the temperature of my home. I gave up, walked down the hall back into the lounge. It was chilly in here too, but at least I could fix that. I kneeled down in front of the open fire, took some of the logs that were supposed to be for decorative purposes out of the vintage scuttle and placed them neatly in the fireplace.

'Give us your lighter, will you, Louise?' I asked over my shoulder. 'And pass me that newspaper.'

She handed them both over, and within a minute I had a fire going. I sat back, gazing at my work, thrilled – though why, I didn't know. It was a simple, household chore. And as I watched the flames flicker, I went back to another time, when Ben and I had gone down to the beach and lit our own fire. He had used only his flint, like a true woodsman, and I remembered thinking that it was almost erotic, watching him create heat and light out of hardly anything.

Louise's hand pressed down on my shoulder, pulling me back to the present. I felt the roughness of her skin, itched to death, her go-to for relief or release, so engrained she didn't even realise she was doing it half the time. 'It's late, come to bed.'

I shook my head as I stared into the flames. 'You go up, make yourself comfortable. I don't want to sleep just yet.'

I heard her take a breath, as though she was going to argue, but she didn't.

'I'll see you in the morning,' I said, not looking at her. 'Goodnight, Louise.'

She stared at me, her eyes wide and hurt, before turning around. To my dismay, she didn't go upstairs. Instead she threw herself into the armchair by the window and crossed her arms over her chest.

'What happened when you escaped from the prison?' she asked.

Despite her question, her need to know, I realised that it was me who still wasn't clear on what had happened – or rather, I didn't know who was to blame for it. And it became suddenly obvious that Louise knew the truth, and it was likely the whole reason for her turning up here in England.

Now that Patrick was gone, she could tell me exactly what had happened eight years ago, when it seemed like everyone had turned against me. Which meant that something had stopped her back then. I leaned forward. This I wanted to hear. All the missing pieces of the puzzle; those I wanted – *needed* – to know.

She wasn't going to just tell me, though, I could see that from her new, hard, unfamiliar exterior. Louise wasn't a pushover any more.

I cast my mind back to that night, before Marco helped me escape. The night they had scooped me up from where I had collapsed next to Alexis's dead body, the poker that had killed her still in my hands.

'Where were you the night she died?' I asked, my voice rougher than I intended. 'You were with me, then you were gone.' I leaned forward, determined now to make her work as hard as she was making me work for the information we were going to trade. 'What happened after the police questioned you, Louise?'

And suddenly feeling much more awake than I had just five minutes ago, I leaned back, my posture mimicking hers as I folded my arms and waited for her to speak. Because we'd never talked about it, not really. She had walked away from me.

She had left me.

Chapter 9

Louise

Then

My world spun in a dizzying spiral. Round I went, then down, down, down.

Hands pulled at me, plucking me from the heap they found me in. I stared dumbly at the mud that streaked my skin and clothes. I looked at it for far too long, but it was better than looking through the French doors. Better to look at the mess I was in than the blood that was in there.

It wouldn't leave me, the sight of *them*, both of them. Jessica looking like she was sleeping. Alexis's eyes open, staring in my direction. Looking not at me, but through me, just the way they always had.

I came awake as the police led me around the front of the house, the images pulsing in my head hard enough to rouse me.

'Jessica… Alexis…' My voice was guttural, low and gravelly. Sagging against the policewoman, I twisted out of her grip. 'Are they… *dead*?'

But she didn't answer.

'Who did this?' A whisper now, so low that I don't think she even heard me. If she did, she ignored me again.

At the police station, she asked me to tell her what had happened. I stumbled through the night's events: the darkness, the deserted house, getting lost in the maze that was the land behind Alexis's home.

'Are they dead?' I asked again, more forcefully this time, finding strength from somewhere, strength that dissipated into sobs that racked me so hard I thought I would choke when she finally deigned to answer me.

'Ms Dubois, yes.' She eyeballed me. 'Jessica Jenson is fine.'

She hadn't looked fine. All that blood, on her hair, her face… But the policewoman would say no more.

Hours later, when the whole night had passed and they finally let me go, I found myself in Andrew's private study, the man himself on one side, while across the room, Marco paced up and down.

'What happened?' I implored, shrugging off the blanket someone had draped around my shoulders and catching Andrew's hand. 'Please…'

Andrew looked down at my hand, a searing gaze, like I was dirty and infecting him with my touch. I dropped my hand, lowered my eyes. Underneath the blanket, I scratched at the skin between my fingers. It felt like it was on fire.

'She found Alexis on the floor, unconscious,' said Andrew. 'She'd been hit on her head. Jessica couldn't see the blood, but she says that when she tried to get Alexis to stand up, she felt it.' He had turned an odd grey colour, and his fingers worked at his mouth. 'Poor girl. Poor, poor girl.'

I wondered who he was talking about, the victim or the witness.

'But Jessica was bleeding too, they were both attacked,' I said urgently. 'Where is Jessica? Has she been taken to hospital? Did she see who did this?'

Andrew's hands fell away from his face. He turned so his back was to me. 'Patrick says the police think it was a fight between the two girls. Jessica won.' He barked out a harsh, humourless laugh. 'It's ridiculous. I mean, Jessica barely knew Alexis.'

'Patrick?' I frowned. What did he have to do with this?

'Jessica's lawyer,' Andrew said absently.

'Jessica wouldn't do anything like—' I stopped, closed my eyes at the vision of the two girls, inert on the floor, the blood...

'Sit down, Louise.' Hands on me again. Marco or Andrew? I didn't know. I let them lead me back to the chair. A silence fell, heavy, like the blanket that was once more placed around me.

'Someone hit Jessica, she needed stitches.' Andrew's words were ragged, panicky. I wondered if he were thinking of his wife, Jessica's mother. He had lost her in tragic circumstances. Was he realising how close he'd come to losing his daughter too?

I wanted to go to him, to comfort him, but who was I to do such a thing? I thought of Jessica, the way she was so open, so loving. She wouldn't have hesitated.

I exchanged a glance with Marco. He sat by the window now, stoic and silent.

'What is this place?' Andrew waved a piece of paper in my face, back to his normal authoritative tone, though it still held an edge of fear. 'Where is Jessica now?'

I looked again at Marco, uncomfortable that Andrew's questions were all directed at me. Marco was up again, pacing the room once more, the cordless landline clamped to his ear, the fingers of his right hand running over his mobile phone.

'Louise!'

I jerked my gaze away from Marco and stared at the paper Andrew held. 'Um, the commissariat on Avenue de Grasse,' I replied.

'And they took you there too? But they let you go?'

My throat tightened at Andrew's accusatory tone; how many emotions must be running through him right now?

I swallowed against the bile. 'I could see her – them – through the glass. The police came through the front door. They saw me, they wanted to know what I'd seen.'

I didn't tell him that they had questioned me as though I was a suspect, having looked dubiously at the makeshift covers I'd placed over my shoes as I was skulking around the back of Alexis's property.

Alexis.

Alexis stretched out on the floor, blood all around her.

Alexis dead.

And Jessica arrested on suspicion of murder.

'I need to speak to Patrick again.' Andrew had fallen away from me, was talking to Marco. Marco tucked the phone between his chin and shoulder, waved an acknowledgement.

I watched him leave, and with Marco still tapping away on his mobile, I felt suddenly very alone, with just my thoughts for company.

How well did I know Jessica Jenson?

I knew her body as well as I knew my own. I knew her preferred choice of drink (vodka, straight up). I knew that coke made her fly and Ecstasy made her dance and weed made her melancholy.

Did I know she was incapable of murder?

Yes. Yes, I knew that. As much as she loathed Alexis, there was no way she would have killed her. She couldn't have killed her, Jessica was bone-thin and brittle, for goodness' sake.

'Walk with me,' commanded Marco, hanging up the phone, pulling me out of my thoughts.

I shrugged the blanket from my shoulders and followed him out of the room and into the bright light of a day that had suddenly turned dark.

I'd not spent time with Marco for a while, not since Jessica had needed me. I gazed at him now, remembering the fantasies I'd had about him before my dreams turned to her.

'Tell me everything, as it happened,' he demanded.

I took a deep breath and opened my mouth to speak. Before I could, Marco held up his hand and placed a finger against my lips. I looked at him, surprised, my mouth tingling at his touch.

'Don't try and remember what you told the police,' he said. 'Actually remember the night, walk yourself through it.'

'But the two are the same,' I replied when he took his finger away. 'What happened and what I told the police are the same thing.'

'I know. I just want you to use the memory of the night when you tell me what happened, instead of the memory of what you said to them.'

'We sat in the car for a bit—'

'How long?' Marco interrupted.

'Five minutes, maybe less.' I paused, waited until he nodded at me to continue. 'We talked about how maybe we had the wrong night, because it was so dark. Then I said maybe the party was outside, at the back of the place, and I got out of the car and went around to the boot to get my camera stuff out.'

'There was a power cut,' he said absently. 'So where was Jessica while you were getting your equipment?'

'I thought she was beside me, but she'd gone. I thought I saw her heading to the front door, so I got my equipment out myself. It took a few minutes, and when I went towards the villa, she was nowhere in sight.'

'What did you do?'

'I decided to go into the garden, see if my hunch about a gazebo was right. It was really dark; not only were all the properties in darkness, but the street lamps were out too. I took...' I stopped, opened my eyes, which I hadn't even realised were closed, and clutched blindly at Marco's hand.

'You took what?' he asked roughly.

'I took photos,' I whispered. I couldn't believe I had forgotten. 'I was clicking as I walked, using my flash to light up the path in front of me.'

'Where are they?'

I looked down at our hands, entwined now, his fingers crushed against mine. 'On my camera. I haven't had a chance to develop anything.' I felt the electricity transfer through our skin. What if I'd inadvertently captured something on film? What if I had a shot of the killer on my camera? I voiced my thoughts to Marco excitedly.

'We need to get them developed,' he said. 'But not in a shop, not anywhere public.'

'Marco, I'm a photographer.' I felt a slow smile creeping over my face as he looked at me blankly. 'I have a darkroom of my own.'

–

My apartment on Rue Léon Noël was small. On the top floor were the living quarters, a kitchen area and lounge that doubled as a bedroom. Below was a tiny basement, which I used as my darkroom. The basement was why I rented on Rue Léon Noël; apartments that contained a basement or cellar in the better areas of town were well out of my budget. As I showed Marco in, I watched him look around. I wished he could see what I saw when I sat in here on my own. I wished he would comment on my extraordinary pieces of feminist art, originals by Victoria Van Dyke and Cindy Sherman, and my favourite, a reproduction of Misty Copeland from Annie Leibovitz's 'Women' collection. But he wouldn't, he couldn't. They only existed in my mind. A lot of my life was fantasy, I couldn't afford the real thing.

Until now, that was, with Jessica and Marco and Andrew. I reminded myself as Marco glanced at my bare room that I was living the real thing now. If I kept in with these guys, maybe one day I *would* have Van Dykes, Leibovitzes and Shermans on my walls.

It was a bigger possibility than it had been a few months ago.

'Where's the darkroom, then?' he asked.

I scurried over to the basement door, wary of the impatient tone of his voice. He followed me down the concrete stairs, stood to one side as I switched on the light.

I waited for the fanfare, for the exclamation of surprise, of wonderment. For this room, though just a small, windowless cellar, this room I was proud of. Here was where all my money went and where all my talent lay. But Marco said nothing of the surroundings. Instead he asked, 'Isn't it all digital now?'

I spoke as I pulled out the first film to prep it for development, working as I talked. This was the one place I was comfortable, speaking about what I knew.

'Mostly, but I still use film. I like the process, this process,' I explained as I retrieved my developing chemicals and trays from the shelf. 'Digital is a great medium, but I still prefer the old way, especially for long-exposure shots. Flick that light switch off for me, will you?'

'What about when you want to Photoshop a picture?' Marco asked, as he moved closer to watch what I was doing.

'You mean retouching? I don't have much cause for that, but if I did, I'd know beforehand and I'd take along my digital equipment.' I could feel him behind me and I tried to concentrate on the job in hand.

I worked jerkily, unsteady, aware of his presence. The tension grew, along with the heat in the little airless room, as I darted back and forth, pegging up the prints. Marco moved forward, squinting to look at the images, which had yet to appear. I watched him, muttering an 'excuse me' when he got in my way. Eventually he retreated into a corner, sat on a little wooden stool. With his face concealed in the shadows, he spoke.

'You know, whatever you have with Jessica, it's not going to last,' he said.

I felt my face grow red. So he had heard the rumours too. The whispers around town that made me proud rather than ashamed. I tucked my chin to my chest, busied my hands.

He let out a little laugh when I didn't reply. It sounded like he was goading me – I didn't like it. His tone changed as he emerged from the shadows to stand beside me:

'You're talented, Lou. You could be something more, something better than Jessica's plaything.'

I looked over at him, not quite meeting his eye. He moved again, in front of me now, blocking me from my work table, filling my vision so I had no option but to look at him. His hand came up, tucked my hair behind my ear, his touch sending my face and chest ablaze.

'Why don't we see what other talents you've got?' He leaned in, his breath tickling my face, his other hand light on my waist, his touch harder as he moved lower.

My heart hammered in my chest at double time. I forced myself to hold his gaze, encouraged him with a smile that was slow in coming. I didn't know why he wanted me, not then, not at that moment.

Later – after – I would find out.

–

Eventually, awkwardly, I dressed and moved over to look at the prints.

I shivered, seeing the images of the path I'd walked that night. The pictures showed nothing; simply hedges, trees, the white brickwork of the villa and the creeping vines, all falsely lit by the flash of my camera.

I laughed to cover my disappointment. 'I really thought there might be something there.'

Marco came to stand by me. I looked away, blushing at his nakedness. 'Maybe there could be something there,' he said, rubbing his chin.

'What… where?'

He turned to me and smiled. My breath caught in my throat.

'You're talented, Louise. Couldn't you *make* someone be in the shots?'

I remembered his earlier comments about Photoshopping and retouching. I thought of what we had just done on the dusty floor of my darkroom, of how I had wondered why on earth he wanted me in that way.

My face felt pinched and tight, my stomach cramped as though someone had punched me. My hands pulsed and stung. I scratched absently at them. Now I knew why he had wanted me, wanted to make love to me.

I should have felt defeated, a failure. I should have felt used. But something twisted inside me, indignation, outrage. *Good old Louise, she'll do this, go there, pick this up, do this, do that. Show her a bit of flattery, some attention, and she'll be so grateful she'll do anything for anyone.*

But I had the power here, this one, single time, I had the skill, the talent. Maybe it was time for me to call the shots for a change. Maybe it was my turn to get what I wanted.

I had Jessica, but for how long? Until Ben came back? Until she tired of me? Until she got banged up for Alexis's murder? Until Andrew's lawyer friend Patrick offered her everything I couldn't? And if she discarded me, as she was bound to do, I'd be right where I was before. Unable to afford my rent, having to go home to England, to live once more with my parents.

My chest tightened at the thought.

I had to hold on to what I had. Her friendship was unstable, precarious. And if I was losing that – *her* – I needed a safety net.

I raised my eyes to meet Marco's. This time I didn't shy away from his gleaming, tanned, naked body.

I licked my lips, which were suddenly dry.

'Give me a few hours,' I murmured. 'I'll come to the casino later.'

He grinned, pulled me to him and crushed his lips down on mine.

I watched him leave, and when I heard the door close, I sat down at the counter and got to work.

-

There was a throng of journalists lining the long driveway when I returned to Jenson Coast later that day. I hovered around the fringes, head down, safe in the knowledge that nobody would know who I was, my invisibility working to my advantage for a change.

Pushing my way through the crowd of paparazzi, I headed to the closed reception door. Someone called my name and I stopped, turned. I ran my eyes over him, the nondescript middle-aged man. I had no idea who he was. But he knew me, he knew my name.

Nobody ever knew my name.

Thrilled and frightened in equal measure, I ran the rest of the way to the hotel. Behind me I heard pounding feet, and I pushed on until someone grabbed my arm.

I batted out my hand, connecting with something solid, then raised my fist to strike again.

'Jesus, Lou, it's me!'

I looked up to see Marco. For a moment I was confused, wondering where he had been, seeing as he'd left my flat hours ago. But there was no time to ask, as he grabbed my hand and pulled me the last few yards to the heavy oak door, which was closed for the first time since the hotel had opened.

'Oh my God, Marco,' I cried as he inserted his key, opened the door and pushed me in, 'it's mental out there!'

'It's only going to get worse,' he replied grimly, before running his eyes over the manila envelope I was clutching. 'Have you heard the latest?'

'No, what?'

Before he could reply, Andrew walked into the reception area and I slipped my faked photographs into my shoulder bag. 'Hi, Andrew, are you okay?'

He looked at Marco.

'I was just going to tell her,' said Marco.

'Tell me what?' I asked, swinging my gaze between the two men.

But neither of them spoke. Another man had appeared, ghost-like, from the shadows. As he looked me up and down, I shrank under his scrutiny.

'This is Patrick King, Jessica's lawyer,' said Andrew, almost wearily. I noticed that he didn't introduce me.

Fearfully, irrationally thinking that this Patrick knew of the fake pictures that were burning a hole in my bag, I turned to Marco.

Marco's mouth worked, his eyes flicking over my head in the direction of the two men.

'The police called,' he said finally as he locked his eyes on mine. 'Jessica escaped.'

Chapter 10

Did he sense I was about to call the wedding off? Did he somehow overhear my conversation with Louise? Was it information he had held onto, kept secret in case I got cold feet? Or had he planned all along to tell me this the day before our wedding?

He told me he was very ill, his words quiet as he looked out of the window of our room. 'I've got a cancer, up here.' He tapped at his head. 'I haven't got very long, I don't think, maybe a year.'

I giggled. Clapped my hands over my mouth. I told him I was sorry for the inappropriate laughter, and asked him what on earth he meant.

'I mean what I just said. I don't have very long left. I want to return to England and live there. I thought we could stay at your father's home, near the sea.'

'What?' I ran my hands through my hair and shook my head. It was a joke, but I couldn't find the punchline. 'What?' I asked again.

At last he turned to face me. The smile was still in place, but now it was more of a grimace. He walked around me and went to stand at the other window.

'Please don't make me keep repeating myself,' he said, his words clipped. 'Do you know how hard it is to say it once, let alone over and over again?'

'What?'

My vocabulary had left me; that single word was all that remained. My lips formed a pucker to say it again, but I stopped myself.

'I have a cancer. It will kill me, I can feel it every day. I want to go to England and stay there, I want to try and continue to work while I have my treatment. Palliative care.'

They were two different things; you either had one or the other, I knew that. But at the time, I didn't question him. My fingers worked at my mouth. I desperately wanted a cigarette, but Patrick didn't like me smoking.

At my silence, his eyes blazed. 'You'll be with me. You'll come to England with me. And we leave tomorrow.'

It wasn't a question, and despite my intentions to walk out of this room and away from Patrick, I found myself nodding. I was suddenly scared, and at that moment, I didn't know what I was so frightened of.

'I can't… What about our stuff?' My head spun; it was all I could think of to say.

'Stuff?' He frowned.

'My clothes… Everything is either at your home or at Jenson Coast.' I gestured to my small suitcase. 'All I brought here is my wedding outfit.'

'Oh, I see what you mean. I'm arranging for everything to be collected. It will be delivered to England, to your father's house. It will probably get there before we do!'

He chuckled. It was an awful sound.

'So tomorrow you'll be my wife, and you'll make me very happy.' He gazed at me expectantly and reached out his arms.

Stunned, I licked at my dry lips. His earlier words resounded inside my head: I haven't got very long. Over and over they repeated on a loop until I caught onto them and clutched them in my mind like a silent mantra.

It's not forever, Jessica, I told myself, and only then could I willingly go into his embrace.

Chapter 11

Jessica

Now

The escape. My moment of infamy. The biggest mistake I could have made, though it seemed like the only option at the time.

'So how did it happen, Jessica?' Louise's voice cut through my reverie, pulling me back to the present. 'Did you ask Marco for his help, or did he offer?'

I cast my mind back again, back to that awful damp concrete prison cell, and I closed my eyes and remembered.

—

When Patrick came to the prison and was led into my cell, in spite of the situation I was in, all I could think was: *This man is no help to me. This man is far too good-looking to be of any use to me at all.* What a stupid, juvenile thing to have thought. But I *was* juvenile back then. I was gullible, too.

In my defence, he didn't say much to change my initial opinion of him; he didn't even ask me what had happened in Alexis Dubois' house that night. Instead he told me what would happen next, that I would be transferred to the courthouse, that I was unlikely to be granted bail, though he would try, that the hearing would be just the start, that I wouldn't be expected to enter a plea at this stage. I stopped listening, sank to the piss-stained floor and began to cry.

'I can't stay here!' I wailed. 'If you can't help me, then you need to tell my father to find someone who can.' My thoughts began to trip over themselves at that point, and I decided that if this Patrick couldn't sort out my situation – legally and quickly – then we needed to explore other options. 'Listen to me, you tell my father and Marco Cooper everything. You let them handle it, okay?'

I sat back, rubbing at my eyes with the sleeve of the shitty prison-issue uniform they'd given me, listening to the sound of Patrick's expensive shoes as they clicked away from me down the concrete corridor.

Soon after Patrick's visit, I found myself in a white minibus with blacked-out windows. I wasn't alone; beside me sat a very young woman. She was dressed in a tank top and a tiny pair of high-waisted denim shorts. Her hair was long, dark and stringy, her fringe falling over her pale blue eyes. She looked at me repeatedly, and shuffled on her seat.

'*Aidez-moi?*' she whispered, her voice breaking. '*Aidez-moi?*'

I shrugged, wondering what she wanted help with. I couldn't even help myself, let alone her.

With just the girl and myself as passengers, plus one bored-looking guard and the driver, we set off. After ten minutes I heard an exclamation from the driver. The guard and I craned forward and my heart thumped in my chest as I spotted a roadblock up ahead. I looked around. We had pulled off the A8 highway; there was nobody behind us on this stretch.

'*Asseyez-vous!*' barked the guard, shouting at me to sit down, even though I hadn't stood up.

He made his way down the aisle, speaking too rapidly for me to understand. I tensed as the minibus slowed to a crawl and then stopped. The girl looked over to me again.

'*Qu'est-ce qui se passe?*'

I shushed her, swore under my breath as the dust from the roadside puffed up around the windscreen, obscuring my view. Then a shout, a thud, and the vehicle seemed to rock in slow motion. I grabbed at the armrest to steady myself. The door bent inwards, buckling under the weight of something or someone as the driver and the guard attempted to blockade it. At the sound of grating metal, the girl beside me screamed, long and loud.

I stood, sidestepped the girl's hands as she reached out for me and hurried down the bus towards the front. It was silent now, and all I could see was the twisted metal of the door. Smoke began to creep in around the bent frame. Through it I could see daylight, and I pushed on, shoving aside pieces of the door, desperate now to get out into the clean air, wondering where the guard was, where the driver had vanished to, who else was out there. My heart thumped and I put my hand on my chest. Was this one of the natural highs Ben was always harping on about? I spat out a laugh that turned into a sob.

There was a black saloon car parked on the verge a hundred yards down the road, and moving like a zombie, I headed for it. It wasn't a car I recognised, and I couldn't see anyone in the vehicle through the black-tinted windows.

Reaching out for the handle of the back door, I paused; then, throwing caution to the wind, I pulled it open and peered inside.

Marco's head appeared between the front seats like a smiling lunatic.

'Get in,' he ordered. 'Quickly.'

But I was frozen. I had known he would come if Patrick followed my instructions to tell my father that I wasn't leaving the prison straight away, that I was being transferred, facing trials and hearings and pleas. Because that was what my father did: he looked out for me. His money had bought my freedom before, back in Spain, but that was on a stupid drugs charge. This was different, this was murder. And it suddenly became clear to me that if I ran now, I was as good as admitting that I was guilty.

'Get in!' urged Marco.

But my procrastinating had wasted time, I saw now, as I glanced back at the bus. My fellow prisoner stood on the steps, hands cuffed in front of her, looking left, looking right, looking dazed. Tentatively she raised her left leg, stepped onto the road and stumbled over towards us.

'Drive,' I instructed Marco as I leaped into the car, my mind suddenly made up by the approach of the girl.

Then she was there, pulling the door handle and sliding into the back seat with me. I gaped at her, shouted at Marco to get her out. In the distance I heard sirens, and I pushed at the girl, leaned over her and opened the car door. She squealed, wrenched my hands off and slammed the door again.

'Fuck!' I cried, and then to Marco, 'Just go!'

I held onto the seat as we sped away and glanced over at the interloper. I wondered what she had done. I wondered how soon we could get her out of the car.

I couldn't see the guard or the driver behind us and I didn't ask Marco about them. I didn't care what had happened to them, if they were hurt, tied up. Did I care that they might be dead? The thought never even crossed my mind. It never occurred to me to think much about their fate, just like I hadn't given too much thought to the fate of Alexis Dubois.

It was me, it was all about me. My life was at stake. Based on this plan of his, Marco had assumed my guilt, and by getting in the car, I had as good as told him that he was right.

And I was sure that I would pay.

—

'I never found out if my father was in on my escape, or if it was just Marco,' I said to Louise.

I imagined that my father hadn't known, for if he had, he wouldn't have moved me just a few kilometres over the border into Italy. No, he'd have got me far, far away, to a place from where I couldn't be extradited.

If that had happened, right now I'd be sunning myself on a Cambodian beach or winding my way through an Indonesian market. I glanced out of the window at the black fields. I wouldn't be here in England, that was for sure.

'And the girl, the other prisoner, Francesca? They never found her,' said Louise.

I shrugged. No, they didn't. They never found Francesca.

Louise pushed herself up from the armchair and moved over to sit beside me. 'But how were *you* found? You were hiding, Marco had arranged for you to stay in Ben's villa. Do you know how the police tracked you down?'

The memory of my second arrest washed over me. I screwed my eyes shut. It didn't help, I still saw it. I still tasted the dirt of the olive grove in my mouth as my face was pushed to the ground.

I'd never known how the police came to descend on me that day. But as Louise's warm hand slipped into my own and I opened my eyes to stare into hers, I realised that she knew.

And she was going to tell me.

Chapter 12

Louise

Then

It was the first time I'd met Patrick, though I'd eaves-dropped on his conversation with Andrew about Jessica that night in the bar. Marco hated Patrick's interference; Jessica thought he was hot. I thought back to the conversation I'd listened to. Someone to take her in hand, Andrew had said. I wondered what Patrick thought of her now, an escaped fugitive, on the run from a murder charge.

I looked to Marco for guidance; I didn't know what to say, how to react. I wondered if he could hear my breathing, see it hitching in my chest. Did he sense my fear about what I'd done, what I carried in my bag? Did he think I was about to produce the faked photos and blow this thing up even bigger? I widened my eyes, opened my mouth. Before I could speak, Marco grabbed my arm and hurried me through to the deserted restaurant.

In a dark corner he waited patiently until my breathing had slowed. After a few minutes he looked meaningfully at my bag.

'I'm scared, Marco,' I blurted out. 'This is… this is a big deal.' I lowered my voice. 'This is illegal.'

His eyes flicked towards the ceiling.

I pushed on regardless. 'Is this really necessary? Don't you think the police will find the real killer, without fake evidence like this?' I paused, indicated the bag. 'By doing this, it looks like we think Jessica killed Alexis Dubois.'

He stared back at me, his expression unfathomable. 'Do you really think she didn't kill her?'

I fell back in my chair. My words came out in a whisper: 'If you believe that, why would you want to get her off the hook?'

Resting his elbows on the table, he put his face very close to mine. 'Because this place took every pound I had to build. I cannot fail at it, do you understand?'

Gone was the happy, cheerful, cheeky man I'd got to know. We were down to the wire now; this was the real Marco, the one behind the smiles. He was afraid too, only his fear was for a different reason.

'My parents remortgaged their house for this. I borrowed in every way I could: banks, family, friends. Louise, if Jenson Coast carries on the way it has been, my debts will be paid off within a year. If not…' Tailing off, he grabbed my hand, brought it to his cheek, rough with a day's stubble. 'I can't lose at this, do you understand?'

'But Jessica is nothing to do with this place—'

'Fucking hell, Louise, don't be naïve!' he hissed. I shrank back from him, but his grip on my hand didn't loosen. 'Her name, her surname is the name of this hotel,' he breathed, his voice a mixture of fury, fire and fear. 'It has to be cleared. It just *has* to be.' Dropping my hand, he raised his own and brushed his knuckles down the side of my face. A different Marco now, wheedling, pleading. 'Help me, Louise.'

It was money. It all came down to money, all the time, everything. It was what I lacked, what I needed to succeed in my life here. I latched onto people who had it. They had it in spades, but it was all fake. Borrowed. On loan from banks and family, buried in buildings and businesses, just to keep them afloat until the real cash came along.

I managed to pull free from his grip. Sitting back in the chair, I crossed my arms across my chest.

'You're not the only one taking a risk here, Marco,' I began. I cleared my throat, spoke more forcefully than was natural for me. 'I need some reassurances too. I need this to be worth my while.'

His eyes flicked from side to side before settling on my face. 'How much?'

I was momentarily dumbfounded. Hurt. Was that what he thought of me, that I would blackmail him? *But isn't that what you've been thinking ever since he made love to you and made you think it was because he actually wanted you?*

'Oh…' I sighed. 'I—'

He interrupted me. 'Let me know, yeah? We'll sort something.' He raised his eyebrows, looked pointedly at my bag.

I kept it clutched against me. Now it was Marco's turn to sigh.

'Lou, we'll be okay. I promise.' He smiled, but his eyes were small and narrow as his hand came around the back of my head, pulling me close to him. He whispered his promise again, this time into my mouth. When we drew apart, I took out the envelope and slid it across the table to him.

I moved my chair around as he pulled out the prints, and pointed out the 'perpetrator' I'd 'unwittingly' caught in the shots. There were six of them in all, four of him by the French doors. One showed just a shadow and the other the smallest portion of a piece of material, just disappearing out of shot, a coat-tail in the breeze.

'Louise, these are excellent.' Marco's grin was like the sun coming out from behind a cloud, so unlike his sombre mood of moments before that I matched his smile with one of my own as he put an arm around me. 'Who is this man?'

I shrugged. 'No idea, just a passer-by in a batch of old photographs.' I was proud as I looked at my work, at this man who really was nobody. He was unidentifiable: a shadow, a ghost.

'I picked him because he's wearing a dinner jacket, see?' I pointed out the coat-tail. 'He was dressed up for something fancy, but he's too out of focus for anyone to actually work out who he is, no matter what technology the police use. These are not digital, and there are no negatives.' I pulled a mock-mournful face. 'I accidentally threw them away.' I sat back at this, biting the side of my nail as worry pushed aside my pride. 'That won't matter, will it? The police won't insist on having an ID?'

He shook his head, no, and I glowed, basking in his obvious pleasure at my work.

'I wish I'd known how skilled you were before...' He tailed off, his smile fading.

'Before what?' I asked, but even before I'd finished speaking the words, I *knew*. I sat upright, felt my eyes widen as it hit me. 'Marco, you helped her escape!'

It wasn't a question, and to his credit he didn't try to deny it. Instead, his eyes still on my prints, he shrugged.

'Where is she?' My whisper came out in a hiss as the fear rose in me again. 'What did you do?'

He rolled his shoulders, sat up straighter in his chair.

'She's in Begato, just outside Genoa. Ben is renting a villa there.'

I sat back, deep in thought. So Jessica was back with Ben. In her rightful place, where she belonged.

It was over, then. What she and I had had was finished.

Surprisingly, the grief didn't drown me, not like I had imagined it would. And I wondered, was it Jessica I had wanted, or just a way to insert myself into this family? And if that was the case, hadn't I done that? Hadn't I proved my worth by jeopardising my name and my career with my illegal Photoshopping of the party prints?

I reached hesitantly for Marco's hand. If Jessica was back with Ben, he was my only chance now. And he *owed* me.

'They'll need to be careful. The police will have passed her details over the border. How safe is Begato? How secluded is the villa? She'll need to stay hidden, at least until we've got these prints to the police.'

As Marco opened his mouth to reply, a door clanged shut behind us. We both sat up, spun around and saw the curtain across the fire exit still moving.

'Andrew?' Marco called, but he was greeted only with silence.

Disentangling his hand from mine, he got up and opened the door, but the brightly lit corridor that led to the casino was empty.

'Just the wind,' he said as he came back to sit beside me.

I searched his face, usually so open and cheerful, and was dismayed to see worry etched across his features.

We sat in silence for a long time.

'Let's take the photos to the police,' I said eventually. 'Maybe after we can get some dinner?'

'We should get them to the detective,' he agreed.

I noticed he ignored my question about dinner. Internally I squirmed. If I were going to keep him onside, I was going to have to work hard. When he made no attempt to get up, I fell back in my chair, deep in thought. How? How could I keep him, how could I broach the subject of my status?

I opened my mouth to speak again, still unsure of what I was going to say, when the door to the reception crashed open and Andrew stumbled in. We looked up as he shouted out for us, not seeing us straight away in the dimly lit corner.

'What is it? What's wrong?' Marco called.

He made his way to our table, leaned over and rested his hands on it before looking up at each of us in turn.

'They've located her,' he muttered. 'They're on their way to arrest her now.'

I exchanged a look with Marco, but before either of us could say anything, the door opened again. Striding through it, mobile clamped to his ear, came Patrick King. My stomach cramped at the sight of him, just the way his eyes raked over Marco and me. He held his hand up, a silent instruction for quiet, even though neither of us had spoken. Finally, he snapped his phone shut, put it in his inside jacket pocket and looked at me again before settling his gaze on Andrew.

'She's been found in a villa near Genoa.' He glanced at Marco. 'I'm going there now, I don't want the police making her talk without me present.'

Marco stepped forward. 'We'll go with you, buddy,' he said easily. 'She'll be glad of some familiar faces.'

And so into Patrick's Mercedes we all climbed, not speaking, surrounded by an ill-fitting awkwardness that I couldn't explain. It was Andrew who broke the silence, angrily spitting out his words.

'What is she doing in Genoa?' He turned around and glared at Marco and me, as though we held all the answers. Which of course we did, but he didn't know that.

I averted my eyes from his angry stare. In the rear-view mirror I saw Patrick scrutinising me. He smiled at me, and I looked away again, this time out of the window.

As we drove, I thought of the door slamming shut earlier, the feeling that someone had been eavesdropping on our conversation.

I looked back at the mirror: Patrick was still watching me.

–

When we turned off the dusty main road onto a track that seemed barely wide enough for the car, we were suddenly joined by four police cars, blue lights flashing, sirens blaring.

Was Jessica really hiding down here? With my face to the window, I looked around. All I could see for miles was acres of olive groves, separated in a haphazard fashion by low stone walls and taller brick structures. Then something else caught my eye.

'It's Ben!' I called. 'Stop the car!'

I felt Patrick's glare on me, but I yanked at the handle, opening the door so he had no option but to screech to a standstill. I jumped out and ran the few feet back to Ben, pulling up sharply at the look on his face.

'She's in the villa,' he hissed as he grabbed my arm. He looked aghast at the police cars that sped down the lane, past our stationary car.

'Someone told them where she was hiding,' I replied grimly. I glanced back at the Mercedes. It had resumed without me, trundling down the track after the police cars. 'Come on,' I said, and tugged on Ben's arm, 'we need to get to her.'

But he pulled away from my grip, his eyes darting left and right, anywhere but at me. 'I'm sorry, Louise,' he said with an apologetic shrug. 'I… I can't be part of this. I have to think of my reputation.' He pulled his hands through his short hair and shook his head. 'I'm so sorry, I need to leave.'

Stunned, I watched as he hurried away. Surely the police would want to speak to him? After all, he'd harboured an escaped fugitive. As he grew smaller and smaller in the distance, I turned around and began the trek after Patrick's car.

'Tell her I'm sorry!' Ben called, his voice tinny and faraway.

But I didn't reply. I didn't even acknowledge that I'd heard him.

I saw that the cars had stopped. A cloud of dust obscured my view, and I stopped and leaned on the low stone wall that ran down the right-hand side of the villa's grove. As I shaded my eyes from the low afternoon sun, I saw a figure streaking through the gnarled olive trees.

'Jessica…' Her name came from my lips in a whisper, and then, louder, 'JESSICA!'

But she wasn't going to stop, and I pushed myself off the wall and ran the last few hundred yards to come to a standstill by Marco.

'She's in the grove,' I wheezed. 'She's running.'

She emerged from the trees now and was sprinting full pelt towards the higher wall that ran down the left side of the property. With a rebel yell, she launched herself at it, and my heart leaped as she clung to the top, her feet scrabbling for purchase.

A scream, shouts from the police, and a heart-wrenching wail that I realised came from Andrew as the police surged. Then she was on the floor, her face buried in the dusty red earth as they twisted her arms behind her and slapped the cuffs on her wrists.

It was the single worst thing I'd ever witnessed, including Alexis's dead and bloodied body. With that, I'd only seen it when it was over. Now, here, I saw it all. And as Jessica struggled to raise her head, she look straight at me. I heard myself gasp at the sight of her face, dirtied with the red soil, the only clean patches made by the tracks of her tears. Subconsciously I moved towards Marco, knowing that now I'd seen this, I'd never be able to look at Jessica the same way.

I glanced at Andrew, who seemed suddenly very old, frail almost. He too couldn't take his eyes off his daughter, and the look on his face was almost worse than Jessica's.

I put my arms around him and led him back to the car. To my surprise, he let me.

Once I'd deposited him in the passenger seat, I returned to Marco. 'It was him, wasn't it? It was Patrick who told the police where Jessica was. But why? He's her lawyer, he's paid to defend her, why would he lead the police here?'

He didn't answer. Instead, clutching my wrist, he moved us towards the police car that Jessica was being loaded into. Patrick swept past, and I shuddered, wondering if he had heard my comment. But he ignored us, and bent down to speak to Jessica through the open window.

'I've got something, Jessica, photos that will get you off, so just hold tight and don't say anything to anyone until I'm with you, okay?'

I stiffened at his words. *Photos that will get you off.* It was true, there were photos, but Patrick didn't know that. Nobody knew yet except Marco and me. I looked at Jessica, at her dirty face from which her emerald eyes shone. Reaching through the window with her restrained hands, she clutched at his, her eyes gleaming with gratitude.

I felt like I could vomit. She was thanking *him*. But it was my work that was getting her off. It was *me*. I was invisible. Again.

'Lou, come on, we need to get to the police in Cannes before he does,' Marco muttered in my ear. 'Come on, now!'

And not knowing what was going on, nor what Patrick's game was, I let myself be led away.

Chapter 13

Jessica

'Patrick told the police where I was?' My voice was dull, blunted. Louise had expected fury and fire, but in all honesty, I had always wondered if my husband had had a hand in my capture. Not at first. No, for a very long time I was exceptionally naïve about him and the games he played. But later, when I opened my eyes to the world around me, then I had suspected.

'You knew it was him?' Louise's exclamation was one of astonishment. Ironically, her tone matched the one she had hoped to hear from me.

'Not then. Not until…' I trailed off, had to be careful of what I said.

'We never knew for sure,' Louise went on, 'but who else could it have been?'

Anger, simmering red-hot rage, swirled in my belly. What was Louise doing here now, eight years after I'd actually needed her? Where had she been then? I swallowed against the bile that rose in my throat. Now she had all the questions – but it was too late for the answers.

'I need to get some sleep,' I muttered. 'Are you taking the couch or upstairs?' I looked away from her as I asked the question, needing to ensure she knew we were not sharing a bed.

And as she flailed around, trying to find words to placate me, I looked at her properly for the first time. She had been so cute back then. A roly-poly, chubby little girl, out in the wide world with no idea of how to handle herself. So young. So innocent. She had loved me. She had idolised me. And I'd enjoyed it, enjoyed having a sidekick who would do anything I wanted.

I patted the sofa around me, searching for my phone before remembering that I'd left it upstairs. I moved to go and retrieve it, but Louise had already stood up, was making her way huffily to the door.

I let her go.

Once again, I felt heavy with fatigue, and I closed my eyes, pressing my fingertips against the lids.

–

Photographs, Patrick had explained, when we were back at the police station and alone in the interview room. Prints taken unwittingly by Louise that proved someone else had been there, that someone else had bludgeoned poor Alexis Dubois over the head.

I was shocked, speechless.

'They've been submitted as evidence in your defence, but here…' He pulled out a phone from his breast pocket, hit a few buttons and spun it to face me. 'These are only photos of the photos, but if you zoom in, you can see.'

I took the phone and stared at it dumbly, not really registering what I was supposed to be looking at. For a long moment there was silence, then the screen went blank in my hand. Still I continued to look at it. I heard the scrape of metal on the concrete floor, then the phone was removed carefully from my hand and I looked up to see Patrick's face inches from mine. He tapped at the screen, held the phone himself this time as he showed me again. For a long time I didn't look at it, I looked at his face instead. Then with his thumb and forefinger he made the picture bigger and *I saw it*. A man, pale and ghostly in the shadow of the porch. I was chilled, suddenly and thoroughly, right down to the bone.

'What does this mean?' I didn't dare hope, couldn't say the words I wanted to.

Patrick smiled at me, placed his hand on my shoulder. 'It means that very soon this will likely be over. Right now, you're free to go.' But his smile vanished so quickly that I blinked in surprise. 'The police don't trust foreigners. They want a killer caught and banged up, it doesn't matter who they are. These photos, don't question them, Jessica. Accept them.'

'What?' I said, not understanding.

He straightened up, put his hands in the pockets of his trousers and walked the length of the room. I watched him, noted how graceful he was.

'You are in a very unusual position, Jessica,' he began as he leaned against the wall. 'Do you have any idea of your wealth, of what your standing could be in society?'

I rolled my eyes. Yes, I knew of our wealth. I knew that it let me lead the life I'd been living up until now.

'Did they find the other girl, the one who was in the police van?' I asked suddenly, and looked over at Patrick.

He shrugged, held out his hands. 'Still missing, I think.' He dropped his hands, came back towards me and leaned on the table. 'Jessica, I'm trying to tell you something.'

I was chastised. Patrick made me feel that way, like he was a real grown-up and I was a silly little girl. I dropped my gaze, muttered an apology.

'It's okay, I know this is a lot to take in. But what I'm trying to say is, there is a lot of interest in you, in your activities. You have to surround yourself with people who have your best interests at heart, and right now, you're not doing that. The people who profess to be your friends have the capacity to damage you and your future.'

My stomach flipped, almost like I'd been winded. He was talking about Marco, of course he was. Marco had orchestrated this whole thing at my behest. But was he telling me that Marco had told the police where I was hiding? I sat back heavily in my chair and pulled the neck-line of my T-shirt away from my throat. I became aware of Patrick still leaning over, still regarding me carefully, and I breathed out slowly.

'It's okay, we got this in time – thank goodness for these photographs, really. And I suppose we have Louise to thank for them, even though she didn't know what she was snapping at the time. I wonder...' Patrick tailed off, stood up and paced back to the far wall. 'I wonder...'

'What?' I asked. 'What do you wonder?'

He shook his head, smiled again. 'It doesn't matter, it's over now. Nobody can extort anything, nobody is going to blackmail you, not while I'm looking after you.'

I stood up then, crossed the room to him. Every single cell was on fire as I grabbed his arm, spun him around to face me. 'You think Marco and Louise were going to blackmail me over this evidence?'

'Oh no, I don't know that.' He shook his head vehemently.

'But you suspect it, right?' I was disbelieving, but the more I thought about it, the more it seemed that it could be true. Louise wouldn't think of it, but with Marco next to her, whispering in her ear... They were going to take these photos to my father and offer them up as evidence in exchange for him handing over his share of Jenson Coast. Because if it were all innocent, why hadn't they showed them to the police straight away? Why break me out and wait until I had been caught before coming up with this proof of my innocence? 'That's it, isn't it, I'm right, aren't I?' My vision blurred, my body shook and bile rose in my throat. I felt my legs trembling and I turned around, arms outstretched, needing to get back to my chair before I fell down. Then, from behind, Patrick's arms closed around me and the fire inside was cooled. We stayed like that for a long while, as he whispered words of comfort.

Marco, Louise, Ben, my father... Eventually they all faded from my mind until all that was left was one name.

Patrick.

Ah, Patrick, he got me all right, just where he wanted me. And for a brief time, I forgot about everyone else. He was my saviour.

My white knight.

My prince.

And like the silly little girl I was back then, I let myself believe the fairy tale he offered me.

Chapter 14

Jessica's Diary
September 2011

As we flew from France to England, I repeated three words to myself constantly: It's not forever. But then, as we drove out of the airport and headed towards the M25, Patrick presented me with another bombshell.

'You realise that when we get to our home, I'm going to have to surrender your passport?'

I froze, in the process of fastening my seat belt. I let go and it pinged back, the clasp hitting the window.

'Careful,' he murmured.

'What the hell do you mean?' I shouted, twisting around in my seat to look at him. 'Why the hell would I need to surrender my passport?'

'Jessica, please.' He winced, stroked at his scalp. 'Don't shout.'

This was me, the woman he had married. The one who shouted, screamed, threw epic tantrums until she got her way. But of course, he didn't know that, did he? Because he didn't really know me. He liked what he saw, he liked what he'd heard from my father, but he didn't know me.

And I didn't know him, not really.

But I was beginning to.

'I'm sorry.' I lowered my voice, contrite. 'But I don't understand why.'

'You're a suspect in a murder case, you know that.' He pulled out onto the motorway and glanced over at me, impatience evident in his expression. 'I did explain this to you, don't you remember?'

I thought back over our conversations, I remembered the odd way he had sold the marriage to me, something about spousal privilege, and him not being able to testify against me in court. I did not recall him ever mentioning that he would have to surrender my passport.

'But how will I be able to go back to France if I don't have a passport?'

He indicated, pulled onto the hard shoulder, put the handbrake on and turned to face me. 'Jessica, you can't go back to France unless they catch the real killer of Alexis Dubois.'

I fell back against the headrest and stared out of the window. I put my hand on my throat, trying to push down the lump that sat there painfully. Patrick waited a beat, and when it became clear that I wasn't going to – or couldn't – speak, he started the car and drove on.

'It's ironic, really,' he said, his voice jolting me in the silence.

'What is?'

'Well, the photos that Louise developed, they may have put the police on the wrong track. They'll be wasting their time seeking someone who quite simply doesn't exist.'

I breathed in sharply and held my breath. I understood that in Louise's eagerness to help get me out of prison, she had inadvertently stashed me away in another jail. I burned with anger towards her then.

–

I watched his retreating back as he went up the stairs of our new home. No carrying me over the threshold, no romantic first night together.

I didn't follow him. Instead I went into the lounge and sat down. Rifling through my shoulder bag, I came across a crumpled pack of cigarettes. I shook one out, saw a box of matches next to the fireplace, grabbed them and lit it with shaking hands. I paced around the room, breathing in deeply, closed my eyes as I felt the burn in my throat. Above me I heard the bedroom door open and a footfall on the landing.

'Jessica, are you smoking down there?'

I looked at my cigarette, the tip glowing mockingly at me in the dusk.

Yes, I was smoking. That was what I did. I smoked, drank, did whatever I wanted to.

But not any more, it seemed.

Without warning, my legs turned to liquid and as they went from under me, I sat down hard on the cold wooden boards, my back to the door. With the cigarette clamped between my lips, I crawled across the floor and dragged myself up onto the sofa. My throat ached, and to try and numb it, I inhaled deeply until the cigarette burned down to the filter. I looked around for an ashtray, could see none within reach, so I spat on the end of the cigarette, squeezed it between finger and thumb and laid it on the coffee table in front of me.

Then I folded my hands in my lap, tilted my head back and opened my mouth in a silent scream.

Chapter 15

Jessica

Now

There was somebody outside. I couldn't hear them, or see them, but I sensed them.

I raised my eyes to the ceiling, safe in the knowledge that Louise was still up there, still sleeping. *Her* I could hear, or her snores, anyway.

Pulling the drapes back just a little, I saw the woman standing in the glow of the porch light, eyes raised as she looked at the CCTV cameras that Patrick had installed.

Detective or constable or officer – I couldn't remember her rank, but I recalled her hard eyes and even harder voice.

Nina Hart.

My heart began to beat faster as she raised her hand and knocked on my front door.

The cottage seemed to still itself around the sound of her firm rap. In the quiet of the too-early dawn, it sounded like a gunshot. I remained where I was, motionless, watching as she glanced up at the camera that trained its red eye on her.

For a moment she was out of sight, then I heard the unmistakable sound of the letter-box flap.

Holding my breath, I moved quietly into the hall and stared at the small white card on the floor.

I couldn't see her any longer, but I knew she was there.

'Why aren't you answering the door?' The voice behind me made me jump. I turned to see Louise halfway down the stairs.

I ignored her and crouched down to pick up the card.

The letter box shot inwards, and a pair of eyes looked straight at me.

'Jessica, I can see you there. Can you open the door, please?' Nina's voice, confident and authoritative, echoed around the hall.

Still I crouched, frozen.

'For God's sake!' Louise ran down the last few stairs, nudged me out of the way and pulled open the door.

'Hello?' she said. 'Can I help you?' Her voice was brisk, commanding. She sounded just like I used to.

Hart's gaze didn't falter as she stared back at her. 'And you are?'

I moved, finally, hauling myself upright with the help of the banister. 'Louise, this is Detective Hart, from the police station.'

Hart fixed her cool eyes on me. 'Constable Hart,' she said.

'Louise is a guest.' I stuttered over the mistake I'd made about the constable's rank, vaguely remembering a time when there was nothing and nobody that could make me falter. 'From France.'

Nina's face changed when I mentioned Louise's name. I knew then that she'd looked into everything: me, her, Patrick, Alexis.

I tried to claw my way back to control. Clearing my throat, I said, 'What can I do for you, Constable?'

'We'll be performing the autopsy on your husband later. You left the station in such a hurry, I didn't get a chance to inform you.'

It seemed a strange thing to come to tell me, seeing as dawn hadn't even yet broken. There was more to her visit. The realisation chilled me. 'Thank you,' I managed. 'Will there be anything else?'

Nina didn't answer as she gazed around the hallway, into the kitchen, up around the ceiling. She kept her face neutral, but I know she had spotted it: another CCTV camera above the door of the kitchen, and yet another inside the kitchen, covering the back door. Behind it, around the fixings, were black score marks that stood out on the white woodwork. I knew what she was thinking: that this camera had been moved, swivelled often to change the direction it was pointing in. Did she know why? To point away from the back door, to conceal at certain times someone coming in or going out?

I moved then, blocking her view, and watched as she mustered a cool smile.

'Thank you for your time, Mrs King,' she said, and with a last glance at Louise, she backed out of the door.

On the sofa again, sleep was surprisingly easy to fall into. I dreamed of a voice that I loved to hear, and willed myself to stay asleep to listen to it. But a hand was on my arm, the voice now whispering urgently in my ear. I shrugged it off, turned over and tried to fall back into my dream, but it was too late: I was awake. I pushed my hair out of my eyes and sat up, and it hadn't been a dream.

'Ben!' I clutched the blanket to me before throwing it aside and grabbing him in a bear hug. 'What are you doing here? You shouldn't be in here!' I glanced frantically around, pushing him away, intending to hustle him out of the house before Patrick woke up.

Then it crashed back at me: Patrick wouldn't be waking up. Ever.

I fell back onto the sofa, rubbed my eyes. 'Sorry, Ben.' I smiled up at him. 'I forgot for a minute there.' Then another thought occurred to me: I hadn't told him that Patrick had died. 'How did you know?'

He grimaced, his beautiful mouth twisting like he was sucking a lemon. 'There are people out there, reporters, I think, hanging around the car park like flies around— Oh, hello, Louise.'

A cold shiver ran through me at the sight of her standing in my pyjamas in the doorway to the lounge. She stared at Ben, clearly shocked to find him in my home. I looked away from her, at my hands folded neatly in my lap.

'Ben, good to see you.' Coolly, she walked over and gave him a perfunctory kiss on both cheeks before sitting next to me and draping my blanket over her knees. 'What were you saying about reporters?'

Ben looked from her to me. I imagined how we appeared, huddled together like lovers underneath a shared blanket. Or was that just my paranoia again?

'No reporters have knocked on the door,' I said.

He glanced at his watch. 'It's still early.' He winked at Louise. 'Even the paparazzi have some standards.'

Louise pulled a cushion out from behind her and chucked it at him. 'Prick,' she said mildly.

I watched their easy banter closely. It was obvious their friendship had grown over the years. I could feel Louise's stare burning into me. I recalled my words to her yesterday, how it'd been years since I'd seen Ben. I avoided looking at her and instead got up from the sofa.

'I came up the side lane and let myself in.' He looked at me suddenly. 'You need to lock your doors, Jessica.'

I nodded guiltily. Patrick had always been responsible for locking up the house. Patrick had been in charge of everything.

'What happened – to Patrick, I mean?'

I half expected Louise to answer Ben's question. I don't know why. I suddenly remembered that I was his wife, this was my home. Too much time following his lead. I'd become unable to think or speak for myself.

'We're not sure,' I murmured. 'They're doing a post-mortem today.'

There was a silence that stretched on so long it was uncomfortable. I heard the squeak of leather as Louise got up.

'Drink, Ben?'

I looked up. 'We'll both have a black coffee, please.'

'Cheers, Louise,' he replied.

When she had left the room, I turned to him again. The sight of him revived me, churned up something that I'd not felt for so long. Happiness, pure and simple. 'Come out for a walk with me? We'll go out of the side door and up the lane into the woods,' I cast a glance at the sound of Louise singing in the kitchen as she made our drinks. 'Come on.'

I slid my feet into my shoes and took Ben's hand. From the lounge we walked briskly down the hall and into the kitchen. I paused, watching Louise scoop out instant crap rather than using Patrick's fancy machine. 'Back in a while,' I called as I opened the back door.

Then we were out before she could reply, moving across the dew-soaked grass and coming out onto the lane that ran alongside the house. As we ran, hand in hand, my tension began to melt away.

I half expected her to come after us, to demand to know where we were going, inviting herself along too, but the lane was empty behind us. It was still early. A mist clung to the land, the birds the only noise we could hear. We walked on in silence, forking off at a footpath, and stopped at an old well, sitting on the concrete edge and looking down into the seemingly endless depths of it.

Ben chucked a pebble in and we listened to the splashing echo. 'What happened with Patrick?'

'I don't know,' I told him. 'Not yet. The post-mortem is—'

'Today, I know. You told me.'

I shrugged, leaned back and let the early-morning sun fall on my face.

'What do you think happened to him?'

I sighed. He wasn't going to let it go. 'I don't know – a heart attack, maybe? I think he thought his damn cancer was back, maybe he ended it. Can we not talk about Patrick?'

Ben looked over at me. 'What do you want to talk about?'

I edged around the well until our legs touched. 'I don't want to talk about anything,' I said, turning to face him. I wrapped my arms around him.

'Jessica,' he said quietly as he disengaged my arms, 'not here.'

I sat back, stung. 'Why? We always do it here.'

He didn't answer. Instead he scooped up another handful of stones and plunked them into the well. When it became clear he wasn't going to reply, I crossed my arms and regarded him through narrowed eyes.

'You don't want to do it any more. Why not? Is it because we don't have to hide any longer? You liked the thrill, the danger, right?' I stood up, straightened my jeans and turned back the way we had come.

'Jessica, wait!' He reached out a hand and grabbed my wrist. 'Don't be stupid, it's not like that.'

'That's what it sounded like. Why did you come at all if you didn't want to see me?'

He pulled me down next to him. 'You texted me, you told me to come.'

So I had, from the mobile phone that I kept in the box with all my other secrets. Well, not all of them. After all, that original box was too small to contain eight years' worth of the secrets that had damned me.

'You've always been the one I turn to, Ben, all these years,' I said, and was aghast to hear the choke in my voice.

'Not always,' he chided softly. 'You made your decision eight years ago when you married Patrick. And yet still I come every time you call me.'

I had no smart comeback for that, because it was true. I had married another man, yet I still expected Ben to be at my beck and call. And he had been. Each time I rang or texted him to tell him the coast was clear, he would make his way from wherever he happened to be at the time and arrive on my doorstep. And all of those times, in the afterglow of our lovemaking, he would listen as I bemoaned my life. He made it clear that I had other options: Dad, when he had still been alive, and friends who would welcome me with open arms; money in my own name. But he never knew how deeply I was trapped here with Patrick, he never knew the ties – and the lies

– that bound me here. He never knew I didn't actually have any of the money that was supposed to be mine. And just like the day he left Jenson Coast all those years ago, he never asked me to go away with him.

'Ben, why don't you want me to be with you?' I swallowed. It was the first time I'd asked him the question that had haunted me for so many years.

'What do you mean?' He took my hand and kissed the tips of my fingers.

'You never ask me to be with you, not back then, not now, not in the years in between. You come here, we have sex, you tell me that you love me, but you never ask me to be with you. You never ask me to come and live your life with you. Why?'

'You never said you wanted to.' He shook his head, gripped my shoulders and looked into my eyes. 'I only ever wanted you, yet you never expressed any interest in being with me on a permanent basis. You didn't even say goodbye when I left at the end of the summer in Cannes. I left you a note asking you to join me in Italy, which you ignored. Then you married Patrick. I just figured that you wanted me on a part-time basis, and I'd rather have you part-time than not at all.'

'Hold on, back up, what note?'

Ben shoved his hands in his pockets. 'I gave Lou a note to pass to you. You didn't have a mobile phone then and you'd pissed off somewhere in a huff.' He reached out and took hold of my hair, ran it through his fingers. 'And you did come, just not in the way I'd planned, you being a fugitive and all.'

I stared into his eyes until I felt like I was in danger of drowning, then I wrenched out of his grasp, my hair snagging painfully in his hand. I stared down into the well and wondered if I could jump in. Was that it? Eight years of thinking he didn't want me, only to discover that all this time he had not only been thinking the very same thing about me, but he had extended an invitation.

'I never got any note,' I whispered. I looked at him sharply. 'Did Louise know what it said?'

He nodded. 'Yep, she read it.'

Of all the people I'd suspected of betraying me over the years, throughout all of the paranoia, this treachery from Louise had never occurred to me. It cut deep, but the pain gave way almost immediately to a seething anger that burned in my veins.

'Fucking hell, Ben,' I whispered, my eyes filling with tears and blurring my vision. 'All that wasted time.' I thought of the near decade that had passed, and the way I'd lived it, unhappily for the most part.

He moved around the well at speed and grabbed my arms forcefully. 'Are you telling me all this time…?' He broke off, still holding my arms. 'You stupid idiot, you silly bitch, why didn't you say anything?' His voice was raw and rasping; his hands, which tugged at my clothes, were rough and demanding. They moved to grip my face and he moaned into my mouth.

I took it as he took me, the violence of our sex, and I gave it back to him, dragging my fingernails across his skin as deeply as I could. Angrily we fucked each other, without restraint or restriction or reserve.

Afterwards, leaning against the side of the well, we were calmer, peaceful, and it felt like a little bit of order had been restored.

We dressed in silence, moving about to find discarded clothing. Clad in just my bra and jeans, I peered into the well and swore softly.

'What's wrong?' Ben paused, pulling on his boot.

'My T-shirt is down there.'

He clutched the side, looked over the edge. A glow of white shone against the dark, dirty water six feet down. I made a strange noise, an unfamiliar feeling boiling high up in my chest. I wondered if I was about to cry, and then, as the sound emerged, I realised that I was laughing properly for the first time in eight years.

Soon I wouldn't be laughing. Soon it would sink in that it was actually Louise who was to blame for everything that had happened to me over the last eight years. And that anger, that tightly compressed rage contained inside of me, would be unleashed.

With me wearing Ben's jacket and him in just a shirt, we began to walk, not back where we had come from, but continuing on over the fields and footpaths. I had never walked this countryside with Patrick. He wasn't – hadn't been – a lover of the land, unlike Ben. I'd grown to appreciate it, had stored up the memories, kept a mental snapshot of the colours, the smells, the feel, all so I could tell Ben when he came next. The sunrises, the sunsets, the deer that occasionally strayed into the field that backed onto our garden. Though I'd only seen the deer once, and I'd never told Ben about that day. After what had happened – after what Patrick had done – the deer had stayed away. I allowed myself a smile; maybe they would come back now.

'Why would Louise not give you my note?' he asked.

I didn't answer him straight away. I had never told him what his leaving had done to me, leading me back into the lifestyle he had helped me escape. It struck me anew that everything that had happened – Alexis's murder and my incarceration, the arrival of Patrick – could have been avoided if Louise had given me Ben's note. I wouldn't ever have gone to the damn party, I'd have been in Italy, with Ben.

I swallowed my anger. 'Don't mention it to her,' I told him. 'I don't want her knowing everything about me and my life.'

He gave me a strange look, but didn't push it.

We turned right, towards a stile that would take us onto the village high street. He helped me over, and kept hold of my hand as we continued our leisurely walk. 'So what happens now?'

I felt a fluttering in my chest, the freedom of being able to speak the words I'd wanted to say for eight long years. 'I want to be with you, always. When you go away, I want to come with you.'

Out of the corner of my eye I saw him smiling.

'Well?' I prompted.

'I want it too. I've got lots of things lined up and I want you with me at all of them.' He stopped walking, turned to face me, his expression guilty now, like his excitement had taken over and he'd forgotten something important. 'Next spring I'm due to go to France and Brazil. I know you can't come with me, so I'll cancel them, I'll work in England, or hell, I won't work in TV at all. I'll stay here with you, Jessica.'

I breathed out slowly, realising why he thought he'd made a faux pas: the passport issue, the licence I was on for the rest of my life with the police that meant I couldn't travel overseas. With the events of the last couple of days I'd forgotten all about it. All about the eight-year lie that I'd been unwittingly, unknowingly living, until recently.

I needed to tell Ben the truth, but there were things to do first. My work here wasn't done. And he couldn't stay with me – I had Louise in my house already.

I checked my watch, calculating how long we had been out. As much as I wanted him to stay by my side, starting right now, it was an impossibility.

I needed to take care of her first.

'Let's not think about that right now,' I said, tugging him along until his stride matched mine. 'We've got plenty of time for planning, the rest of our lives, right?'

He smiled, cautiously at first, then properly, as I pulled his arm around me and we started to head home.

As we prepared to angle off across the back field, he put a hand on my shoulder. 'Jessica,' he said, and pointed in the direction of the nature reserve, 'look.'

But I'd already seen it, a police car parked right outside my cottage.

I thought of Louise inside. When we'd left, she had been making coffee. I drew in a sharp breath. What would the police find?

And then I saw. Robinson was leaving the house, carrying a cardboard box. Hart followed closely behind, head down as she looked at the clipboard she was holding. I hung back, slipped the hood of Ben's top over my head and turned away as the police car began to move off. It crawled past us without stopping. I scuffed my feet in the dirt of the lane. What were they looking for? What had they taken away in that box?

As I turned back towards the house, I saw Ben stepping into the bushes. I remembered another time, another country where he had left me to face the police on my own.

It's all right, I told myself, he'll come back when it's clear. He has to think of his status, his career. Besides, he can't be seen here right now.

But it still hurt.

When I reached my doorstep, I took a deep breath. Before I could let myself in, though, Louise was on the threshold, catching at my arm and pulling me inside. The door slammed shut behind me.

I pulled the hood down and double-bolted the door. 'What were the police doing here?' I demanded. 'What did they want?'

She drew me into the kitchen. 'Where were you?' she asked, her eyes huge and round. 'And why are you wearing Ben's coat?'

I looked at her coffee cup, clean and empty beside the sink, the tell-tale wine bottle next to it.

I sighed, shook my head, crossed my arms over my chest, realising it was obvious that beneath Ben's coat I was naked from the waist up. 'It doesn't matter. What did they take away?'

And then I remembered, a horrible thought – one that could do me serious damage, especially if that sneaky Hart had got her hands on it.

'They took your laptop,' Louise said; then, as I flew to the bookcase and began pulling random items off, 'What are you doing?'

'It was Patrick's laptop,' I said, not caring about the computer but frantically conducting a search of my own. 'I never even logged onto the damn thing. Did they take anything else? God, where *is* it?'

'Is this what you're looking for?'

I abandoned my search, spun around to face Louise. She smiled coldly, but she was intrigued, I could tell. She held the book aloft, one eyebrow raised, and tapped a long blood-red nail on the cover.

My heart sank and I leaned against the bookcase.

She turned the book to face her, flicked through the pages. The silence was long and I reverted back to my days with Patrick, unsure of what I was supposed to say, better just to remain silent until it was made clear to me.

'*Symptoms and Effects of Drugs and Poisons*,' she read out loud. 'Now why on earth would you need this kind of book, Jessica?' Suddenly her smile was wide and open. 'And more importantly, why would you be so keen on the police not discovering it?'

Suddenly the pressure of the silence was deafening.

Chapter 16

Louise

Jessica was a free woman, but she wasn't coming home to Jenson Coast.

'Why is she staying with Patrick?' I whispered to Marco after Andrew had told us of her plans. 'This is her home, she should be here; his job is over now.'

'The media presence,' replied Marco with a shrug. 'That's what Andrew says, anyway.'

'But the paparazzi only get as far as the door. We don't have to let them in,' I reasoned. Privately I thought it wouldn't hurt for Jessica to do an interview or two, to specifically chosen media outlets. The press didn't let things lie, after all. It was all over, but they were still here – she should be controlling them, not the other way around.

'She'll be okay with Patrick,' replied Andrew mildly as he walked back into the room. 'In fact, I encouraged it. Jessica isn't a little girl any more, it's high time she settled down, remained in one place, with one man.' Did his eyes flick over me when he spoke those words; was there an emphasis on the word *man*? 'And I can't think of a finer man to stand by her side.'

'What about Ben?' I asked.

'Ben is far from settled down, and he hasn't exactly helped her by hiding her out in his villa.' Andrew's nostrils flared in annoyance.

I glanced at Marco, knowing that it was he who had sent her to Italy – Ben had been a reluctant accomplice.

'But listen, Andrew, someone has to speak to the press,' said Marco, hurriedly changing the subject. 'And the exposure for the hotel wouldn't hurt. If we don't give them something, they'll only make it up.'

Andrew pulled back the blinds and peered out at the paparazzi lining the driveway. 'Fine, you do it then,' he said, his back to us.

Marco gestured to me to follow him. Obediently I let him lead me to his suite, where I stood by the window that overlooked the lemon groves. Just a few days ago, the grounds out there had been heaving with happy holiday-makers.

'It's already had an impact on the hotel.' I swept my arm in an arc. 'Look at this place. All the guests have gone, and if you don't fix this, they won't come back.'

And if you lose everything, I'll be as badly off as I was before.

'I know,' he snapped. He breathed deeply, softened his tone. 'I've got a plan. Those front doors are not going to be closed for much longer. Once they learn of the new executive penthouse suite we're offering for five thousand euros a night, we'll be raking in the money.'

I listened to him, wondered about the 'we' he referred to. Was I included in it? Tilting my face up to his, I saw the gleam in his eyes.

'Go on,' I said. 'I'm listening.'

He laid it all out, his plans for the penthouse renovation. It didn't really involve much construction work – more than anything, it was simply a name change.

'What do you reckon?' he asked.

'It might be seen as distasteful,' I said. At the look on his face, I backtracked hurriedly. 'It's a really good idea, it just needs to be handled right.'

'It's one hell of a great angle, publicity-wise,' he countered. 'And I want you by my side when we do the interview.'

'Me?'

'Yes. It was your photos that got her off the hook, it would be weird if you weren't there. And they might ask some technical questions, about photography and stuff.'

I should have been flattered, but all his words had served to do was remind me that I was the one who'd broken the law when it came to the photos. If they were found to be fake by the authorities, he could deny all knowledge of it.

'Okay,' I whispered, 'but we still need to talk.'

He glanced over at me. 'What about?'

I swallowed. 'I need assurances, Marco. Be it money or...' I raised my head, looked him in the eye. 'I need something.'

He nodded, once. Looked away. 'We'll arrange something,' he said.

His eyes lingered on me before he came at me, pulled me into his embrace, divested me of my clothes, as though he could silence my thoughts and fears and financial demands with his body. I went to him willingly. But I wouldn't forget what I needed. I had to think some more about what he could do for me in return for my photos. For now, though, I had other things on my mind.

'Marco?' I whispered his name as he lit a cigarette.

'Yeah?' He rolled to face me, held the cigarette to my lips and I inhaled.

'It was Patrick who told the police where Jessica was, wasn't it? He overheard us talking in the restaurant.'

In the dim light of the setting sun, I saw his face darken. 'Yeah, I can't see who else could have called them.'

'Why, though?' I sat up against the pillows. 'What's he playing at?'

Marco shrugged, reached over me for an ashtray. 'I don't know. He wants her for himself. Money, maybe…' He tailed off, shrugged again and shook his head.

'He's a lawyer, an expensive one. He lives in a villa in Antibes, Andrew told us all this. He surely has enough money of his own,' I exclaimed.

'Louise,' Marco touched my face, unusually tender, 'is there any such thing as enough money?'

He was right. To people like Marco and Andrew and Patrick, there was no such thing. Me, I'd be happy if I had enough just to live on. But was that what Patrick wanted from Jessica, money? Or a beautiful woman on his arm and Andrew's name behind him to propel him further up the ladder, both socially and professionally?

'You do care an awful lot about Jessica, don't you?'

Marco's voice pulled me back from my thoughts and I glanced over at him.

'Of course, she's my friend.'

'Just a friend?' he murmured as he ground the cigarette out and reached for me again.

I nestled close to him, the smoke from the cigarette swirling around our smiles, my confidence boosted momentarily by the afterglow of the sex. 'Are you jealous?' I asked softly, playfully, hopefully.

He laughed long and loud as he pulled me on top of him, as though it was the silliest thing he'd ever heard.

Two days later, with Andrew watching from the wings as the sun began to set over the horizon, Marco and I were the epitome of a young professional couple as we positioned ourselves on the lawn in front of the reporter. I had chosen the recipient of the exclusive that we were to give with care, finally settling on *Le Figaro*. It was the oldest national daily newspaper in France, and the second biggest in the country. I knew of the reporter as well, and his reputation as a bold but fair journalist. He was middle-aged, French by birth but schooled in England, which lent him an arrogant public-schoolboy air. I would have to handle him carefully. My breath caught in my throat. My talents lay behind the lens of a camera, not in fielding difficult questions by a renowned journalist. Discreetly, I wiped my palms on my skirt, scratched at my eczema-scarred hands one last time before folding them in my lap, wondering why on earth I'd agreed to this.

'So let's start from the beginning, make it as pain-free as possible, yes?' Jean-Henri's smile was like that of a crocodile before it eats its prey. 'Take us through that night...'

And so I did, just the way I'd told the police. I added in information that I'd since learned of, such as Alexis's head injury, the power cut, the partygoers who had been moved to a house a few streets over while Mr Dubois called the electricity company. It still wasn't clear why Alexis was the only person who remained in the house.

As I told him about the lucky shots I'd happened to take outside, Jean-Henri's eyes widened in an encouraging manner.

'Just test shots,' I said quickly, spreading my hands wide and nodding to Terry, Jean-Henri's photographer. 'We do them all the time, right, Terry? To assess the light and the background before we start an actual photo shoot.' I smiled shyly at Marco. 'It was Marco's idea to develop them, I hadn't even thought about them.'

'Really?' Jean-Henri glanced over at Marco. 'What a lucky break! What made *you* think of them?'

Keep it natural, keep it easy, I prompted in my head.

'We were exploring every avenue,' replied Marco smoothly. 'The police are so busy, we were keen to do anything we could to help them.'

'You think the police were too busy to conduct a proper investigation?'

I winced inwardly but didn't interrupt. I had faith that Marco could talk his way out of anything, much better than I could.

'The police are always up to their eyes in it, we were happy to help in any small way,' he replied.

'Help the police, or help Jessica Jenson?' Jean-Henri fired back.

Marco held out his hands, palms up. 'Help everyone.'

'But the killer hasn't been caught.'

Marco shook his head, sadness evident in his eyes. 'No, and that's the most important thing, to be honest, because though the innocent party has indeed been proven innocent, the murderer is still out there, which is why we should take this opportunity to ask your readers to study the photos Louise took, look closely, and if anybody has even the slightest inkling of recognition, to tell the police.'

I sat back, my mouth open in awe of his performance. He was a natural; he could have handled this interview on his own, without me. There was a moment of silence, and I pulled myself out of my trance, sat up straight and turned back to Jean-Henri.

'And of course, we mustn't forget the victim in all this. That's why we wanted to commemorate her life and her name in some way. So Jenson Coast is very proud to announce that a penthouse suite will shortly be opened here at the hotel, in the name of Alexis Dubois.'

I bowed my head, aiming for halfway between sympathy and respect. Jean-Henri scribbled furiously in his notebook and subtly, I squeezed Marco's hand.

'Impressive, but also extraordinary. What does Jessica think of her father's hotel being a permanent reminder of her incarceration?' Jean-Henri's words were sharp and quick. Brutal.

'Like everyone else, Jessica mourns the loss of a life. Alexis was the same age as her, you know. It's a tragedy, and Jessica stands with Jenson Coast on this decision.' My answer was instantaneous, my words were spoken with a confidence I didn't feel.

Jean-Henri made a show of flicking through his notes, though it was unnecessary. 'Didn't Jessica and Alexis clash over a man, Ben Albin? And Ben is a rather high-profile guy, popular in these parts especially.'

I shook my head. 'Not really. Jessica spent some time with Ben when he was here, as we all did, actually. He's a friend of all of us.' I paused as a waiter came along with lime sodas and took one off the tray, waited for Jean-Henri, Marco and Terry to accept a glass. 'I can see the story in that, two women fighting over a man, but Jessica's friendship with Ben was just that, a friendship.'

'And you two?' Jean-Henri's expression was wicked, his tone gossipy, and I breathed out now that the spotlight was on us rather than Jessica.

I looked over at Marco. His smile was slipping. 'We're friends,' I said, but it sounded false. 'Just friends.'

When it was over, I walked Jean-Henri and Terry to the car park. As we said our goodbyes, I slipped a sealed envelope into Jean-Henri's hand.

'Our invoice,' I said. 'The fee we agreed on. I've put my bank details in there, if you wouldn't mind passing it on to your accounts department?'

'Your bank details, right,' Jean-Henri said.

Was that a sneer on his face? I wondered as he drove away. Or was it simply my paranoia coming out to play?

Chapter 17

Jessica's Diary
September 2011

'I have to go to London for a few nights,' Patrick said, a couple of days into our 'honeymoon'.

I nodded, relieved that I would have some time to myself. I thought of what I could do without him by my side. I could drink, smoke, find someone to buy some weed from, maybe something stronger. I needed oblivion, just for a while, for as long as it took me to adapt.

'Can you leave me a bank card?' I asked.

At my words, he stopped carefully folding his shirts and turned to me. 'What do you need money for?'

'Food,' I said, thinking quickly.

He resumed packing the bag. 'I've done a shop, there's plenty of food. There are some nice steaks in the fridge, milk, bread…'

My mouth hung slack. 'I… I can't have any money?' I thought of my father, of my card that was always loaded with instant cash and topped up frequently, no questions asked.

'What if I want something else? Clothes or…
something.' Suddenly I couldn't think what
on earth I could buy that would be acceptable
in Patrick's eyes.

He laughed, but it was cold, quiet. 'All
your clothes arrived from France. I hung
them in the wardrobe.'

I forced a smile, nodded and drifted back
downstairs. On the hook in the hallway
hung Patrick's coat. Checking that he wasn't
behind me, I delved into his pockets and
came up with a handful of loose change.
I shoved four pound coins into my pocket
with a grimace. I couldn't even get twenty
cigarettes for that.

Then I remembered my currency card.
It must be here, somewhere among all my
things that had been delivered from France.
When Patrick had left, I would find it.
I'd go to the nearest cashpoint and with-
draw enough money to buy me everything
I needed.

I turned the house upside down after
he wished me a cordial goodbye. He had
unpacked all the boxes that had been
delivered; everything had a neat home.
Everything was there except my cash card.
I drew in a shuddering breath. I didn't live
like this. Correction: I never used to live like
this.

Chapter 18

Jessica

Now

My body was gripped with fear as I looked at Louise sitting like she belonged in my kitchen, holding the book of poisons. I'd known fear before, in small doses, like the time I took a ya ba pill when I was in Thailand aged eighteen. Ya ba are small red tablets made from a mixture of methamphetamine and caffeine, which produce a hallucinatory effect – like mushrooms, I'd thought, when I was offered one by a young Spaniard at a beach party on Koh Samui. In reality, it was nothing like the relatively harmless mushrooms; with them I didn't experience nausea, the sweats, a random clicking that made me fear my brain was collapsing inside my skull, and an immense anger. I directed my displaced fury at the pill giver, battering him with my fists, hurling rocks at him until I was restrained by other partygoers.

I was travelling with my father, and I couldn't go back to the hotel to meet him in that state. Instead I curled up under a towel on the beach as my friends stood sentry around me and the others partied on. During the time I was under the influence, I felt panicked and cornered, just like I did now as Louise stood in front of me brandishing my book of illegal drugs.

'It's… it's j–just a book,' I stammered. 'I didn't… I haven't…'

She put the book on the table behind her and moved to stand in front of me.

'Jessica, I was just kidding. I wasn't accusing you of anything, it was a joke.'

Laugh now, I instructed myself silently. *Do it right now before you make an even bigger fool of yourself and dig yourself an even bigger hole.* From somewhere, I found it, my acting skill that no matter how hard I'd tried over the years I'd never quite perfected, but I threw my head back and laughed anyway. It felt forced and fake, nothing like my laughter with Ben earlier.

Louise looked at me weirdly, and I quickly changed the subject.

'What did the police say? Did they just take Patrick's laptop? Why did you let them in? Didn't you tell them I'd gone out?'

'I had no choice. They weren't neighbours coming round to borrow something, Jessica. They're the *police*. You can't say no to them, or have you forgotten your past experiences with them, cooped up here in your nice safe little home?'

There was that change again, the brief flash of confidence that Louise never used to have. Back then, she wouldn't have spoken to me so sharply. She'd always agreed with me, even if she felt differently inside.

We stared at each other. Eventually, I felt rather than saw her relent. 'They went upstairs, looked in the bathroom for a long time, at the bath… Was that where it happened, where he died?' She shook her head, strawberry hair once the deepest red flying around her face. 'Never mind. Where's Ben? And why did you run off with him?'

'I didn't run off with him, we went for a walk. He saw that the police were here. He'll come back when the coast is clear.'

'So he doesn't see you for years, and when he finally shows up, he bolts at the first sign of trouble? Some friend! I don't know what he's even doing here.' Turning on her heel, she walked into the conservatory.

Her put-down of Ben was the trigger for my fury. It was quick to come these days, my anger, though I'd been used to controlling it in front of Patrick. But Patrick wasn't here any longer. And I hadn't forgot that Louise had kept the biggest secret of all from me.

Her lie... it blinded me.

And as I followed her, I unleashed my temper.

'What do you mean by that remark?' I looked around the conservatory, noting that the blinds were closed. 'And why did you shut my blinds?' I stalked around the room, lifting them all so that the sunlight blazed through.

'If he was any sort of friend, he wouldn't be sneaking off through the woods at the first sign of the police turning up. He'd be here, supporting you.'

'He's on the television, he's got a career to think about!' I was really shouting now, my voice raised in the old way, a way I hadn't dared speak for years. 'I understand that, why can't you?'

She spun on her heel, came up to me fast. 'And why did you lie when I asked when you last saw him? You didn't seem very surprised when he turned up here. It's obvious you've been in contact all these years. Why did you lie, Jessica? Have you been cheating on Patrick all this time?'

All of a sudden, the answer to her questions was obvious. It was what I'd wanted to say so many times when I'd been questioned – no, interrogated – by my husband during our marriage, but had never dared. Now I dared, and it felt so good to finally say it.

'It's none of your business. My life has never been any of your business, yet you were always there, sticking your nose in where it didn't belong. Hanging onto me, following me, copying me. *Stalking* me!' I clamped my mouth shut before I could scream at her for withholding Ben's note all those years ago. That would come later. I needed time to digest it first, to work out exactly what I wanted to say when I confronted her.

And just as I'd returned to my old self, so did Louise. Her eyes, moments ago blazing with anger, were now hurt, tear-filled.

It didn't stop me, though; when the heat rose in me, nothing could stop me. As I backed up to the conservatory door, I saw Louise's wine glass from last night still on the windowsill. Without hesitating, I picked it up, pulled my arm back and threw it as hard as I could in her general direction. It whizzed past her face and hit the wall, tiny shards of the £60-a-piece Riedel stemware landing on the carpet.

She moved then, backing into the kitchen, head down, compliant. Taking a deep breath, I followed.

She was sitting at the table, smoking furiously. I sat down opposite her, the anger gone, all the wind vanished from my sails, even though I'd not said half of what I wanted to.

'Give me one of those,' I said, as I reached across and tapped out a Marlboro onto the table.

Louise slid her lighter towards me and I lit the cigarette, put the lighter gently back in her hand. None of it was an apology, but for now, it was enough.

'Did Patrick know you were in contact with Ben?' Louise asked.

'I think he suspected,' I said. 'But he never knew for sure.'

It was another lie, but I didn't want to tell Louise the whole story. I was beginning to realise that the more I told about my life with Patrick, the more motive it seemed I had for killing him. I'd been there before; I'd learned my lesson.

The two of us smoked silently for a while before she spoke again, 'You know I'm behind you, right? I mean, you can tell me anything.'

I smoked my cigarette down to the butt and then crushed it out in the ashtray. She was behind me. Right, but where had she been for the last eight years when I really needed her? She'd been behind me all right, so far behind I couldn't even see her.

'Thanks, Louise, but I'm fine, I'll be fine.' I stood up, went through to the conservatory and peered through the window. The road outside was empty, but for how long? I closed my eyes, remembered Jenson Coast, the way the reporters had swarmed the car park eight years ago. Would it happen again? Probably not. Patrick wasn't as big news as Alexis Dubois.

But you are, a little voice whispered.

'I hope the press don't come here,' I said. 'I can't deal with them – with all that – again.'

'You know, it wouldn't hurt to speak to a reporter. All they would want is a few lines from you.'

I looked at her as though she'd gone mad. 'It's all right for you, you can speak to them and be the hero. You're not standing in my shoes, you don't know what it's like. I'm not speaking to them.' I sank into a chair.

'Fine,' she said, a weary tone in her voice.

I pressed my lips together. Why did she think she knew best? She didn't know anything. Why couldn't everyone leave me alone to live my life in whatever way I saw fit?

'It worked before,' she said. 'When Marco and I did the interview, it got the hotel back up and running like it was before.'

She got up and headed to the door. I blinked at her back. What was she doing? Leaving to find some journalist to speak to, to make money off my misery? Again?

Faster than it ever had before, the heat returned to me. It burned in me, a volcano, churning, a pot of water boiling up, over. I planted my hands on the arms of the chair, pushed myself up and lurched after her, grabbing her arm and swinging her around to face me. 'No, just leave it! You're not speaking to them, not about me, not about my life, not again!'

She wrenched her arm free but I caught hold of her wrist. We struggled silently, ridiculously, in the hallway. I felt the fire all over my body as I grabbed her hair and pulled her head backwards. She shrieked, breaking the silence, scratched at my neck with her nails.

Distantly I heard her shouting my name. The fear in her voice registered, but dimly, too far away. I couldn't even see her any more, I had no control, no way of stopping, just strength born of years of silent, smothered fury that was only occasionally allowed a release, and never when someone else was there. But now I had someone, an actual person I could use.

I twisted her body; she caught her foot on the bottom stair and went down. Though she was now helpless, still I didn't stop. My left arm came around her neck and I pulled my forearm back. I saw her face, but her pain didn't stop me. I didn't realise how purple it was, that her eyes were watering, bulging, the blood vessels in them standing to attention. I didn't hear her wheezing, gasping for breath. All I concentrated on was keeping my arm in place. Then, just as she was weakening, flopping forward, something crashed into my back, knocking me sideways to lie next to Louise on the floor.

I looked up, shielding my face from the blows that I was sure were coming, and through my hands I saw Ben, kicking the door closed as he stared down at me, looking for all the world like he didn't know me, like he'd just discovered that he had no idea who I really was, or what I was capable of.

'I wasn't even going to talk to them,' Louise whimpered. 'What did you think I was going to do? Go to the nearest town and find a reporter to speak to about something that nobody has even got any interest in?'

I closed my eyes, wrapped my arms around myself as though it would keep me safe.

As though it would keep my anger and lack of self-control inside me.

Chapter 19

Louise

Then

The days rolled past; Jean-Henri's article appeared. I read it, over and over, alone in my apartment. I received the fee that we'd agreed for the interview. I banked it, returned to my small flat and logged on to my bank account to look at it.

It was good; it would cover my rent for about three months.

But it wasn't enough.

I sat alone, the television off, the curtains drawn for the first time. I thought, I plotted. I waited for someone to call: Andrew, Marco.

Nobody got in touch with me.

I worried that my life was slipping away from me again.

Since the night of Alexis's murder, the weather had turned. All summer we had bathed in glorious sunshine, searing temperatures keeping us awake at night, the need to seek the shadows growing urgent in the late morning, staying in the shade practically until the sun went down. But that night, the night Alexis died, a violent, horrible death, the sky grew dark, and though a couple of weeks had passed, the sun had not made a return.

There was no rain, not yet. People had started to comment on it, complain that the mercury was still in the searing nineties, it was bound to break soon, the rain would come, a good storm was needed and then all would return to normal.

But the storm stayed away.

The grey sky remained.

And things were far from normal.

For the first time, I had no reason to go to Jenson Coast. I had no idea if Jessica had returned. I'd not heard from Marco, or Andrew. Our work was done; they had no need to call me and I could find no excuse to visit them.

The life that I'd had over the summer was gone, just like the sun. It seemed appropriate that the grey cloud hovered, but I couldn't stand to look at it, so I kept the curtains closed.

I ordered food online, sat in front of the dark television and watched my empty walls as I ate. Periodically I logged on to my bank account, my heart dropping the same way as my balance was. Thoughts of England rushed at me, but they no longer panicked me so much. After all, I was living the same life here as I would if I had to go back home. Already I was experiencing it, holed up here in my shitty flat.

But the more I hibernated, the longer the cloud hung and didn't break, the angrier I got. Marco had promised he would take care of me in return for the photos I had faked. It was typical: as soon as I'd done my bit, I'd been dropped. I was used to that, but this time it was different. This time I'd risked everything.

And I hadn't spoken to Marco in weeks.

Slowly, but with the lethargy falling away from me, I pulled the curtain aside and looked out onto the street.

It was dull out there, the cloud still low and thick. But I didn't need the sunshine to motivate me, my decreasing bank balance was doing that all on its own.

Yanking the curtains open, I pushed the window wide and retreated to the bathroom. I opened that window too, grimacing at the smell of my own body. I couldn't remember the last time I'd showered. I'd had no need. I'd seen nobody. Nobody had been to see me.

But that would change now. This would be my last shot, I would get what I was owed.

No ifs.

No buts.

I would have the life I needed.

The heat was oppressive, like a warning of impending doom, as I made my way towards the future that was slipping out of my grasp. My eczema scars seemed to pop and fizz, a mixture of the heat and my stress. But I heaved a sigh of relief as I walked up the driveway and saw the doors to Jenson Coast standing open. People roamed the grounds and gardens again. The hotel was back in business; Jean-Henri's article had worked.

I came across Andrew first, and greeted him as coolly as I was able.

'Lou,' he said. 'Glad you're here.' He moved towards me, no questions about where I'd been, no 'long time no see'. But he looked relieved, pleased to see me. I softened; I'd been missed by Andrew at least.

But as he approached, I saw that he was holding the landline phone.

'It's Jessica,' he said. 'She wants to see us.' He passed the phone to me. 'Set something up.'

I frowned. Why couldn't he arrange to see her himself? And did that mean she was still hiding out at Patrick's house? Hadn't Andrew seen her since she'd been cleared?

I lifted the phone and opened my mouth to greet her, but in typical Jessica fashion, she was already talking.

'Louise, Patrick told me you've done an interview about me. How could you?'

I held the phone away from my ear and winced.

I waited until there was silence on the line before I spoke tentatively.

'Someone needed to tell them something, Jessica.' I lowered my voice and walked a few feet away from Andrew. 'Your dad thought it was the right thing to do.'

I sensed the smile in her voice when she spoke again. 'I'm sleeping with Patrick.'

The change of subject, the suddenness in both the new direction of the conversation and the difference in her voice, from anger to gossip-filled glee, threw me. And hold on, wasn't that my line, my news, only about Marco instead of Patrick?

'W-what?'

'He really likes me, Lou. He wants me to stay with him. You need to come over, see this place for yourself. It makes Jenson Coast look like a toilet.'

I glanced around the breakfast room that I was in, taking in the floor-to-ceiling windows with the spectacular view of the gardens and the sea beyond. Everything in this place was immaculate, no expense spared, from the gold-edged plates to the hand-embroidered linen tablecloths. It occurred to me that this was how Jessica got in trouble: talking and yakking away without pause for thought.

On Andrew and Marco's behalf I was suddenly offended. And for the very first time, Jessica's shallow nature bothered me.

'What about Ben?' I felt my face growing hot. I'd been about to say *What about me?* before remembering I was in no position to get high and mighty. After all, I had slept with Marco. And she didn't know. Before she could reply, I spoke again: 'Listen, Jessica, I have to tell you something—'

'Save it,' she said, cutting me off. 'Come over tonight, all of you. I'll arrange dinner, it'll be a thank you to Patrick from all of us. Daddy has the address.'

Click.

I stared dumbly at the phone, the dial tone ringing in my ear, and handed it back to Andrew as he strode towards me.

'We're going to Patrick's tonight for dinner,' I said. 'All of us.' I stressed this last part, in case they didn't yet realise that I was now one of them.

'Excellent,' he replied. 'I'll make sure there's cover here.'

As he began to walk away, I called him back: 'Andrew, what do you know about Patrick? Where do you know him from?'

'I've known him for years. He was working as a junior at the law firm I used to set up businesses over the years. I never had cause to use Patrick, as he went into criminal law, then of course he was made partner and seemed the obvious choice to represent Jessica when...' He tailed off, and I didn't fill in the gap for him – there was no need. 'You don't like him, do you?' Andrew smiled, his tone kind. 'Why is that?'

'I...' I stalled. How could I tell him that I suspected Patrick had overheard Marco and me talking about the faked photos? To say that was to admit that we had broken the law.

'You don't trust him.' Andrew tilted his head to one side. 'But he's not the one who lied, is he?'

I felt the blood freeze in my cheeks. 'What do you mean?'

'I mean the photographs that got Jessica off the charge. Patrick told me what you did.'

So it must have been Patrick eavesdropping on Marco and me that day. And surely that meant that it was Patrick who called the police and told them where Jessica was hiding out. Marco had told me the address of the villa, we had heard the slam of a door; another person *had been there*. Patrick had heard us, heard where Jessica was hiding. He had obviously left out that little bit of information when he grassed on us to Andrew. But why would he disclose Jessica's hideout location? She was his client, he was supposed to protect her. Or had this been what he wanted all along, to whisk her away and turn her against us, her family and friends? The ones who loved her.

I pushed my chair back and stood up. I needed to tell Marco this latest revelation. He and I were the only ones who were supposed to know the truth about the pictures; anybody else in the loop, even Jessica, was too dangerous.

'Louise...' Andrew caught my hand as I walked past. 'I know Jessica didn't kill Alexis Dubois, she's not got it in her, but I also know it didn't look good for her. Whatever you did, however you did it, I'm very grateful.'

I nodded, and he released my hand. With my head down, I left the room and walked back outside into the cloudy day.

'Road trip,' yawned Marco, winking at me as we waited out front for the valet to bring his car round.

It was the first time I'd seen him today. He'd only appeared when it was time to leave to visit Jessica. He greeted me as if the last weeks hadn't happened, as if he'd only seen me yesterday, as if he hadn't been ignoring me and my monetary demands.

I chewed on a nail as I observed him. He looked tired, rough. He had obviously not been sitting alone in his suite, pining and worrying the way I had. Where had he been? Who had he been with? Was I nothing but a distant memory?

I needed to speak to him about my fee. Not the one from the article, which was fast dissipating, but the money he had promised me. But first, I needed to tell him my thoughts about Patrick. As he drove, I filled him in on my earlier conversation with Andrew.

'I'm worried. What if Patrick tells everyone what I did with the photos?'

Marco reached across and adjusted the rear-view mirror. 'Why would he? Jessica is his client. If he did that, he'd send her straight back to prison.'

Marco was right. It didn't make sense, any of it. And he didn't seem to be as worried as I was. I let the subject fall, wondered how to approach the other issue that weighed heavy on my mind.

'Marco, that thing you said…'

'What thing?' he asked, juggling his cigarettes out of his pocket, clumsily pulling at the seal before handing them to me. 'Light us up, will you?'

I did as he asked, took one for myself.

'I need security, basically,' I said. 'I would have charged a decent fee for the photos I took. The fakes,' I clarified, in case he didn't know what I was talking about.

'It had an impact on the business,' he said, staring straight ahead. 'But we're getting back on our feet.' He looked over at me, gave me a smile that didn't quite meet his eyes. 'I won't forget you, Lou. I won't forget what you did for us.'

I sat back in the passenger seat, watched France as it whizzed past. In the town centre, everyone carried umbrellas – a talisman against the cloud that still refused to break.

'I won't forget either, Marco,' I said quietly. 'But I understand you need time.'

Mollified, he grinned at me, then reached over and squeezed my thigh. My body reacted to his touch, just like it always did.

His hand remained on my leg. I stared at it for the entire journey.

As we pulled up outside Patrick's place, my jaw dropped. I let my gaze rest on the large outdoor pool set in an even larger expanse of land. Overlooking the pool was an outdoor dining area supported by natural stone columns. The gardens that surrounded the villa were lush and green, evidence of care and maintenance everywhere. It wasn't at all what I'd expected and I couldn't believe that the stuffy, weird man I'd met lived in a beautiful place like this. Grudgingly I conceded that it was just as nice as Jenson Coast.

'Nice digs,' Marco said.

Shading my eyes from the low sun, I peered at the woman who stood on the porch steps. Who was this, an assistant? No, too classy-looking for an employee, wearing what I knew to be a dress from Gucci's fall collection. I'd seen it on model Marija Vujović at the Cannes fashion show back in May, where I'd managed to blag my way in with a press pass. Gucci's autumn ready-to-wear line wasn't even in the store on Boulevard de la Croisette yet. I knew; I window-shopped there every time I passed it. And then I did a classic double-take. Now that I was closer, I could see that it certainly wasn't an assistant standing there loftily.

'Wow, it's Jessica!' I broke into a trot, Marco moving more slowly, still taking in the opulent gardens. When I reached her, I stopped, looked her up and down. A memory of the last time I'd seen her came back to me; of her face and clothes covered in the red dirt of the olive grove, of her arms straining against the cuffs that bound her. I blinked away the vision.

'Jessica, you look… amazing.'

She grinned and reached out. I allowed myself to be pulled into a hug, realising as she stumbled against me that she was drunk.

'Do you like it?' she breathed into my ear. 'It was a present from Patrick.'

I pulled back, studied her again. Yes, the straight black below-knee-length skirt was beautifully tailored, the matching fitted jacket with the wide purple belt and the fur collar was a piece of clothing that I, personally, would dream about owning. But I saw that Patrick had been careful to choose an outfit that covered her body completely. There was no doubt that Jessica looked stunning, but she didn't look like… Jessica. Though she always dressed impeccably, and unlike me could afford the latest designer dresses, this styling was a whole other level. And as I regarded her, I realised she looked familiar. She looked like… Alexis Dubois. I swallowed as Jessica's image swam and merged into that of the dead girl.

'You don't look like you,' was all I could think of to say.

'Thank goodness for that. Maybe I can go out without being pounced on by the fucking photographers,' she retorted. 'They're like leeches, absolutely unbelievable. Come in, Patrick's inside.'

Without waiting for me, she turned and went into the house. I hung back, stinging from her words. Didn't she realise she was talking about me, about my work, my life?

'Take it easy,' Marco murmured in my ear, and took my hand.

I looked in surprise at his fingers entwined with mine as we followed Jessica inside.

'Where's my dad?' Jessica asked as she poured us wine.

As Marco dropped my hand and wandered out of the patio doors, I looked around the kitchen, at the chequered flagstone floor, the beamed ceiling, the double range oven. Peering around one of the columns, I saw that the stairs that rose from the hallway were of whitewashed stone, lined by a crudely constructed mahogany banister.

'Andrew's on his way,' I replied, still awestruck by the house.

Jessica passed me my wine just as Patrick came into the kitchen. There was no greeting – it was as though he didn't even see me – and as he walked over to Jessica, I backed out into the hallway. I needed to find Marco, needed to stay glued to his side, didn't want to risk getting caught alone with Patrick. There was something about the man, something about his cold, calculating persona, that frightened me.

But before I could retreat outside, I heard Jessica speak. I recognised from the high pitch of her voice just how drunk she was.

'Did you do all this, Patrick?'

'Did you not expect us to feed our guests?' Patrick's voice, quiet and controlled, echoed around the hall. 'Or did you think the food would fix itself?'

My eyes widened. Jessica would never allow anyone to speak to her that way. With a flare of excitement in my chest, I waited for the inevitable outburst. To my surprise, it didn't come.

'I'm sorry I didn't help.' Her reply was a whisper, so unlike the Jessica I knew that I wondered if there was someone else in the kitchen, a maid or a hired help.

'I told you it wasn't in your best interests to have them over. I told you I would look out for you, but in order to do that, I need your cooperation.'

Look out for her? Why would she need protecting? Alexis's killer hadn't been caught, but Jessica was in the clear, wasn't she?

As I heard the clatter of plates and cutlery, I slunk outside and took a seat next to Marco.

–

Dinner was a stilted affair. Talk of the murder, the only reason we all found ourselves here at Patrick's place, was off limits. But we had nothing else to speak about.

'Jessica, I brought the interview if you want to read it,' I said, digging in my bag and pulling out the newspaper.

She glanced at Patrick, and though I saw no response from him, she shrugged and offered me a small smile. 'No, thanks.'

Confused, feeling small and slighted, I placed it on the table. Marco's meaty paw found its way into my mine. Again I looked at it, my hand tiny in his. Why was he being so affectionate to me? Did he sense my nervousness, or was he holding on to me in case I said the wrong thing and he needed to give me a warning?

But I didn't pull away from him. I was grateful for his touch, for the sense that someone seemed to be on my side.

As Andrew and Patrick began to talk among themselves, I felt myself relaxing a little. Until Jessica's shriek pierced the air:

'Are you two *together*?'

Marco's hand disengaged from mine, fast. I shrugged, looking from him to Jessica, feeling the heat in my face.

In the distance, I registered a car crunching over the gravel in the driveway, but I paid it no heed. Instead I locked my eyes on Jessica's: 'We've been seeing a bit of each other.' I gazed down at my lap, not daring to look at Marco. 'Seeing each other' was a stretch. Sleeping together a couple of times was the extent of our relationship, but I'd had to say something.

I waited for the explosion. Why there would be one, I didn't know. But I'd spent enough time with Jessica to know there would be a reaction. When it came, it floored me.

'Patrick has asked me to marry him.' She tucked her arm in his, looked at each of us in turn, a self-satisfied expression on her face.

I stared at her, glanced at Patrick, impassive by her side. The silence was broken by an awkward 'Congratulations.'

I looked at Andrew, expected him to be beaming, pleased as Punch, reaching for the ice bucket that held the champagne, but it wasn't him who had spoken. Coming across the lawn, clutching a bottle of wine, was Ben.

'Ben…'

I'd heard his name on Jessica's lips many times. She had screeched at him happily, moaned his name when they were making love. Never had I heard it the way she said it tonight. With regret, with remorse.

As Andrew and Marco stood up to greet the newcomer, I saw Jessica rise in her chair. Unseen by anyone else but me, Patrick yanked her arm sharply, forcing her back in her seat. Slowly he released her hand, then gave an almost imperceptible nod, and she stood up alongside him. Together they made their way over to Ben, me trailing behind.

'I didn't know we were expecting further company.' Patrick cast his eyes in my direction as though *I'd* invited Ben. He peered down the driveway. 'Any more coming? Should I prepare more food?'

'Just me,' said Ben weakly. 'Congratulations, both of you.'

'So, come, sit, drink, we've plenty to celebrate.' Patrick enclosed Jessica in his arms and herded her back to the table.

Lagging behind, I heard Andrew mutter in Ben's ear, 'Sorry, lad, I didn't know. I wouldn't have called you to come along if I had.'

So Andrew had invited Ben. Why? Was he having second thoughts about pushing Jessica into Patrick's arms? Had he too discovered that there was something off about the man? That he was a liar? That he was playing a game nobody could work out?

–

As the night went on, the evening turned from uncomfortable into excruciating. Finally, when the subject could be avoided no longer, Andrew turned to Ben.

'Any repercussions from the police, about this young lady hiding in your villa?'

Ben's face flushed a deep shade of red. He looked down at the ground as though he'd been caught in a lie. I watched his reaction with bemusement, wondering about his apparent guilt. He had no need to be embarrassed, it was common knowledge that it had all been Marco's idea.

He began to stutter out a reply: 'No, there would have been, but what with her being released without charge...' He tailed off, took a long swallow of his drink.

Andrew shook his head, narrowed his eyes. 'I don't know what the pair of you were playing at, holing up like that. You're lucky, you could both have been compromised: your career, Ben, Jessica's future.'

Guiltily I stared down at my feet. I reminded myself I wasn't responsible, that it had been Marco's plan. I peeped at him, but if his conscience was pricked, his face didn't betray it.

'So what about this wedding, then?' Andrew forced joviality into his voice. 'When and where? Soon, I hope. God knows, we could do with a celebration after everything that's happened.'

Everyone looked expectantly to Jessica. For a long moment there was silence, until she stood up.

'We're out of vodka,' she said, ignoring her father's question as she held aloft the empty bottle. 'I'll get some more.'

Patrick, silent up until now, touched her arm. 'Do you think we need to open another? It's getting late, our guests are probably thinking about leaving.'

I glanced at my watch. It wasn't even ten p.m. Social meals and gatherings like this one didn't start winding up until the early hours.

Jessica stared at Patrick. 'I want another drink,' she said, and with a flick of her wrist, she shook off his hand and stumbled towards the house.

'Excuse me,' said Patrick, pushing back his chair and making to follow her.

'You're right, we should be making a move.' Andrew stood up too, Marco and Ben following suit.

'I'm going to use the bathroom,' I said. But nobody heard me.

In the hallway, I paused, looked around. Upstairs? Downstairs? Who knew? Heading towards the kitchen, I pulled open a door only to find a storage cupboard. As I turned back to the stairs, I heard Jessica's voice coming from the kitchen, loud and slurred.

'I think I wanna go home with my dad.'

I waited, one hand on the banister, for Patrick's reaction.

'No, Jessica,' he replied, quiet but firm.

'No?' Jessica's voice rose an octave.

Realising my invisibility had its uses, I edged to the door and peeked into the room.

Jessica stood in front of the sink, looking up at him.

'No,' Patrick continued. He shook his head, regretfully almost. 'The police haven't found Alexis's killer yet. Though you're not being charged, you're still a suspect. If you go away from here, I can't protect you, not like I can when you're under my roof. You need to listen to me on this one, okay?'

Jessica was still a suspect?

She turned to the window, gripping the edge of the sink. I saw her throat hitching, knew her well enough to know what was coming next. The aroma of the litre bottle that she'd drunk almost entirely on her own flooded the air as it splashed onto the porcelain. I waited for Patrick to do the job that had once been mine; to rub her back, sweep her hair away from her face and hold it there. Instead, his mouth twisted, and he watched her for a second before stepping around her and out the back door.

I should have gone to her then, comforted her, encouraged her to come back to Jenson Coast with us, regardless of what he said. But I didn't. Instead, I watched as her head rose, and she looked through the window at the others, who had moved towards their cars. Patrick was shaking hands with Andrew, Marco and Ben. Then he gestured back to the house, no doubt apologising for Jessica's drunken behaviour.

Edging back to the door, I slipped outside and ran around the house, passing Patrick on the way.

'Bye, Patrick,' I said softly.

He didn't reply, he didn't even look at me.

Chapter 20

Louise

Then

A week after the abortive dinner party with Patrick and Jessica, Marco and I headed inland to pay our respects at the memorial for Alexis Dubois. Cannes was still covered by grey cloud. The temperature had dropped, and although summer wasn't over, there was a definite chill in the air.

'How's the business doing?' I asked Marco, determined to let him know I'd not forgotten the money he owed me.

'Steady,' he responded. 'Getting a bit better, anyway,' he added quickly, casting a sideways glance at me.

'How long until we reach the church?' I asked.

'Not far now.'

The funeral, when the police finally released her body, would be a private, family affair. I didn't particularly want to go to the memorial, but Marco had said that if we were using her name on the penthouse suite in Jenson Coast, we had to show our faces.

I looked out of the window at the slow-moving traffic. It seemed like everyone in Cannes was headed in the same direction as us.

'Did I tell you what I heard Patrick say? That when Jessica said she wanted to go back to Jenson Coast, he said no.'

'You did.' He nodded. 'It's not our business, don't let it worry you.'

I changed tack, eager to keep a dialogue between us. 'Do you think they'll really get married?'

'Nope,' he said. 'Jessica's got a new toy in Patrick. As soon as she tires of him, she'll be back.' I felt his eyes on me. 'That's what she does: gets bored and moves on to the next fad.'

I stared out of the passenger-side window. Was that what I'd been to her, a fad? A stopgap between men?

I regarded Marco in the driver's seat, envied him his ability to just shrug things off. But there was one thing he wouldn't shrug off, I promised myself.

My money.

'Here we are,' he announced as he turned into Le Grand Jas cemetery grounds. 'Jesus, look at it!'

I gaped through the window, grateful for the black-tinted windows. The journalists and photographers who had slowly drifted away from Jenson Coast were all here, and the crowd of paparazzi had doubled in size. Police cars lined the route to the church, and I saw Maron, the officer who had questioned me after Alexis's death, scrutinising every mourner who passed her.

I scanned the crowd for Nathan Saint. I'd not heard nor seen anything of him lately. The drugs trade in Cannes had faded away; no longer was Marco dealing so blatantly in the casino. Maybe Nathan was doing the same. Perhaps he had left town or been told to lie low. Maybe he was running or hiding, scared that his dealing would be connected to the death of the seemingly unblemished girl who had been the princess of this town.

We parked well away from the glare of both the police and the reporters and blended into the crowd as we made our way to the church.

The service was dismal and very, very long. Alexis's family were among the most popular in this region, and ministers, politicians, friends, socialites and family members stood up and talked about the girl whose life had been taken far too soon. For the first time, the devastation resonated with me. Since that awful night, I had been concentrating on Jessica, on the injustice of her arrest, making sure that Marco and I were in the clear and that Jenson Coast didn't suffer. Then there was the interview and the plans for ways to cash in on the tragedy and make it work for us. I felt suddenly sick, actually nauseous, and so I stood up and made my way out of the church, thankful that we were seated at the back and nobody saw me fleeing.

I bent over the stone wall that lined the graveyard as I waited for the queasiness to pass.

To distract myself, I walked up to the flowers that were on display at the entrance to the church. There were hundreds of bouquets, but I found the one Andrew had asked me to order quite easily. It was showy but classy, with a card that simply read: *From all at Jenson Coast.*

Eventually Marco came up behind me.

'You all right?' he asked gruffly.

I shrugged, my eyes blurred with tears. Who was I crying for? Alexis? Me? The summer holding the promise of a new life that had been snatched away from me? My memories were tarnished, black, just like the sky that swelled and ballooned above us. Dark like the blood that had pooled around Alexis's body.

'I think I'll go home,' I said, straightening up and attempting a smile.

Suddenly I was very, very tired. I'd got no further with my attempts at extracting my money from him, but right now, all I wanted to do was lock the door of my flat behind me and crawl into bed.

He gave a half-wave, then lowered his shades to cover his eyes. 'You'll be all right getting back?' he asked.

I nodded. 'I'll be fine,' I whispered, but he'd already turned back towards the church.

I watched him go, my face wet now with tears.

On the long bus journey home, I finally admitted it: I was losing him, I was losing everything. I dabbed at my eyes behind my shades and sighed as finally I arrived in my familiar cobbled street. As I pushed open my door, I thought of the service, and the sadness, and the blackness that surrounded all of us. Perhaps Cannes was cursed, I thought; without Alexis Dubois, the brightest star, maybe we were doomed to live in darkness now.

I was pulling down my fold-out bed before it struck me. My brain ran backwards, retracing my steps, the realisation hitting me that I'd not unlocked my front door; that it had in fact been left ajar.

Leaving the bed, I glanced around. Nothing seemed out of the ordinary. My tiny television was still in place; a little pile of money sat on the arm of the sofa where I'd left it. My laptop lay on the kitchen counter, untouched, unopened. I looked over at the door that led to my darkroom in the basement and let out a strangled cry as I saw that, like the front door, it was slightly open. Any concerns I had that somebody else might be in the apartment left my mind as I darted over and yanked the door wide open. Staring down into the gloom, I reached out and flicked on the strip lighting. Then I walked slowly down the stairs, my heart sinking with each step that I took.

I stood in the middle of the room and slowly turned in a full circle. Years of film had been ripped from their cartridges to be spooled on the floor and draped over the few bits of furniture I had down here. Prints had been torn into little pieces and hurled like confetti. I thought immediately of the pictures of Alexis Dubois' house that I'd doctored, poring over them painstakingly, printing and discarding and reworking from the laptop until I was at last satisfied with the resulting ghostly figure. I'd kept them all, each and every stage of the faked pictures. They were my safety net, a reminder that I could show Marco if he wasn't forthcoming with my money. I sank to the floor.

Had Marco done this? Had he destroyed the evidence of what I'd done so he wouldn't have to pay me?

But no, he couldn't, could he? He had been with me at the memorial service; he was still there now, as far as I knew. Though it had taken me ages to get home on the bus. He could have driven here, done whatever he needed to and been gone before I was even halfway home.

The cabinet where I had stored the faked photos was an old-fashioned metal four-drawer unit, which now lay upended on its side, dozens of files and photos spilling out. I rushed over and squatted down, knowing I'd never lift it upright, but aware of exactly where I'd left the file that contained my forged work of art. It wasn't there, and though I pulled out every file that remained, the prints that could condemn me to my own prison sentence were gone.

I kicked out at the cabinet and sat with my back to the wall, looking around at my ruined work and equipment. I gazed at the room until my eyes began to sting, then eventually, I dragged myself back upstairs and into the kitchen.

I pulled everything out of my big shoulder bag, even though I knew I didn't carry the file of forgeries with me. But my notepad was there, a battered old thing I'd had for years, recording every job that I'd done and also, helpfully, documenting where I filed my proofs. Picking it up, I headed back into the basement.

Two hours and half a bottle of wine later, I finished my stock-take. I'd matched up every single shot for each job I'd been booked for over the last year. I stared at the notebook and the stack of files that I'd placed next to me on the floor. I wanted to double-check and then check again, but I knew I'd come up with the same answer.

I sat for hours in the darkroom. When night fell, I dragged myself back upstairs and called Marco, telling him to come to my apartment.

I returned downstairs to wait.

'Lou?' His voice pierced through the haze.

I looked towards the door above me. 'I'm down here.'

Heavy footsteps. His shadow filled the doorway. 'Jesus, Louise, what happened?'

'I've been burgled,' I said, more evenly than I felt.

He jogged down the stairs and looked around the room. 'When did this happen? Did they take a lot?'

I shrugged, kicked at a spool of film on the floor. 'Today, while I was at the service.' I paused. 'Whoever did this took the prints I faked.'

'It's okay, the police have the originals. We don't need them any more – Jessica's free now.' He lowered himself to sit beside me.

I shook my head. 'You don't understand, they took the whole file. The prints before I Photoshopped them, the copies in between that I wasn't satisfied with. They took all of it,' I reached into my bag and pulled out my cigarettes, lit one and sucked at it greedily. 'And that's not the worst. That was the *only* file they took, everything else is still here. Whoever did this knew what they were looking for.'

I watched him carefully as he surveyed the trashed room. His face was ashen. Could he have done this himself and still be shocked? Was he that good an actor?

I didn't know. I didn't know him well enough.

'They took everything?' he asked. 'All of it?'

Was that his mind working that I saw now? Were the cogs whirring, thinking that even if he hadn't done this himself, it could still get him off the hook for paying what he owed me?

'Well, not all of it,' I said, standing up and dusting down my skirt. 'Obviously, I kept a set for myself, just in case anything ever happened.' I waited a beat. 'I paid for a security box, stored them in there.'

He nodded distractedly. 'Good thinking, Lou,' he said. 'So… what do we do now? We can't call the police, can we?'

I moved into the shadows so I had the opportunity to study him unseen. My lie about the copies didn't seem to have worried him. But who else would know exactly what I had been hiding down here?

'Do you think…?' I let my sentence hang in the air between us, trailing off. Immediately, Marco spoke up.

'Patrick?' His mouth set in a grim line.

Emotion rushed at me. Relief that Marco hadn't double-crossed me. Fear that Patrick had been in here and could come back at any time.

I dissolved into tears that I had been determined not to shed. Suddenly everything was too much and I folded into myself, cried like I would never stop. And then, just like *that* night, the night I'd seen Alexis's broken and bloodied body, arms encircled me, pulled me up, pulled me in.

'S'all right,' Marco said, his tone awkward but his grip strong. 'Come on, let's get out of here. You can't stay here tonight.'

I packed a few clothes, my camera and my notebook, Marco watching me. When I was done, he took the bag from me and we made our way out to his car.

'Thanks for this,' I muttered. 'I… I really don't want to put you out, but I appreciate it.' I gazed back at my flat as we pulled away. 'Just the thought of being in there, if he came back…'

Marco cleared his throat. 'Don't think about it. You'll stay at Jenson Coast.' He flashed me a smile. 'Everything will be fine.'

I nodded, leaned my head back and closed my eyes.

Chapter 21

Jessica

Now

After attacking Louise, I could have stayed on the hallway carpet forever, just closed my eyes and drifted off, and maybe when I opened them both, Ben and Louise would have gone, Patrick's funeral would have taken place, the police would have decided to leave me alone and I could just live here quietly and sedately in my house.

But that was wishful thinking, childish dreams that came from my old life, before Patrick and before Alexis Dubois, when if I had a problem I could go to Daddy and he would make it all okay again. Jesus Christ, I didn't even have my father to see me through this.

I made a noise in my throat, halfway between a sob and a laugh, that bordered on the hysterical. I became aware of Louise still retching beside me, and I rolled over and looked at her. I felt nothing as I watched her sit up, one hand wiping her watering eyes, the other rubbing her neck.

I looked over at Ben, who stood in front of the door, leaning against it, both palms flat on the wood, his back to me.

Why were they here? Were they both somehow wanting to cash in on my life?

Louise had courted publicity since she realised the life-style it could bring her; she had used my situation back in Cannes and Alexis's death to her own advantage, for financial gain, starting with that damned interview for the gossip rag. And Ben, he was practically a national treasure these days with his nature and wildlife programmes and his long-term contract with the BBC. He was, and always had been, the boy next door, but sometimes even the boy next door needed a little controversial notoriety.

And if my thoughts were correct, there would be reporters turning up on the doorstep at any minute.

'I think you should both leave,' I said, in a voice that sounded far stronger than I felt. 'Ben, take Louise back to your hotel. Leave me the number and I'll contact the pair of you tomorrow.' I wasn't used to issuing demands any more, and it gave me a spark of strength.

They both began to talk at once, my name falling in an identical whine from their mouths. I held my hand up to silence them.

'Leave the number and go.' I would have said 'please'; usually I would have tagged that word on the end of any request, but not now, not any more. Never again, I told myself fiercely.

Louise remained silent as she hauled herself off the floor and slowly made her way up the stairs. I watched her, for no reason except to avoid looking at Ben. He cleared his throat, but before he could speak, I held up my hand again.

'Just… just for tonight, Ben. I have to be on my own tonight.'

I retreated into the kitchen and he didn't follow me. I moved through to the conservatory, slumped into a chair, closed my eyes and waited for Louise to finish packing.

That was when I heard it: a very faint but detectable squeak that came from above. I snapped my eyes open, looked up towards the ceiling.

When you live in a house for enough years, and spend those years in an almost permanent state of gently simmering fear, you learn to recognise each and every sound, especially those you associate with an event you'd rather forget but never will in case you need to identify the sign again at a later date. I got up and moved back into the hallway, brushing past Ben, barely seeing him, taking no notice of him as he stood statue-like by the door. As I put one foot on the bottom stair and rested my hand on the banister, Louise appeared in the doorway of my bedroom. She carried her bag and her coat, and as she descended, I stood back and let her pass. But when she reached for the door, I put my hand on her arm.

'Wait, please,' I said.

From her expression, I knew she was anticipating the apology she assumed I was about to make. I took her bag off her arm; she relaxed more, a smile even forming on her lips now. Eager to forgive me for half strangling her, eager to forgive me anything.

But instead of pleading with her to stay, I yanked open her big shoulder bag and upended its contents onto the floor. She gasped, and Ben stepped forward. I paid no attention to either of them as I crouched down and rifled through Louise's things. Once I could see there was nothing of interest to me among them, I put them back one by one with more care than I'd removed them, then stood up and handed the bag to her.

She snatched it from my hand, her eyes tear-filled again as she pulled open the front door. 'Jessica...'

I ignored her plea, her pathetic small voice.

Ben looked at me and said nothing. It was interesting: we didn't really need words, Ben and I. Ours was a relationship of the body, not just in sex, but in the way he would sling his arm across my shoulders and in return I would fit perfectly into his chest. We could hold hands for hours without becoming uncomfortable, or sit side by side with just my foot touching his knee or his hand resting on my arm. And there were no words now. I dared not speak mine and it seemed he couldn't find any. I nodded at him, and bleakly, he nodded back and went outside to stand by Louise.

I closed the door quietly and locked it. Then I switched off all the lights, retrieved a couple of items from the kitchen and went upstairs. In the bedroom, I opened the drawers in both bedside tables. Patrick had been a neat freak, with literally everything that was stored anywhere lined up, labels facing forward. I had got into this habit myself over the years – sometimes tidiness seemed to help keep the fear at bay – and I knew straight away that both these drawers had been opened and the contents moved. Everything was still there, almost where it should be, but the papers were not totally straight and parallel to each other.

I looked at the cupboard door. Louise had left it ajar; she couldn't have known the noise it made before she opened it, and she wouldn't have wanted to risk it happening again as she closed it. Pulling a chair across, I clambered up on it, ran my hand over the uppermost shelf. Blindly, I found what I was seeking and pulled it out. It was time to move it to a safer place.

In recent years, the life I lived had become a puzzle. Sometimes I would happen upon clues, little red flags that led me to believe that nothing was quite as it appeared. I left these clues where I found them, until Patrick's death, when I knew people from outside would want to poke over our lives and our home, and then I'd collected most of them and placed them behind the side panel underneath the bathtub. Not just behind the panel, but underneath the two loosened floorboards that sat three and four planks back, for if I'd learned anything during the last eight years, it was to conceal absolutely anything that should not be found.

I recalled Louise's words, how Nina Hart had stood here, her gaze lingering on the bath. She had not looked beneath it, though. Why would she?

I looked now, on my knees, with the panel removed, the marks of the screws evident on it, the floorboards levered up and resting in the bath, and I took out my red flags, one by one. The shotgun. Patrick's laptop, the one he used every day, not the one I'd left in the kitchen for the world and the police to see. I held my biggest, boldest red flag, the clue that proved tenfold that my life wasn't all it was cracked up to be, yet also that it wasn't over, and stroked at the cover, then opened it up and shook my head, in awe each time I looked at it that it could still be used, was still valid, though only just. Finally I put everything back, soothed by the action, soothed by everything I'd looked at, letting my gaze rest on them before I put the floorboards back, and then the bath panel, and checked it from every angle with a critical eye.

It had taken years and it might take some time still, but slowly the puzzle pieces were falling into place.

I stood up and was dusting off my knees when I heard a short, sharp rap at the door. I froze, still hunched over, and willed myself to stay still and quiet.

Was it Louise returning with a mouthful of excuses, or Ben, perhaps, having dropped her off at his hotel? Or – and oh God, the worst one – was it Hart back again, wanting to chip away at me further?

I heard the letter box squeak open, and then a tiny, reed-thin voice came floating through and up the stairs.

'Jessica? Jessica, can you let me in? It's me, it's Sally.'

I remained in the bathroom, feeling my forehead wrinkle in confusion. Sally? I didn't know anyone called Sally.

And then I realised, and I straightened up so fast my spine cracked. With one last glance at the bath panel, I hurried down the stairs and wrenched open the front door. She moved forward hesitantly. I pushed the door shut behind her.

I switched on the light in the hallway and turned to study the stranger in my home. She was nothing like I'd imagined her to be. She wore a strangely old-fashioned raincoat, the colour of it almost matching her mousy hair, beneath it white linen trousers and sensible flat brown shoes, and she stood in the hallway with her hands in her pockets and looked down at the floor. I caught a scent from her, one that clung to her breath and her clothes, an aroma I couldn't quite decipher, something sweet, something sickly.

'I'm sorry to disturb you,' she said, her voice meek and quiet and low. 'I had to come, though. I'm Sally—'

'I know, you said,' I replied. She raised her eyes then, looking at me properly for the first time since I'd pulled her inside. And even if she hadn't told me her name, I'd have known just by looking into those rich chocolate-brown eyes, eyes I'd seen before, eyes that had seen me, that had cast fear into my soul. 'You're Sally King,' I stated. 'Patrick's mother.'

Chapter 22

Jessica's Diary
October 2011

I stumbled through my new life in England moving neither forwards nor backwards. Then came the deer, and my life swivelled on the axis where it hung with so much fragility, and changed again.

It came out of the trees, grazed around the field that bordered the cottage. I watched for a while, not daring to speak, but as it seemed not to even see me, I called out in a hissed whisper to Patrick.

'What?' he said, coming through to the conservatory, knotting his tie.

'Look,' I whispered. 'Out there, the deer.'

I watched him, saw his mouth twitch a little. This is it, I thought, something that can bind us to this house, a first experience for both of us, one that we can look back on and build on. I reached my hand tentatively towards him and felt a hopeful surge as I saw his hand come up too. But instead of taking mine, he moved backwards to the hallway. His quiet tread could be heard on the stairs, and then, from our room, I heard the grate of the cupboard door as it opened. I smiled, imagining him retrieving the camera. We never took photos, never even thought of it, and that he was going to record this moment made me almost happy. No, not happy; it made me hopeful.

But when he returned, it was not with a camera in his hand, but something wrapped in brown burlap. He edged out of the door towards the deer, and I sat up in the chair, watched him as he moved down the field. I held my breath as he got within a few feet of the animal, touched my fingertips to the window pane as he shook something out of the sack. I watched his arm as it came up, and when the shot rang out, I let out a strangled cry and ran for the door.

It was an old gun, it must have been to have belched out so much smoke. When I reached him, I saw that the deer was gone, and I breathed out in relief. But the bullet must have caught the animal, for when Patrick turned to face me, he had flecks of blood on his face. He wiped the back of his hand across his mouth, and I knew that the smudged bloodstain on his jaw would be something I would never forget. I didn't move, couldn't move, couldn't even speak, and I stood in that spot as Patrick wrapped up the gun I'd never known he had and walked back to the house.

When he left for work, I gathered together all the money I'd taken from him and bought a pay-as-you-go mobile phone. Then I visited the local library and used the internet on their public computer. It was easy to track Ben down through his agent. And when I had the number, I called him.

Chapter 23

Louise

Then

We slipped into something indefinable, Marco and me. After the break-in at my flat, I remained not only at Jenson Coast, but in Marco's suite. We fell into a weird routine. He came and went, tending to hotel business. More often than not we ate dinner together. Sometimes we had sex. I didn't know what we were, I didn't ask.

Still I waited for the right time to broach the subject of the money he had promised me. At times, though, it didn't seem so important. I didn't have any rent to pay at Jenson Coast, and the food was free. I thought of my old flat. I'd let the rent go into arrears. Any time now the lease would expire or be taken from me. Previously, this would have worried me senseless, but the more time I spent at Jenson Coast, the more I felt like I belonged with these people. Marco surely wouldn't see me homeless.

Would he?

So I let it go, always keeping in my mind that I had backed myself up with the pretend batch of prints in the make-believe security box.

And then, in the first week of September, two things happened. First, the cloud that had hung over us for weeks, threatening but never delivering, finally broke. Secondly, Jessica got married.

As thunder rumbled and rain lashed down, a convoy travelled just over two hours from Cannes to the wedding location in Provence. I sat in the passenger seat next to Marco, while Jessica and Patrick headed up the line of cars with Andrew flying solo behind.

As I watched the back of Jessica's blonde head, I found myself still as disbelieving now as I was one week ago when we received the wedding invitation.

'I can't believe they're doing it,' I commented to Marco. 'I mean, is it even this easy to get married in France if you're not a citizen? Or is she? Has she got dual nationality or something?'

'I'll tell you something, he must have pulled some strings to get the Chateau Villermaux at short notice.' Marco ignored my question and looked over at me. 'Has Jessica said why there's such a rush?'

But I hadn't spoken to her at all. I hadn't seen her since I'd been staying at Jenson Coast. I'd seen nobody, only Marco and, on occasion, Andrew.

I'd spoken tentatively to Andrew, mentioned if maybe it wasn't a little soon for a wedding. In reply, he had said the oddest thing.

'According to Andrew,' I told Marco now, 'Patrick said that once they're married, he can never be called upon to give evidence about her. Spousal privilege, he called it.'

'Patrick knows the photos are fake.' Marco's knuckles turned white as he clutched the steering wheel, his mouth set in a grim line. 'He's covering himself.'

It was as I had thought. And yet neither of us could work out what he was playing at.

'Do you think we should speak to him?'

Marco heaved a great sigh. 'I don't know. I just... I don't know how to read him.'

'Do you reckon anyone will be at the wedding from Patrick's side? I've never heard anything about his personal life.'

'I don't think he has anyone, from what Andrew's said. There's a mother back in England, I think, but it doesn't seem like they keep in touch.' Marco clicked on the indicator. 'Here we are.'

We pulled up next to Patrick's car and I got out.

'I'll check us in,' said Patrick to Jessica, ignoring me as I approached. With an unfathomable black look at me, he put his head down and strode towards the reception, Marco following behind with our cases.

I looked at Jessica, not knowing what to say to her. How could it be that just a matter of weeks ago, I'd felt like I knew her better than I even knew myself? We had spoken about everything, nothing was off limits. Now there was nothing but silence.

'Are you excited?' I asked after a stilted, awkward moment. Hidden as she was behind her impossibly large shades I couldn't tell.

She shrugged, offered me a tight, pinched smile.

'Do you want to take a walk while the men are checking in?' I gestured to the grounds. 'It's beautiful here and the rain has almost stopped.'

I watched her as we walked. Jessica didn't look how a bride should: she looked pale, drawn, anxious.

'Jessica, do you want to do this?' My words came out in a rush, as though if I didn't speak fast, I'd lose my nerve. 'Do you want to be married to Patrick?'

She looked at me properly for the first time. With a shaking hand she removed her shades. I scrutinised her face, the purple shadows under her eyes. With a tiny, almost imperceptible shake of her head, she whispered her answer:

'No.'

Robotically, she walked on, head down now, and I looked on in horror at the tear that tracked down her face.

Tentatively, I took her hand and led her to a nearby bench. 'Jessica, you don't have to do it if you don't want to. This is really huge, and if you're not sure…'

'It didn't seem real until now, it's all happening too fast.' Her words were clipped, sharp. She stared straight ahead.

'So slow it down, talk to him.' I made a face. Personally I wouldn't fancy talking to Patrick about calling off the wedding if I were in Jessica's position.

'It's too soon for marriage. It's been, what, six weeks?' She shook her head again, dazed now. She looked like she was lost.

I replayed her words in my head.

Six weeks…

I sat up straight on the bench. 'Six weeks, really? Has it been that long?'

She clicked her tongue, fixed me with a stare, a little of the old Jessica coming back. 'Six weeks isn't long, that's my point. Louise? Are you listening to me?'

'What?' I tried to concentrate on what she was saying, but suddenly I had to get out of there. I stood up. 'Tell him it's over. We'll be here, your dad, Marco and me.' I patted her hand, nodded reassuringly and darted back along the veranda to the hotel.

Marco never had much interest in what I was doing. Sometimes I didn't think he noticed if I was with him or not, so it was easy to slip out with his car keys and make the drive into Aix-en-Provence. I cleared my mind, thinking of nothing as I drove – not Jessica, not the life-changing thing that had occurred to me as we were talking – and after an hour, I pulled up outside my destination.

Inside, as I waited in line, a tub of camomile lotion caught my eye. I remembered my mum buying the stuff, slathering it over my blistering, flaking skin until the scent made my stomach churn. I flexed my fingers, blinking in astonishment as the skin on my knuckles for once didn't split and bleed at the motion.

My hands were healed. As I paid for my purchase with eyes downcast, I thought of old wives' tales I'd heard: how, in the situation I was in, ailments and conditions cleared up as if by a miracle.

I made my purchase quickly, dumped the brown paper bag on the passenger seat and broke the speed limit all the way back to Chateau Villermaux. When I let myself back into the room, Marco was reclining on the bed, sipping at a beer and flicking through the channels on the television. I walked past him into the bathroom and removed the pregnancy test from the box.

I did what needed to be done quickly and set it on the side to wait. Before the minute was even up, the blue line had appeared.

It felt into the sink. I fell back onto the floor.

A baby.

Marco's baby.

I was nineteen years old. I hadn't planned on a baby, I hadn't even lived yet.

I sat there, my skin freezing on the cold tiles. I stayed there for a long time. Eventually a knock came on the door.

'Lou, you in there?' Marco shouted.

He's going to think I did it on purpose. He's going to think I did it to get the money he promised me. Because this way I'd be set up for life. Well, for eighteen years at least.

I pulled open the door. He filled the doorway, staring at me blankly, the bottle of beer hanging loosely in his fingers.

'Can I have some of that?' I whispered, not waiting for a reply as I grabbed it and gulped greedily.

'What the…? Louise?'

I looked up at him with half-closed eyes. But he wasn't looking at me, he was looking into the sink.

I shrugged, swallowed, bit back the tears. What was there to say?

Marco vanished from the doorway, retreated to the bed. He sat with his back to me. I looked away from him, pushed the door closed again with my foot.

I stayed in the bathroom for what seemed like hours, until I forced myself to stagger back out into the suite. He was still on the bed, the television playing in front of his unseeing eyes.

'What do you wanna do?' he asked softly.

I caught sight of myself in the mirror on the wall. My reflection startled me. My skin was clear and smooth, the flakes gone, the scratches and eczema scars fading. This pregnancy, though it couldn't be very far along, had done that.

'I want to keep it,' I replied. It was automatic. I hadn't even thought about it. My answer was instinctual.

'So…' he said as he tilted his head, regarding me with an expression I couldn't read.

'So,' I confirmed.

To his credit, he didn't ask if it was his. I was sure he knew me well enough to know my lifestyle, to know me, to know that no other man had so much as looked at me while I'd been in France.

I burned with shame at my shortcomings.

Silence enveloped us again until Marco spoke up:

'Have we got to meet the others tonight for dinner?'

I jerked upright. 'Jessica! I'd forgotten. Marco, I think she's calling off the wedding.'

He looked at me over his shoulder, a questioning look on his face.

'I should call her,' I said, reaching for my phone.

Just as I put my hand on it, the telephone on the nightstand rang. I snatched it up.

'Jessica?'

'Change of plan,' she whispered, her voice so low I could barely hear her. 'Well, same plan actually. I'm getting married tomorrow.'

'Oh…' I twisted the phone cord in my fingers, my mind still on my pregnancy, on Marco, on money. I didn't even wonder why or how she'd had such a sudden change of heart. 'So, are we eating tonight or will we see you tomorrow at the ceremony?'

With a gentle click, the phone line went dead. I looked at the handset before replacing it on the receiver.

'I guess we'll see her tomorrow,' I said to Marco.

He nodded, his mouth thin and tight as he snatched up his car keys.

'Back later,' he muttered, and slammed out of the room.

I moved over to the window and watched as he got in his car and roared off. The rain continued to beat down.

–

The sun cracked through the grey as we gathered outside the following day. The castle formed a beautiful backdrop as the small group stood around the happy couple.

Neither of them looked particularly happy, however. I cast a sideways glance at Marco. Would this be us one day? Shunted into a future together because I hadn't given him a choice? A small fire of irritation burned in my stomach. Birth control took two people. I'd been careless with my pill, but he'd never even asked me about it.

'She looks happy, doesn't she?' Andrew leaned in to me, interrupting my sour thoughts. He was seeking reassurance, I thought, rather than making a statement.

I put my arm through his and squeezed. 'She'll be very happy,' I whispered back to him. I didn't sound convincing.

In the bar afterwards, I hung back, watching Jessica as she skirted around the outside of the small group. It was so out of character. She was always in the centre, not falling back to lurk in the shadows as she was doing now.

I thought how good it would be to confide in her. After all, she had shared her wedding fears with me yesterday – not that I had been much use, I thought guiltily. But this, my secret, it could be something that could bring her back to me.

Edging up to her, I pulled her aside.

'I have to tell you something. I'm having Marco's baby!' I hissed in her ear, my words coming out in a rush, my face flushing as I said them out loud for the first time.

She stared through me, her eyes bleak and dark, and my heart dropped. 'Jessica...?'

Her large green eyes pooled with sudden tears. She moved her lips to my ear, but before she could speak, I felt her stiffen.

I turned around and took a step back as Patrick loomed over me. I wouldn't have thought he could loom over anyone – he wasn't as big as Marco – but I instinctively moved back a step and covered my stomach protectively with my hand. Patrick didn't miss this action; his eyes travelled down the bodice of my summer dress and he smiled and licked his lips.

'Louise, why don't you dance with me?'

I blanched. Surely his first dance should be with his new wife? Why would he want to dance with me? He never even spoke to me. But Jessica flicked her wrist at us and moved back to the bar. I let Patrick lead me on to the dance floor.

'Marco told me your news,' he said, his breath hot in my ear. 'Congratulations.'

'Thanks,' I replied uncomfortably, wondering what Marco had actually said. His reaction to me wasn't exactly like he wanted to break open the cigars.

'But you have to be careful these early days of pregnancy.' His left hand gripped mine so tightly, I gasped.

'What do you mean?' I asked.

He kept moving, twirling us around the floor. I heard my knuckles crack before I felt it, and I whimpered as the fingers of his right hand dug painfully into my waist.

'Keep away from Jessica, she doesn't need you advising her on anything.' He pulled away, looked down into my eyes. He appeared mournful, sad even, his expression so out of keeping with his words and the way he squeezed my hand that I was momentarily confused, sure that I hadn't heard him correctly. 'Keep your little family safe, Louise. It's all in your hands.'

If I opened my mouth I would scream, or cry. I wasn't sure what would be worse. Frozen, I looked over Patrick's shoulder. I saw Marco laughing in the corner with Andrew, unaware of me, unaware of Patrick. I saw his hand swiping at his face, his fingers pinching his nostrils. I knew he had snorted coke to get him through a boring day. I knew him that well, at least.

'I don't know what you mean,' I whispered. 'Please, you're hurting me.'

'Come, have a glass of champagne,' Patrick replied softly, and still holding my hand in his and with his arm around my waist, he led me to a table away from everyone else.

'Jessica and I are returning to England for a while. There will be no need for you to contact her. It's time you left us alone now. We're married, your life has moved on. Your friendship is done, she's had enough of your games.'

'Games?' My voice wobbled horribly and I pressed the back of my hand to my mouth. Patrick was the game-player, not me.

'Your disgusting sexual advances,' he fired back. 'She hates it, she's told me how uncomfortable it makes her. Leave my wife alone, neither of us wants you around.' He paused. I watched as he reached elegantly into the ice bucket, plucked out an ice pick and touched the sharp end with his finger. 'For your own sake, for your baby's sake, leave it.'

Had Jessica really said that to him? I'd never been in love with her, I'd never wanted her to be my girlfriend. Sure, I did love her; if I was truthful, I was slightly obsessional about her. She was beautiful and wild and free and everything I'd never be – I adored her.

I thought of dark fantasies I'd had: the feel of her hair, the touch of her skin. The contradiction between my personal protests and my true feelings seared my face.

I heard a small whimper, understood it came from me. 'I didn't… It was never like that…'

I clamped my mouth shut. Patrick wasn't interested in reasoning or excuses. He didn't want me in Jessica's life, not even as a friend. He was taking her to live in England, separating her from her loved ones. Piece by piece, he was breaking up the group.

I leaned heavily on the table and looked over at Andrew, still talking jovially with Marco. Did he know about England? Had he encouraged it, to stop Jessica's wild, free-living, troublemaking ways? Would he rather she was with strict, no-nonsense Patrick?

I sagged at the thought of Cannes without her. Even though we'd not spent time together lately, I had always been sure she would return to the fold.

Jessica living in dark and gloomy England, the place I was determined never to return to. It was like clipping a bird's wings.

And with Patrick's words and his actions he was asking me to make a choice between Jessica and my baby.

The choice was obvious.

There was no choice. Not only for the safety of my unborn child, but for me, for the life I was desperate to lead.

Marco and I returned to Cannes the next morning.

And I wouldn't see Jessica again for another eight years.

Chapter 24

Jessica

Now

I made instant coffee for my unexpected guest, with a hefty helping of milk. Sally didn't strike me as someone who would require freshly ground beans from the fancy machine. She took the mug gratefully, wrapped her hands around it and stared down into the pale brown liquid.

'I'm sorry I didn't call you, but I didn't know how to reach you,' I said. 'How did you find out about Patrick?'

'The police called me. It was a shock. Nobody expects their children to go first.' Her voice wobbled dangerously and I lowered my gaze and looked down at the table.

Please don't cry, I begged silently.

She took a tissue out of her pocket and dabbed at her eyes before picking up her cup again and taking a sip. I watched her carefully.

If you had put a line-up of women in front of me and asked me to decide which one was Patrick's mother, I'd never have chosen the one who sat in front of me now. And just as I had that thought, I realised why Sally King had never been a part of our lives: it was because she didn't fit.

Patrick had been money-driven and ambitious. He wanted to be regarded as upper class. That was evident in the clothes he wore, the restaurants he ate in and the social circle he mingled with. It was clear in the clothes that he made me wear, the way he dissuaded me from finding employment except for volunteering, because that was appropriate for a woman of my means; I could give back charitably, but not be seen to take a wage. It was why he had selected me as his wife, because my father owned a hotel in the South of France and because my family had decades-old money. Yet I wasn't the normal high-society wife; I had a past, a blemish that only served to heighten the interest in me, and it made Patrick look a little less staid.

Sally didn't fit his mould. I didn't either, not really, but he thought he could change me, and he very nearly succeeded.

'I didn't see much of Patrick once he left home to go to university.' She spoke up suddenly.

'That must have been hard. He was your only child, right?' I asked, trying to sound interested, trying to inject warmth into my tone.

Sally laughed. She put her head back and brayed, showing silver fillings in her back teeth. It was such a startling change from the demure, mouse-like creature who had sat opposite me only moments before. She covered her mouth with her fingers to smother the sound.

'I'm sorry, that must have seemed really inappropriate.' She coughed and wiped at her eyes again. 'But it wasn't hard, my dear. When Patrick left home, I relaxed for the first time since he was born.'

As her mirth fell away, her words came out hard and brittle, and I leaned forward and put my elbows on the table, intrigued now by this woman I'd never known but had often wondered about.

'What do you mean?' I demanded.

Gone was the timid, reticent Sally, a gleaming-eyed, abrupt woman in her place. 'How was he with you, Jessica?'

Her question was a challenge and it was one that I rose to.

'Controlling, possessive, frightening, domineering,' I replied, listing his faults in a monotone.

She made a noise in her throat, a murmur of agreement, maybe.

'So, like me, do you feel a little relief?'

'Oh God, Sally!' I laughed to break the tension. 'I mean, come on...'

'Poor girl.' She reached over the table, patted my hand almost absent-mindedly. 'It's a shame we were kept apart, we could have been friends, allies, even.'

In that moment, I saw that she was speaking the truth. With two of us to keep Patrick in line, keep his peculiar idiosyncrasies at bay, we might have made it work. It *was* a shame, and I felt guilty that I hadn't tried harder, hadn't insisted that I meet her. But maybe he'd foreseen what the pair of us together would have been like and had forbidden it.

Sally went to sip her coffee. I took it away from her and avoided her look of surprise as I turned and poured it down the sink.

'Forget the coffee, Sally,' I said, brightly. 'Let's have something stronger. We'll toast Patrick, raise a glass to him. What would you like?'

She looked around the kitchen as though a bar stocked with liqueur was suddenly going to appear. When none did, she looked over at me, her eyes twinkling.

'Do you have any beer?'

I was about to say no when I remembered the boxed crate that Patrick had received from a client last Christmas. I opened the under-stairs cupboard and brought the box into the kitchen.

'Pale ale, locally brewed.' I read the label as I pulled out a bottle and handed it across to Sally. 'Glass?'

She shook her head, popped the cap off and drank greedily. It foamed up, and I looked away as she covered the bottle top with her lips. I realised now that the smell that emitted from her was alcohol – not the beer I'd just served, but something stronger, like gin or vodka. It was an aroma that seeped from her pores like sweat, and I knew then that she drank every day, every night. She probably hadn't always been an alcoholic, but something or someone had pushed her to it, and now she drank spirits freely, the same way other people would think nothing of having a morning coffee or afternoon tea.

'Patrick hated beer,' she stated, her eyes flat now, no longer gleaming like they'd been a moment ago.

I nodded in agreement and joined her at the kitchen table. 'I never saw him drink alcohol.'

We sat in silence for a few moments until I could stand the sound of her slurping no longer. I got up to switch the radio on. A local station blared out a traffic report.

'Have you come far?' I asked politely. The thought occurred that if she had too much to drink, she might want to stay with me. I'd already got rid of one unwanted house guest, I didn't want to have to discourage another.

'Colchester,' she replied with a wave of her arm.

I frowned and came back to the table. 'Why were you there?'

She looked up, surprise on her face. 'That's where I live.'

I sat down heavily and slumped in my chair, picked at the label on the beer bottle. Colchester, just a half-hour drive away, not hundreds of miles up north like Patrick had led me to believe.

'Where did he tell you I lived?'

I shook my head, embarrassed smile fixed in place. 'I'm not sure he mentioned, really, not that I can remember anyway.'

She barked out a laugh, which quickly became a sob, though her eyes were dry. Suddenly I hated Patrick for shunning her. Hadn't he realised that regardless of her flaws, he was lucky to have a mother?

'Would you like to organise Patrick's funeral, Sally?' I spoke the words quickly and without thinking.

She paused, beer bottle clamped between her lips, and stared wide-eyed at me. 'Wh-wh-why?' She bleated the word, and I could tell that her throat was coated with tears.

'I think it would be good for you to finally be able to do something for him, the most important thing you'll ever do.' I was thinking as I was speaking now, a plan forming that would not only help Sally in the long run, but would also mean I didn't have to be responsible for a job I didn't want to do.

'Oh God,' she choked. The beer bottle crashed to the table, wobbling dangerously before tipping over onto its side. Nothing spilled out, however; it was already empty.

She was coming towards me now, over the table, not around it, stretching out her arms, and I stood up and embraced her awkwardly. I clamped my mouth closed against the smell, not only of alcoholic spirits, but a greasy, unwashed scent and the underlying aroma of sickly lavender. Gently I pushed her back and she fell into her chair, her arms hanging down towards the floor. She looked exhausted.

I glanced outside and then at my watch. 'Maybe you should be getting off before it's dark.'

She stood up immediately, pulled her coat tightly around her and nodded. 'Yes, you're right. I'm so sorry, my dear, I didn't mean to keep you.'

'Oh, you didn't, you haven't kept me from anything.' I pushed my chair away and rose so we were on the same level. 'I don't know when the police will release the body... I mean Patrick. They're doing an autopsy...' I let my words tail off.

'Um, may I take one?' Sally's hand hovered above the crate of beer that I'd left on the table. A wave of empathy flooded through me, nearly flooring me with the intensity. I wasn't used to feeling much of anything in recent years, except a strictly controlled rage that simmered beneath the constant blanket of misery that I wore. Sympathy was a new one to me, compassion was long dead. But drunken Sally had evoked something in me. Something, I thought now, ironically, that her son had stolen.

'Please, take one.' I pushed the crate towards her. 'Take them all.'

'Oh.' She smiled, picking up the box and cradling it to her chest.

Together, we walked down the hallway. As we stood by the door, she shifted the crate to one arm and took my hand. 'Jessica, could I... might I be able to see where he died?'

I recalled when my father had died how little information Patrick would give me: how it had happened, where, why. I understood Sally's request. With a nod, I gestured for her to follow me upstairs.

'Just there, on his side of the bed,' I said, standing beside her.

She turned towards me, lurched forward and buried her face in my neck. I recoiled, then forced myself to return her hug. Her scent had dissipated now, or perhaps I'd just got used to it, and I found that I didn't want to let go of her. Except for Ben, nobody had touched me tenderly for such a long time, and I got the feeling that the same was true for Sally. But she moved out of my grasp towards the bed, and I let my arms fall to my sides.

'Was he… gone when you found him?'

I closed my eyes, scrambled around to tell her what I'd told the police. 'He looked like he was sleeping,' I said eventually.

She nodded, then bent forward and touched the sheet that covered the bed. Palm flat, she rubbed her hand up and down it. The feeling of distaste was back in an instant, along with the thought that I definitely wouldn't sleep in that bed now.

As though sensing my thoughts, she straightened up and looked over at me.

'Thank you, Jessica,' she whispered as she walked past me back down the stairs.

I didn't follow her, and after a moment, I heard the front door open and close behind her.

Chapter 25

Jessica's Diary
December 2011

I spoke to my father regularly, faithfully, albeit reluctantly. I knew he had encouraged Patrick to take me away. I knew he was tired of getting me out of scrapes. Before, in Germany or Spain or wherever I was, my escapades had been little misdemeanours, brushes with the law for disorderly conduct. Alexis Dubois and the subsequent threat to his livelihood had been the last straw for him. I understood, but still I burned with hurt that he had sent me away.

'Does my father know why we're here, the real reason, I mean?' I asked Patrick one evening. 'I mean, is he aware that my passport has been revoked and that you've got... that you're ill?'

'Do you want me to tell him?' Patrick asked.

Yes. Yes, I did. I wanted my father to know what his pushing us here to England had done. He had effectively closed and bolted the door to France behind me.

I listened in on the extension, after their boring business small talk, as Patrick told my father about my revoked passport.

I felt a bite of satisfaction as my father's voice wavered. Patrick placated him, told him that he would not stop fighting for my freedom to travel, he would never stop fighting to clear my name. My father bought his lies, hook, line and sinker.

I listened to Patrick's closing statement, a request that my father didn't tell anyone else that I was to remain in England.

'It could hurt your business, and from what I gather, you've just got it back on its feet,' he said smoothly. 'And while we're trying to sort it out, it's best if it's just kept between us three.'

'Why didn't you tell my dad about your... cancer?' I asked when the call ended, grimacing at the unspeakable word.

Patrick shrugged. I thought his pride had prevented him. Nobody would ever know if he could help it; he wouldn't even let me go to his hospital appointments when I made a half-hearted offer.

I let it go.

–

This morning I was sitting with Patrick in the conservatory. He was reading a newspaper, I was looking out over the fields. I liked to sit here surveying the land before me, though I was in fact anywhere else but England, reliving my summer and the years prior before my life turned upside down.

'Patrick,' I said suddenly, 'why aren't the dock cranes moving?' We could see them clearly from our home, huge, metal robots that moved side to side, offloading the cargo from the container ships.

Patrick looked at me from over his newspaper. 'It's Christmas, the docks are closed today,' he remarked, turning his head to look at the steel giants, motionless and idle.

I put my hands on the arm of the chair and half stood up. 'Christmas? It's Christmas Day?'

He had a look of amusement on his face, but said nothing, simply snapped his newspaper and went back to reading it.

I remained still, halfway between standing up and slouching back in my comfortable chair. How could it be Christmas? Had I really been here for three whole months? It seemed like three weeks to me, and the realisation chilled me. I had been walking dead for a whole season, numb, detached and apathetic. And now it was Christmas Day, and there were no presents, no tree adorned with baubles, no turkey, no relatives or friends to come in out of the cold. And Patrick hadn't mentioned the festive season at all.

I sat back down, but perched on the edge of the chair as I regarded him out of the corner of my eye. Was he happy? All these months that I had been dying inside, I had barely spared him a thought. He went to work, he came home, ate dinner, read a newspaper and went to bed. Did he even talk to me, and if so, had I responded? Had I put on an act for him the same way I did for my father over the telephone? He looked content enough, sitting in his chair, reading intently.

Three months, the tail end of autumn and the start of winter, and I'd missed it all. And then a little breath tickled around the back of my neck and I felt my eyes widen as I realised something.

We were three months into Patrick's terminal diagnosis of a year. He wouldn't see another winter, or another Christmas. My hand flew to my mouth to try and stifle the yelp that escaped anyway. He looked up at the noise and tilted his head to one side.

'What is it, Jessica?'

I swallowed, breathed deeply, and with each exhalation I felt myself thawing. I stood up on legs as wobbly as a newborn foal's.

'Can I borrow your car keys?' I asked. 'Can you give me some money?'

He set the newspaper carefully on his lap. Regarded me with suspicion. 'Why?'

'Because it's Christmas Day and I didn't…' I stopped, shook my head and tried again. 'I want to make us a Christmas dinner, I want to make this Christmas…' I broke off again, realising that it was excruciatingly difficult to tell my husband that I wanted to do something for him, for his last Christmas. I wanted to tell him that I was sorry, because although I couldn't return to France, or travel anywhere out of England, I now realised that I wasn't the one who was actually dying here.

'I don't think you'll find anywhere open, love,' he said, but he reached into his pocket and passed me his keys anyway.

I didn't break eye contact with him as I took them out of his hand. He had never called me 'love' before.

Since I had arrived in England, I had felt like I was rotting away. That single word, spoken softly, made me smile, and it was a real smile, not the clenched-teeth grimace that I painted on when I talked to my father.

'I'll find somewhere,' I promised, and left the house before I could break down.

There was a Spar shop in the town centre that wasn't only open, it also hadn't run out of meat, vegetables and potatoes. Determinedly, I heaped as much into my basket as I could carry, and even shyly wished the bored-looking server on the till a happy Christmas. Almost as an afterthought, I bought two miniature bottles of wine and a packet of cigarettes.

I drove home through the deserted streets, looking around my home town for the first time. At the last second I turned left and detoured through the roads until I came to the seafront. I parked up, got out of the car and walked down to the pebbled beach. It was a world away from La Bocca in Cannes. That beach – my beach – was lined with the softest golden sand upon which one could stand in the shade of the palm trees and look out on miles of water of the deepest blue. Here, shingle poked through the soles of my thin shoes and the sea was a murky, dirty brown. But it was still the ocean; not the Mediterranean, but an ocean all the same. La Bocca wasn't my beach any more, this one was.

I breathed deeply, wondering if I could make this work.

And this time when I rubbed away my tears, I knew they were from the chill of the ocean wind and not, as they had been that first night, from utter misery.

–

When I reached home, I waved as I saw Patrick standing in the doorway of the cottage. He wasn't wearing shoes, and he moved from foot to foot as he waited. I parked up, pulled the shopping out of the car and struggled up the path with the bags.

'Did you think I'd done a runner?' I asked, grinning as I held up the bags of food.

He made a noise in his throat, snorted a small laugh. He didn't take the bags, but he held the door open as I went through.

'You can't, can you?' he murmured as he closed the door behind me. 'Do a runner, I mean.'

I froze in the kitchen doorway, his words settling over me like snowflakes. And then, as he brushed past me, he slapped my backside. It was another first.

I turned to study him, as this time he did take the bags from me. And as he busied himself emptying them, I allowed myself a smile.

Had Patrick just made his first attempt at humour?

I didn't cook the dinner, Patrick did. But I did sit with him in the kitchen, nursing a small sherry and passing him items when he asked. We didn't talk, though somehow it wasn't uncomfortable, and I complimented him as he served up the turkey crown.

'Good job,' I said quietly as I shovelled great forkfuls of food in.

I was ravenous; I hadn't been eating, a fact verified by the extra holes I'd had to make in my belt. Had I even been cooking these past few months? I wasn't much of a cook, I never had been and had never had the need to learn. Patrick had probably been fixing us dinner when he came home, I imagined. A wave of guilt had me looking down at my plate. He was sick, seriously, terminally ill, and yet he'd been taking care of me all these months.

'Did you enjoy that?' His tone was hopeful, matching my spirit, and I nodded as I finally pushed my plate away.

'I'll do the next meal,' I whispered, more to myself than to him.

It was a silent promise, a vow that for the next nine months I would step up to the plate, I would rise to the challenge. My circumstances hadn't changed, I was still seen as a criminal, and I still couldn't leave the country, but there would be time to think about my own mess later. The next nine months would be for Patrick. I would try and get to know this stranger I was married to.

I heard his exclamation of delight as he spotted the trifle I had bought and watched as he opened a carton of custard and poured it into a pan.

He had certainly been eating while my own mind was elsewhere, I noted, as I saw how his stomach, once washboard flat, had expanded over the top of his trousers. I narrowed my eyes as I looked at him closely for the first time in months. His hair was still dark and thick, his arm muscles rippled underneath his shirt, and his hands as they lifted the pan were nimble. He had always been pale, but his cheeks were rosy and he seemed effervescent and resilient.

As he placed a bowl of trifle in front of me, I picked up a spoon and forced it down my throat, which seemed suddenly to have closed up. Despite the warmth from the oven, a shiver passed through me.

In spite of having less than a year to live, to me Patrick looked healthier than I'd ever seen him.

Chapter 26

Louise

Then

It seemed fitting that as we drove away from Jessica and Patrick's wedding, we left the storm behind us. When we arrived back in Cannes, the weather was as it should have been: hot, sunny, the coconut scent of summer back on the breeze. But as Marco drove through the narrow streets that led to my flat, my anxiety grew. Why was he bringing me back here when I'd been staying at Jenson Coast since I'd been burgled?

He slowed to a stop, kept the engine running as I stared at my apartment.

'Do you need help with your bag?' he asked, grudgingly it seemed to me.

I felt my eyes fill with tears. It was starting, he was banishing me. Did he think that if he left me at my flat, I'd leave him alone? That I'd deny my child its father? Did he think I was going to go away, that I wouldn't need help with this baby when it arrived? That I'd be fine on my own, penniless and soon to be homeless when I couldn't afford the rent?

And I didn't want to go back into the flat. It was sullied, tainted by the ruin that used to be my darkroom.

I stayed in my seat, staring out at the depressing place that was my home.

'What is it?' Marco asked, a hint of impatience showing now.

'I'm scared – you know, after the burglary,' I replied honestly. 'Would you mind coming in with me?'

'It was Patrick, we know that now. And he's leaving, anyway,' replied Marco, staring forward out of the windscreen.

Still I didn't move.

Finally he sighed and looked across the street at my home. Did he see what I saw? The flimsy wooden shutters at street level? The door that would take no more than a gentle shoulder shove to break down? He glanced at me, his eyes narrowing as he watched the tears that spilled over onto my cheeks and the uncontrollable shaking of my hands. I didn't have to fake the emotion.

I felt it.

But for good measure, I rested my hands on my not-yet-showing baby bump.

Marco cleared his throat. 'I've got a house that I've been renovating. It's nearly finished, you can stay there.'

I stifled a gasp, wiped my tears away and gave him a shaky smile.

As he put the car into gear and drove on, I wondered about this house of his. I had never heard about it before, not in all the time that we had hung out together. And what of money? He had told me he had scraped together the funds to purchase his share of Jenson Coast, how could he afford a house as well? And why bother? He had lived at the hotel since I had known him.

Where was this house? Knowing Marco, I imagined it in the hills, in the vicinity of Alexis's place, a neighbouring house to the murder scene. My breath came faster and my head swirled at the thought of living *there*. But soon the sign for the hills was behind us, and we were moving away from the sea into the denser countryside outside central Cannes. Finally he pulled off the main road, taking the bends with ease as we climbed above sea level to the village of Biot. As the road narrowed to a single lane, he carefully guided the car through a concealed pair of wooden posts and continued at a crawl down a muddy track until he finally slowed to a stop.

I leaned out of the window, craning to see past a small copse of trees.

Wordlessly, Marco got out. I followed, walking as fast as the uneven ground would allow, until we pushed through the undergrowth and I stared at the tiny whitewashed cottage.

It was nothing like I would have imagined he would buy, or even want. Single-storey, the walls only showing here and there through the thick curtain of bougainvillea. I touched a deep purple petal.

'I haven't finished the outside yet,' he said, almost apologetically.

My breath caught in my throat. 'It's beautiful.' I turned a full circle, unable to believe that he owned a place like this. 'Marco, this is stunning.'

'Come in.'

The spell broken, we moved on. He pushed the door open and walked through first, flicking on lights, inspecting a panel on the wall, hitting a few buttons, switching on what I didn't know.

It was simple inside, a lot more uncomplicated than I would have imagined for Marco. The downstairs was an open-plan living area and kitchen space. The appliances were new and shiny, all ready to go, but, I suspected, unused thus far.

'Two bedrooms upstairs, one bathroom.' He shrugged, offered me a tight smile.

'Were you planning on living here?' I asked as I followed him up the narrow staircase.

'It was an investment – a fixer-upper, they call it.' He walked over to the window, hunched down to peer outside. 'I got it for a fraction of what it could be worth.' He glanced at me, could that be embarrassment on his face? 'Just something to work on away from the hotel.'

The view was fantastic, and the privacy and solitude this house offered made my heart race with excitement. I stopped, my hands on the stone windowsill, and looked outside. When had I started craving isolation? Since I had been in Cannes, all I'd wanted was to fit in, join in, be one of the crowd. But now…

I stared harder. I could see no evidence of life, not even that anyone lived near.

I loved it.

I felt… safe. Calm.

It was since the night of the murder, I knew that now. Before then I'd been running all over town with Jessica and Ben, even Marco. But I'd stalled, and all I wanted now was to be secluded.

I smiled. This place would do just fine.

I turned to him, watched as he ran his hand up and down the whitewashed wall. I leaned forward so I could look into his eyes.

'And I can stay here?' I asked, doubtfully.

'We'll arrange to get your stuff picked up. There's nothing you need right away, is there?' he asked as he glanced at his watch, no doubt eager to get back to work.

I shook my head. I'd happily leave everything I owned back in that shitty flat if it meant I didn't have to go into Cannes.

'Okay.' He looked uncomfortable as he backed away towards the stairs. 'I'll be back later.'

'Marco,' I called as he began to descend.

He paused, turned around.

'Thank you,' I whispered.

With a nod and another one of those strange pinched smiles, he vanished.

I waited a beat, lost at the sudden absence of him. This wasn't like my crummy flat. I couldn't treat this place like a bedsit where I lounged around all day eating, sleeping. So I set to work. Tentatively at first, unsure if Marco would mind. But, I reasoned, the internal walls were half painted, the brushes and tins cleaned and stacked. And I wanted to stay here. I didn't know if the way I was feeling would vanish as time went by, but right now this cottage in the middle of nowhere was exactly what I needed.

By the time Marco returned, so late into the night it was almost the following morning, I'd nearly finished the first layer on the downstairs walls.

'Wow,' he said, surveying my handiwork with a critical eye.

'Is it okay?' I asked nervously. 'I thought I could be of use.'

'Yeah, it's cool,' he responded.

I had walked to the end of the track, cautious, nervous, but had forced myself on until I came to the centre of Biot and found a simple grocer and butcher. I showed Marco my wares now, sweeping my hand over to the kitchen table. 'I made some chicken, a salad. I went down to the village.'

I didn't know what I expected. Praise for shunting my new-found fear down deep inside and forcing myself to perform the simple act of going to the shops? But he just nodded, sat himself down and pushed the chicken around his plate.

We were like strangers, dancing around each other, thrown together by circumstance. Was this how it was with Jessica and Patrick?

I washed up the saucepans as he ate in silence.

It was far from perfect, and as he went up to bed, leaving his empty plate on the table, I wondered if there was any chance of making this work.

–

As the days stretched into weeks, I allowed my hopes to grow.

'Maybe we should invite Andrew over, Ben too,' said Marco after we'd been in the cottage for a while.

I was delighted at the chance to see Andrew and find out how Jessica was faring in England. Some company other than Marco without me having to leave what I had begun to think of as 'the compound'.

And so on a hot evening as we headed fast into autumn, we gathered on the patio that I'd swept clear of debris and ate our first meal with our guests.

'Looking good, Marco,' said Andrew as he surveyed the gardens that I'd been working on since finishing painting inside. 'I like what you've done with the place.'

'I can't take credit, I'm afraid,' replied Marco as he cracked open a beer. 'It's all Lou's work.'

Andrew grinned, patted me on the back. 'A woman's touch, Marco, that's what's needed.'

In the dusk I watched Marco's face for his reaction. He said nothing, swallowed his beer instead. Disappointed, I turned to Andrew.

'How is Jessica?' I asked as I poured brandy for the men. I looked balefully at the orange juice I had to stick with.

Andrew stared down into his glass, swirling it around and around for so long that I thought he might not answer. Then, just as I was about to change the subject, he finally began to talk.

'She seems happy enough in England.' He took a sip of brandy, paused with the glass still held to his lips and then downed it all at once. 'She's not coming back to France, neither of them are.'

I leaned forward and touched his knee. 'What, never?'

He reached for the brandy bottle, poured a double measure, then put it back on the table without offering it around. He seemed to be deep in thought, as though he were carefully practising his words before he said them out loud.

'I spoke to Patrick this morning, actually. He said that Jessica is adamant that she won't return. Apparently she's had a lot of nightmares, some sort of post-traumatic disorder, the whole Alexis Dubois thing…'

I tried to conceal the look of distaste on my face. It wasn't a 'thing'. Alexis Dubois had been murdered, brutally robbed of her young life. Jessica still had hers, surely she should count herself lucky? I turned away, filled with a sudden dislike. Didn't Andrew realise the serious-ness of what had happened? If he'd been there like I was, if he'd seen the blood… I swallowed hard against the taste of vomit that suddenly filled my mouth.

I was about to make my excuses and return inside for a glass of water when Andrew spoke again.

'Patrick told me that he's going to work out of the London branch of the firm and they're going to stay where they are permanently.'

I felt my nails digging into my palms and looked down at my clenched fists. Nothing had changed, it was still 'Patrick says, Patrick thinks'. Patrick this, Patrick that, Patrick. Patrick. Patrick! If I never heard his name again it would be too soon. And what of Jessica? Was she, like me, feeling the after-effects of that night? Was she too haunted by visions of Alexis, and the spreading pool of blood? Did she closet herself away in her little home in England? Had she put up the same wall I had? Had she shunned the parties she and Patrick were invited to in London, the same way I'd turned my back on Cannes?

Suddenly I felt closer to her than I had in months, even though she wasn't even here.

In the silence that followed, I realised that Marco was watching me closely. I wouldn't go to her. I couldn't – I found it hard to walk to the village, let alone get on a plane and travel overseas. I pulled my shawl tighter around me, and busied myself collecting the empty glasses. I pretended not to notice Marco's thin-eyed gaze, which followed me as I excused myself and went indoors.

Later, Marco cornered me in the kitchen. 'I asked the estate agent if Patrick's letting out his villa in Antibes while he's over in England, just out of interest,' he said, his voice low and gossipy. 'Guess what she told me?'

'What?' I asked as I grabbed another bottle out of the fridge.

He leaned closer. 'It's not his, either to sublet or sell. He was renting it himself.'

I shivered. Patrick had told us that he owned the place.

'Do you think we should tell Andrew? He's misled everyone.'

I thought for a moment, mulling it over as I wrestled with the corkscrew. If we told Andrew, and it got back to Patrick that the information had come from Marco... I rested my hand on my stomach.

'Actually, I think we should leave it,' I said. 'I don't want to get involved. The less we hear of Patrick, the better. And Jessica, come to think of it.' I glanced at Marco as I added my last words for his benefit.

And I wondered, as he nodded and left the room, was that relief I saw on his face or was it just wishful thinking on my part?

Chapter 27

Jessica

Now

The day after Patrick's mother came to see me, I awoke to find the fields covered in a ground frost. I opened all the windows in the house. The cottage was beginning to smell, not just of stale air, but a strange aroma of alcohol, unwanted and unwashed people, and above all, death. It didn't really; I was sure that the rotting scent that clogged my nostrils was all in my head. Or rather, it just clung to me as opposed to my house. It would follow me wherever I went.

That thought popped into my head before I could stop it, but I chased it away with the breeze as I flung the windows wide.

The next job on my list was the bed. I couldn't face lying on it, night after night. I recalled Patrick sleeping in it, dying in it, and the sight of his mother rubbing her hands over it. I wondered what she had been thinking about, stooped over the place where her son had taken his last breath. And then I dismissed that thought too and got to work.

I stuffed the sheets, pillowcases and quilt into bin liners, and with an Allen key that I'd found in one of the kitchen drawers, I began the mammoth task of dismantling the bed itself. It was an expensive frame, heavy solid oak, and it took an age to take it all apart. I switched to the claw end of a hammer to prise some of the parts off. They splintered free, heavy metal nails still protruding from the wood. When I'd stacked the last of the wood at the side of the room, I stood up and dusted my hands off.

I felt as though I'd been productive, like the time a couple of nights ago when I'd lit the fire. Again, I realised how little I'd done in the last eight years to help myself. I'd wallowed; I'd been sinking for years. Ben had been my buoy, my life jacket, and I'd clung to him the same way I'd clung to Louise all those years ago when he had left me.

How strange it was, the way I had turned to people whenever things hadn't gone my way. Never had I turned to myself for help. It was time to change that; time to stand on my own two feet and figure out what I wanted. There would be no more leaning on people – my father, Louise, Marco, Patrick. They were either gone or in my past, I was on my own now.

I realised I hadn't included Ben in the list of people I was saying a metaphorical goodbye to. Could I say goodbye to him? Did I need to? Couldn't I finally be with the one person who had never hounded me, never wanted anything from me except what I was prepared to give him? Without the complications that had previously beset us, couldn't we now be together? Wherever he went, I could not only follow, but go with him, at his side.

And then I remembered: as far as Ben was concerned, I was still bound by law to England. I had to be able to explain myself and the whole issue if I were to leave with him. Perhaps I could make up an extravagant story, tell him a lie. I'd had enough practice, after all.

I was suddenly exhausted, even though it wasn't even yet ten o'clock in the morning. Slumping down to the floor, I leaned back against the wall, my head falling to the side so I was looking into the en suite. I needed to get my energy levels back up, so I crawled into the bathroom, pulling at the side of the bath panel and then lifting the floorboards up.

Like Gollum, I took out my treasures and pored over them, one by one. I let the laughter out when I felt it rising inside me and patted the items fondly. They never failed to light the spark and remind me that everything I had done was for a damn good reason.

They pardoned me for everything; when I was feeling low or doubtful or guilty, these items exonerated me.

Just as I was starting to climb upwards again into the light and the future, the doorbell rang.

I tiptoed to the top of the stairs, clinging to the banister as I peered down. The letter box rattled, a voice called my name. I dug my fingers harder into the wood; it was Nina Hart, Detective Sergeant Richard Robinson's sidekick from the police station. Remembering her first visit, when she had waited outside until I answered, I drifted reluctantly down the stairs.

When I reached the bottom, I could see the letter-box flap still moving, and I knew she would be peeping through it. Sure enough, when I wrenched the door open, she straightened up in a hurry.

'Hello,' I greeted her coolly.

'Hi, Jessica.' She smiled, and I noticed she was clasping her hands together against the cold. 'I hope I'm not disturbing you?'

'Is the Detective Sergeant not with you?' I peered behind her.

My mouth went very dry as another thought struck me: had Louise reported me for the scuffle we'd had yesterday? Was that why Hart was here?

Hart shook her head. 'I'm on my own. I'm actually on my way home, but we've got the results of the post-mortem and I'd like to talk to you about them. I thought I'd stop in en route, save you coming into the station again.'

Unless Hart lived in a tent in the nature reserve, my house wasn't on the way to hers. I didn't say this, though. Wordlessly, I stepped back, letting her in.

'Come through,' I said, leading the way to the kitchen.

'Is your friend still here?' Hart asked, looking surreptitiously into the lounge as she walked past.

'Not right at the moment,' I replied as I pulled a chair out for her at the table. Then curiosity got the better of me: 'Where do you live, if this is on your way home?'

She looked down and fiddled with the clasp of her handbag. 'Near the town centre,' she said. In other words, she had lied: the town was in the opposite direction.

In our previous meetings, she had been whip-sharp, probing, almost accusing in her tone, giving off a vibe that she thought I was guilty of something and she wanted me to know that she knew. I'd not seen her like this, troubled, subservient and uncomfortable – it was like looking at myself over the last eight years.

I glanced away.

'What did you find in the post-mortem?' I asked.

She took a deep breath, laid her hands flat on the table and looked me dead in the eye.

'It wasn't the post-mortem that gave us the most interesting information.' A pause, a beat, and then it tumbled from her. 'We looked at Patrick's laptop and we also spoke to some of your neighbours. You… you also dropped this the other day, at the station.' She pulled a red leather notebook from her bag and laid it on the table. I glanced at her face. At least she had the grace to blush. She had read my diary.

Hurriedly she went on, her final words spoken softly: 'I think there was a victim in this house all along, but I don't think it was Patrick.'

I blinked at her, averted my eyes and looked out of the window. 'What do you mean?' I asked dully.

'It's our job to piece together events when we suspect there may have been a crime committed. We did, and we came up with some very interesting conclusions.' Her fingers twitched on the table, and for a moment I thought she was going to reach over and take my hand. 'Were you a victim of domestic abuse, Jessica?'

'What?' I let out a nervous laugh.

'We checked your CCTV hard drive and saw some pretty disturbing footage. And this,' she tapped her nail on my diary, 'this tells its own story.' Her tone was gentle, such a difference from what I'd experienced before that my eyes swam with unshed tears.

Angrily, I dashed them away.

'Patrick was… complicated. He liked to be in control, but he never laid a finger on me,' I said truthfully.

Hart smiled wryly. 'Maybe he didn't raise his fists to you, but does it seem right that he shoved you out of the front door on a freezing-cold night in just your underwear?'

My mouth dropped open and I covered my face with my hands. I remembered that night, freezing through to my very bones, my chest rising and falling as I heaved dry sobs, crouching like a wounded animal on the path outside the front door. 'You know about that? Did… did someone see me?'

This time she did touch my hand. Pulling it away from my face, she covered it with both of hers and squeezed gently. 'It was on your home CCTV; we looked at it, hours of it.'

'Oh God,' I whispered, disentangling my fingers from hers and hiding my face once more.

She spoke up again, her voice sterner this time, as though she had to get through to me and straight-talking was the only way to go. 'There was a lot of activity in Patrick's browser history, where he had searched and participated in various dominant websites. He had also researched submissive behaviour, muscle relaxant drugs and doping practices, private detectives, BDSM, rape fantasies—'

'STOP!' I rubbed my face and slumped back in my chair. 'Please, stop.' I lowered my voice and looked out of the window again.

We were silent for an age, the only sound an occasional sob that I buried deep in my throat. To her credit, Hart didn't try and speak. Instead she got up and moved behind me. I heard the clattering of mugs and the sound of the kettle being switched on.

'You thought I had something to do with Patrick's death,' I said eventually, a little bit of irritability evident in my tone. 'All this you've just said, it makes it even more likely that I had something to do with it.' I swivelled around to face her. 'Yet I can tell you now don't believe me to be guilty. Why?'

Leaving the mugs, she came back to her seat, sat down and leaned forward. 'I think Patrick's mental health went into severe decline. From what you told me about the illness he thought he had – which he didn't, by the way – I think he'd had a complete breakdown. He had researched suicide in many different ways and very thoroughly. From the methods he was looking at online, we were able to know more or less what we were looking for in the toxicology tests.' She paused almost dramatically before going on. 'We found a large quantity of the drug GHB in his system, along with varying amounts of antidepressants.'

'GHB, I've never even heard of that!' My voice was high and I coughed to try and get it back to a normal pitch. 'What is it?'

'It was first developed as a sleep aid, but it gained a reputation for being a hardcore drug of choice at raves. Taken alone, it can cause euphoria, a bit like Ecstasy. But Patrick didn't have that in mind. He mixed it with a combination of Xanax and Valium, both of which we found he had ordered online and received from India. We don't know where he got the GHB, but sadly, it's not hard to purchase on the streets.'

'And that's what he took, that combination? And it killed him. And he didn't have cancer?' I breathed out slowly, looked over at Hart. 'He wasn't happy, you know, no matter what I did. I really tried...'

She nodded. Her lips parted like she was going to say more, then the kettle clicked off and we both looked at it. 'I'll make the tea,' I said. 'Unless you need to get home?'

She smiled, oh so gently, and for a brief moment I hated the sympathy in her eyes. 'I don't have anyone at home,' she replied. 'This job is the career equivalent of marriage and children, there's not enough hours in the day to merge all three.' She smiled ruefully, but I understood that she'd made her choice and she had chosen her work. I envied her the option to choose.

She stood up at the same time as me. 'Can I use your loo?'

I nodded. 'Through there,' I said, and watched as she left the kitchen, closing the door quietly behind her.

I didn't tend to the drinks; instead I sank back down in my chair and dragged my fingers through my hair. I hoped she wouldn't remember that I had offered, and she would go swiftly on her way. I was shaking, but now it was from elation rather than fear. It was so nearly over; the last eight years were coming to an end, and I was so close to freedom that I could taste it.

Drained and bone-tired, I sat still for a while. I thought again about leaving, wondered where my backpack was, my faithful friend, the one thing I still had from those good old days. If I slipped it on, would it instantly transport me back a decade in time to when my life was filled with frivolity and fun instead of littered with police charges, accusations and dead bodies? I thought I'd caught a glimpse of it when I'd gone into the cupboard under the stairs to get the crate of beer out for Sally yesterday.

I got up, noticing my step was lighter. Gone was the shuffling, stooped walk I'd adopted for so long. As I pulled open the kitchen door, I remembered that Hart was still in the toilet. But the bathroom was at the end of the hall, near the front door. I could see from where I stood that the door was ajar and the room was in darkness. And just as I realised that, I heard the small but very audible squeak of a floorboard upstairs.

I fell back against the door frame and wrapped my arms around myself. My new feeling of buoyancy vanished instantly. I closed my eyes, but all I could see behind my eyelids was my treasures laid out on the floor upstairs for anyone to look at.

Another footstep above me had the effect of a starting pistol. I pushed myself off the wall, flew down the hall and took the stairs two at a time. I was silent as I ran. I was an animal, stalking, knowing exactly where to tread so my footsteps went unheard. At the door-less doorway, I came to an abrupt halt as I surveyed the scene in front of me.

Hart was visible just inside the door of the en suite, on her knees, one hand at her throat, working the slim gold chain that hung around her neck, the other clutching a bottle. Her fingers were shaking, but the tremors weren't confined to her hand, her whole arm seemed to quake.

She didn't look up; did she even know I was there? Was it too late to run? Could I leave in the same silent way I'd arrived? No, I needed one of the items that was right in front of her. Without it, I was trapped on this island forever, and I'd already been imprisoned for far too many years.

I remained motionless, I let my eyes linger on all the items on the bathroom floor: on Patrick's laptop, his real one, not the one I had bought and loaded myself with the incriminating search history, emails and online orders. I saw the photographs of Alexis Dubois' home in France, before, during and after they had been doctored. I looked at the shotgun, the box of bullets, the book entitled *The Symptoms and Effects of Drugs and Poisons* that had been my bible. I focused my gaze on the printout of combinations of both illegal and legal drugs that could kill, the syringes, both new and old, the pots of liquid GHB and the packets of Valium and Xanax. Finally I looked at my passport. It seemed to glare back, dark red and mocking me: *You were so close, Jessica, so damn close.*

The bed, which I'd taken apart, lay neatly stacked beside me. Softly, slowly, I reached out and picked up a plank of wood. It was one of the last pieces I'd dismantled, the nails protruding jagged and wicked from the end.

I weighted it in my hands, then, taking a deep breath, I approached the bathroom steadily.

Chapter 28

Jessica's Diary
October 2015

Patrick came to me in the kitchen and told me bluntly that my father had died.

He passed his hand across his mouth, reminding me in that moment of the day he'd shot the deer, but when his hand came away and there was no blood smudged across his face, I was surprised. And then I realised what he had said, but he had already retreated into his study. I stood, chopping knife in hand, motionless, before drifting down the hall to find answers. Where, how, why, all counteracted with Patrick's 'I don't know', 'we'll have to wait', 'I'll try and find out'. Until finally he snapped at my constant questions, grabbed me by my shoulders and shook me, told me he didn't know anything else.

I slipped out of his grasp, sprang towards the phone and told him I was going to ring Louise. I was panting breathlessly, feeling like my life was ending, yet strangely more alive than I'd felt in years.

He wrenched the receiver from my grasp, slamming it down into its cradle, and then pulled the wire from the wall.

A chink of metal cut through the silence and I stared down at my hand. I was still holding the knife, and in my shaking fingers it was knocking against the door handle behind me. I could see the seeds of the pepper caught on the blade, and I raised it, held it in front of me and steadied it with my left hand. Patrick moved around his desk, sidled past me out of the room, and I heard him walk upstairs.

I waited; the only sound in the room was my breathing, hitching in my chest. And then I heard it: the grate of the door upstairs being opened, the sound of the wood catching where the door had dropped, the sound that I now associated with the appearance of the shotgun. I sagged, might have fallen over if I hadn't landed heavily against the door. How many times was the shotgun going to appear before it was finally pointed in my direction? The sound came again, the door grinding shut now, and it propelled me into action. I dropped the knife, swung out of the study and yanked open the front door. At the end of the path I hesitated. Where could I go? I didn't have any location or safe house or friendly face to head towards, but I didn't want to go back inside. I didn't want to hear that grating sound or see that damn gun. So I perched on the wall that lined the front of our house. I spotted Mr Lavery opposite, and he saw me too. He was pruning, as usual. At the sight of me he packed up his secateurs and his trowel, and with his head down, he picked up the handles of his wheelbarrow and moved down the side of his house.

Patrick came out eventually, and with his hands on my shoulders he steered me back inside. I let myself be led; the danger had passed, the cupboard door had been closed.

–

My father's death awakened something in me that only Ben's sporadic visits over the years had come close to touching. I was reminded of Christmas and the impromptu dinner that Patrick and I had made. That day had been almost pleasant, hopeful, and for me, a light at the end of the tunnel. It had ended on a sour note, though, as I had wondered about how damn healthy Patrick looked, and with the realisation that nothing would change in the immediate future, I'd sunk back into my previous deep, dark hole.

I thought often of Louise now. I imagined her life, flying high in Cannes, the popular one now that Alexis and I were gone, backed up by the stature and status of Marco. She would be so happy, I knew that.

Living high.

Flying high.

I'd been doing my research at the library, finding cases of people whose passports had been revoked getting a temporary visa, like a compassionate leave to travel.

Patrick had smiled at me, as though humouring me, before reminding me that this was what he did for a living, and didn't I think he'd have already looked into it?

He moved on, as he always did, throwing me with the sudden change in subject as he reminded me about the Law Association Gala on Tuesday evening, and advised me which dress he thought would be most suitable for me to wear.

–

On Tuesday evening we drove to London. I feigned sleep on the journey – I didn't want to look out of the window and see everything my life was missing.

On the red carpet he instructed me to smile for the camera. My mouth wouldn't work, though, and in the end he wrapped his hand around mine, squeezed until it felt like my bones were breaking, then leaned in close and whispered in my ear, 'Just fucking smile.'

One final squeeze, and something that crunched in my hand acted as an electrode. I bared my teeth, smiling so wide I felt my gums go dry.

At the gala, through dinner and beyond, I nursed my bruised hand and drank heavily, in a manner that I had become accustomed to. The only difference was I usually drank like this in secret, certainly not in front of a room full of important people, and never while Patrick was with me.

I found a corner away from the laser beam of Patrick's stare and there I located a friendly barman. I settled myself in for the night and drank steadily.

Later, I found myself back in his car. I didn't remember walking to it; in fact, I recalled nothing of the evening since our bone-crushing arrival. I wondered if I had embarrassed him.

A quick glance sideways. He was staring ahead, not talking, his mouth a thin line of fury.

I looked down at my lap. Yes, I had embarrassed him.

My old friend the black hole was back. I could see it within reach, somewhere in the footwell of the car. I leaned forward and slipped quietly into it.

I woke, climbing sleepily upward, dragging my sticky eyelids open and trying to swallow down my nausea. I was sitting upright, and I glanced at the clock illuminating the darkness. It was 6:01 in the morning, and I was still in the car.

I was still in the car.

I was cold, freezing to my very bones, wearing nothing except the thin black dress Patrick had told me to wear. What time had we got home? No later than one a.m., I was sure. Dinner had finished at eight and I was certain it wasn't that late when Patrick had plucked me out of the party and driven me home in silence. I rubbed at the windscreen, peering out at the distant sky that was just beginning to grow light.

He had left me in the car, outside our house, on an autumn night in which the temperature was dipping into single figures.

I muttered to myself, cursing as I tried to find the will to get out of the car and go into the house. But I had no strength, and instead I searched again for the black hole to slip into.

Chapter 29

Louise

We always want what we can't have. That's what they say, and in my case it was true. Marco and I slipped into a life of unease, so different to what our friendship of the summer had been. Now I was… what? Neither girlfriend nor friend. Just the mother-to-be of his unplanned child.

My shitty little flat and the half-life I'd lived in it was long gone. It was undeniable that I had a better life now. I was safe here in the compound, surrounded by dense, thick forest. I didn't wonder where my next pay cheque was coming from.

I no longer needed a pay cheque.

I had everything I had ever dreamed of.

Except a friend.

Except Jessica.

As my bump grew, so did my feeling of loss. Her name was on my mind, on my lips, in my heart all day long. I thought of her constantly. Was she sad and lonely in the little seaside village of her incarceration? Or was she back to her old self, bar-hopping and in with the locals? I thought she might be lonely. After all, Suffolk was hardly London or Cannes or Berlin, was it?

243

I fancied turning up at her door, Jessica gazing at me, her gorgeous eyes full of gratitude that I had come for her, for surely she never wanted to be with Patrick, right? I would take her hand and we would leave. With her father's money we would be fine; we wouldn't need anyone else.

A kick from deep inside me usually pulled me from my fantasies. Guiltily I would force myself to think of other things.

Guiltily because this child never figured in my day-dreams.

This unborn child never figured in many of my thoughts at all.

Marco was indifferent to what was happening. We found ourselves increasingly civil to one another. We were like roommates, or neighbours who were polite when they passed.

But we had no neighbours. I had no friends except for Ben and Andrew, and they were both so busy. Sometimes I went for weeks without seeing anyone except Marco.

In the final month of my pregnancy, I gave in.

I calculated the time in England, waited until mid-morning on a weekday, when I was sure that Patrick would be at work. Then I sat in the window seat, staring unseeingly out of the window, and dialled the number I'd got by going through Andrew's phone while he was in the bathroom the last time he came to visit.

As the phone rang, my breath hitched in my throat. I was going to talk to Jessica! After so long, too long. I clutched at the window frame, my knuckles white with the effort of trying to contain my excitement.

'Come on, pick up, pick up,' I hissed to myself.

Silence.

I blinked.

'Jessica?' I spoke tentatively. 'Jessica, are you there?'

A single intake of breath.

A click.

A dead line.

I stared dumbly at the phone.

Cold spread through my body, replacing the heat of only moments earlier.

It hadn't been Jessica on the other end of the line.

It had been Patrick.

I moved through the next few days as though in a fog. And then, before I could begin to formulate another plan for contacting her, the baby came.

–

I loved him – Robbie – at first sight. I was astounded, shocked, seeing as throughout my pregnancy I'd not thought much about him at all.

'He looks like me,' whispered Marco as he peered over the side of the cot at our child. 'He's dark, and look at that hair!' It was the most he'd spoken to me in months.

'I love him so much,' I whispered back. 'I mean, I never knew…'

Marco turned to face me, sat heavily on the side of the hospital bed. 'Of course you love him, he's your son.'

My hand crept across the bed to encircle Marco's fingers with mine. '*Our* son.'

He nodded, gazed over at the baby again.

I thought his fingers squeezed mine, but I might have imagined it.

'Let's go home,' he said gruffly.

At the compound, another surprise awaited. Gifts lined the lounge, a banner proclaiming *BABY BOY* had been hung. Underneath it stood Andrew and the biggest shock of all was the people standing beside him.

My parents.

My mind flew back to the awkward phone call I had made to them months ago. If the truth be known, I couldn't even remember much about it, how they'd reacted, how I'd sounded. But now they were here, smiling and looking totally unlike their normal selves.

'Mum, Dad?' Clutching Robbie to me, I made my way towards them.

As I stood in front of them, I blinked. Gone were the brown and beige clothes, the button-up cardigans and long skirts. The couple in front of me looked… normal. As though they were just a husband and wife on holiday.

'I never thought you'd come all the way out here!' I smiled, hit by unexpected delight at seeing them.

'It's not far,' replied my mum as she reached for Robbie. 'We took a plane from Manchester and your lovely Marco arranged a fancy car to pick us up.'

She turned and simpered at Andrew. 'And the hotel, oh my, Louise…'

My parents were staying at Jenson Coast, Marco had organised their travel plans.

I looked at him, my mouth an open O of shock.

He smiled, shrugged like it was no big deal.

'Thank you,' I mouthed. It seemed so inadequate.

For four days, the house was filled with people and chatter and gifts. When they left, I looked around: the tiny cottage suddenly felt huge.

It felt empty.

I had enjoyed myself, I realised. Perhaps, at last, it was time to try going out into the world again. I had made it to the hospital to deliver Robbie. That was in Cannes. And it had been okay.

That night I sat in the lounge and surveyed the gifts that had been left for us. Reading some of the tags, I realised I didn't even know half these people. But obviously Marco did, as did Andrew. They held the weight here, they had the contacts and the power.

And through them, so did I. Through them, I was able to lead this sort of life. A life I'd never thought could be mine in a million years. I had to hold onto it, I reminded myself. I should write thank you cards to these people, maybe deliver them myself.

I should get back out there.

Vigour renewed, diving in like a child at Christmas, with my new son beside me and my man pottering across the room in the kitchen, I got lost for hours as I began to open the gifts.

The sky had darkened to a deep purple when Marco came in.

'I made coffee,' he said, setting the mugs carefully on the table. 'Have you been having fun?'

I smiled up at him, regarding this new Marco with an appreciative eye. The last months had been lonely, I could admit that to myself now. I had seen nobody; Marco had been distant and uncommunicative. I couldn't blame him, didn't blame him. Who wanted a pregnant woman who had only been a casual fling, if that? I wondered about the difference in him. Was he so taken by his child that his whole outlook had changed? I hadn't been trying very hard with Marco, and I should. After all, he was why I was here, living this life, opening these expensive gifts from his friends.

Sipping at his coffee, he stroked a finger down our sleeping son's face.

'I'm glad he looks like me,' he said, so softly I almost didn't hear him.

My breath caught in my throat. It could have been a slight, intended for me, but for all Marco's traits, cruelty wasn't one of them. I gazed at him. Was that it? Had he been worried that Robbie wasn't his child? All this time… all these months… I looked down at myself, my post-pregnancy body not much different to how it had been since I'd known him. Did he really think another man would want me? Was his rough, tough exterior a cover for a man who might be just as insecure as me?

'Do you want to open some?' I asked shyly, presenting a gift like a peace offering.

His eyes held mine for a moment, then 'Gimme that!' he said, grabbing it and ripping the paper off.

I heaved a sigh as I watched him. Maybe this could work. Maybe… if I got out and about, lost some weight, stopped thinking about other people and what might have been. If I stopped chasing the past, stopped chasing *her*…

I got up from the floor, walked the length of the room to stretch my legs as I sipped at the hot drink. As I walked, I looked around at my home. It hadn't been my money, but I had whitewashed these walls, I had hung the photographs of the French scenery I had taken.

'What the—?' Marco's exclamation startled me, and I looked over at him.

'What?' I asked.

'This is a fucking weird gift for a baby,' he said.

He held it aloft, the silver glinting as it nestled among the blue tissue paper in his hands. I edged closer, my breath quickening with each step I took.

'There's no gift tag,' he said, rifling through the paper. 'Must be a late present for the new house.' Shrugging, he put it on the floor, moved to the next brightly coloured gift box.

I looked at the blue tissue paper, the item mocking me inside it, shiny and new. Threatening.

I remembered before, when an item just like this one had been twirled around a table.

For your own sake, for your baby's sake, leave it.

Leave my wife alone.

All the while twirling the ice pick, touching the sharp point with his finger. Finally spinning it so the blade was aimed at my stomach.

Patrick had sent it. And the ice pick that lay in the expensive paper in front of me wasn't a house-warming present at all.

It was a warning.

A silent message that only I would understand.

My hands, for months smooth and unburdened by pain, suddenly began to itch. A heat within me, deep under my skin. Automatically I reached for my cream, one that I hadn't needed to use, one that I could afford now. I slavered it on, quelling and diminishing the fire within me. Dulling it until I could no longer feel the pain.

Chapter 30

Jessica

Back in the kitchen, I lifted my eyes to the ceiling and imagined I heard a thump on the floorboards. I washed my hands over and over, rinsing the claret stains, averting my eyes as the water swirled down the plughole.

I closed my eyes. This was never supposed to be a part of it.

As if pulled by an invisible string, I drifted eventually to the bottom of the stairs. Walked up them ghost-like, treading in the way that was as familiar as breathing to me now, stepping where I knew my feet would make no sound. I didn't go straight into the bathroom. Instead I sat outside, next to the piece of wood that now lay discarded on the tiles. I reached through the door and rifled through my things: all the things that Nina had found.

No need to hide them now. Nobody else was coming here. The police had already taken everything they thought was of interest. A thought: had Nina told anyone she was coming here? DS Robinson, perhaps?

I thought of the little I knew of her. She was young, eager; was this her first big case? Was she looking to prove herself to her superiors, hence the pre-dawn visits, snooping around outside my home, devouring my diary that she'd found when I 'accidentally' dropped my bag, losing all the contents back at the police station?

I was almost certain that Robinson didn't know she was here.

I began to breathe a little easier. My heart beat a little slower.

In the dark shadows of my senses, I became aware of a sharp inhalation, jagged, wheezing. A scratch deep in an unseen corner of the bathroom.

I worked fast then. I had a little time to spare, but the disappearance of a police officer wouldn't go unnoticed for long. Mixing the solution, I filled a syringe. Hopefully it would be the last time.

–

Hours later, when I heard the clatter at the door, I took a deep breath. Ben or Louise were the only ones who would call round now.

They were the only ones left.

Opening the door, I left it ajar and moved back to the kitchen. She followed me, all anger gone. She was quiet, contrite, the way she used to be.

'I've been talking to Ben.' She paused. 'He told me some stuff I didn't know.'

'Oh yeah, what's that then?'

I sat at the kitchen table, didn't offer her a chair. Folded my arms. Waited.

She glanced around, her gaze lingering on the pile of post and papers that lay on the worktop, before perching nervously on the edge of a chair. 'I always wondered, I mean we did, why you didn't come to your dad's funeral.'

She looked down at her hands in her lap, picked at a nail. 'I was angry when you didn't show. And then Marco saw a photo of you and Patrick in that damn lawyer magazine, just days afterwards.' Placing her hands flat on the table, she made eye contact for the first time. 'You looked so happy in that picture.'

I inhaled, looked away. I hadn't been happy. I'd been devastated, the stuffing knocked out of me. I'd seen that photo, I'd seen that if you looked closely, you could spot the fear in my eyes, that my smile wasn't one of happiness but was forced, manic even. I thought Louise knew me well enough to see that for herself. I thought it would be as clear as day to her. Now she'll come, her and Marco, I'd thought when I looked at the photo. Now they'll see, and they'll come and rescue me from my prison, just like they did once before.

But they didn't.

'Ben told me that your passport had been revoked, that you couldn't leave England, not unless Alexis's killer was found and charged,' she went on. Her hand moved across the table towards me. It looked like an insect approaching. 'When I heard that, everything fell into place. When your dad had his heart attack, he was trying to tell me something. I couldn't work it out, I thought he was talking about his counsellor, but he wasn't. He was saying "consulate". He'd phoned them, hadn't he? Something had happened to make him check for himself, or maybe he was calling them to implore on your behalf. Either way, they told him the truth: that your passport had never been revoked, that they didn't know what he was talking about.' Her eyes shone with her discovery. 'The shock was so great that it killed him.' She lowered her gaze, waited a beat before looking back at me. 'I think you found out too, maybe before, maybe after your dad died. But I think you knew. What did you do when you discovered that Patrick had lied to you, Jessica?'

She had never spoken to me so directly before and I thought about answering her, but before I could, she reached towards me again.

'And when you still thought it was true about your passport being revoked, why did you tell Ben and not me? Did you think he'd tell us, was that what you wanted?'

'I knew he wouldn't tell anyone. He had no idea that it was a lie, neither of us did then. And he was too wrapped up in his own career to be my saviour,' I said, my voice hard and dull.

It was true. I'd told Ben because I knew he wouldn't fight it. He wouldn't start a petition against the injustice – that wasn't his style. Besides, I'd thought that having me part-time was what he wanted; it fitted in nicely with his career jetting off all over the world. He had taken the passport bombshell and believed it; he had no reason not to. Just like me. Just like my dad. And when I thought it was true and my dad thought it was true, we had done what Patrick had told us to: we had kept our mouths shut.

'But we could have helped, we could have come to see you,' Louise went on, plaintive now, her voice almost a whine.

'You still could have come to see me. *Your* pass-port wasn't revoked,' I snapped, moving my chair backwards, away from her oncoming hands. I didn't want her comfort, her support. Not any more. It was too late now. Now was the time for answers. I levelled my gaze at her. 'I needed you. I expected you. I thought I could rely on you. Why didn't you come and see me, Louise?'

'I did.'

I hadn't expected those words.

'What? When?'

She shrugged. 'I got as far as Folkestone.' She rubbed her face, shoved her chair back and stood up. 'Do you mind if I get a drink?'

'I'll do it.' Moving around the table, I put my hands on her shoulders. Our first contact that had been initiated by me. 'Sit down, Lou. You're my guest, after all.'

The relief at my words, kindly spoken, was evident on her face. She had always been so easily placated. She relaxed visibly as I clattered around the kitchen, pulling out mugs, milk and coffee.

'Tell me what happened, Lou,' I said. 'Tell me why you abandoned me. You could have rescued me from this hell but instead you decided to plan a big wedding of your own.'

Chapter 31

Louise

After the ice-pick delivery from Patrick, I tried to put Jessica out of my mind. When Robbie got a little older, I began going into Cannes more and more, starting with our marriage at the city hall. It wasn't a romantic day, it didn't take place with a castle in the backdrop like Jessica and Patrick's. It was a civil ceremony, businesslike and brisk, probably only brought about by my request to Marco that we – he, me and our son – share the same name. I didn't put forth the real reason: my need for security, both financial and personal. Throughout the day, Jessica was on my mind. I wondered what she would think of my marrying Marco. I wondered if she even cared.

Afterwards, I declined Marco's suggestion of an early night. I pretended not to notice his look of disappointment when I turned back to the window, waiting for the card, the flowers, the good wishes she would surely send and which would show she hadn't forgotten me.

When it became clear that no deliveries were going to arrive, I eventually went to bed. Marco was sleeping. Robbie was beside him. I climbed into bed with my boys and told myself how happy I was.

After I became Marco's wife, a part of me wanted to remain in the compound, in the sanctuary I'd created there, but I forced myself out into the world. I hovered on the outskirts at first, not going into the centre where all the action was, avoiding the area of Alexis's home in the hills, until I was ready to stand in the bullseye.

I thought it would hit me that I *had* missed it, but as I walked the cobbled streets, I realised everything had changed.

It seemed duller, like it had been when the cloud that refused to become the storm it was supposed to had hung over the town. Alexis and Jessica were gone, and the beauty had vanished with them. Or maybe I had changed. The light I'd felt briefly, for the first and only time that summer, had been stripped away.

I made myself walk the streets we'd once claimed as our own. I pushed Robbie's stroller for miles until my back was damp with sweat. I sat heavily on a bench overlooking the sea.

My compound was better than here. In the cottage grounds, I sweated with the heat of the sunshine, not with nerves. Never with fear.

But what was I so fearful of?

I took a deep breath, leaned my head back and closed my eyes. The landscape of the sea vanished. The scenes of that night came rushing back at me.

The two women, one of them my best friend, lying inert on the floor.

The blood that pooled around them.

The blood.

So much blood…

The magic of Cannes was gone. Drowned in an ocean of blood that only I could see.

I let go of Robbie's stroller as I gasped for breath. I put my hands to my eyes, but the image burned an imprint on my lids. I would never un-see it. I would never forget it. It would be there forever. Triggered every time I came here, to this city that I had adored.

'*Excusez-moi?*' The voice was rich and deep. I whipped my head up, staring blankly into the eyes of the stranger who had spoken. '*C'est votre bébé?*'

The woman had one hand on the handle of Robbie's stroller. It must have rolled away from me.

I grabbed it from her, muttered a hasty apology in French. She pulled up the collar of her fur coat, gave me a haughty glare. A look that travelled from my trainers up to my red, bloated face.

I turned the stroller round, pushed it past her. And then the tears came. When I wiped my face, I was surprised to find they came away clear and not coloured red like the blood in my nightmares.

–

I stopped going into Cannes.

I hadn't thought Marco had noticed, or, if I were honest, that he cared how I spent my days. Until the day he forced me out.

'I need you to bring a portfolio to the hotel.'

His voice came down the phone. I looked at Robbie as he followed the stray cat we had taken in around the kitchen. He was almost four years old now. We enjoyed our life here in the cottage, surrounded by the wilderness that I felt shielded us. The trees and shrubs had grown wild. Marco was always threatening to get someone in to maintain the grounds, but I liked it. With the green curtain I couldn't see down the hill into Cannes. I rarely left the security and peace of the cottage. And I liked it that way.

'Lou?' His voice was impatient as he barked down the line again.

'You want me to come to Jenson Coast?' I twisted the phone cord. 'But what about Robbie?'

'Bring him with you, Andrew will like to see him.' He went on to tell me the exact location of the portfolio he had forgotten to take with him that morning, but I already knew where it was: I could see it on the kitchen table.

'The Panerai Yachts Challenge is on today.' Marco's voice softened as though he sensed the tension inside me. 'Why don't you bring your camera, check it out? It's been a while since you've taken pictures.'

He was right. I had exhausted the scenery in and around the cottage. I thought for a moment, wondered if I could, wondered if it was about time I got a hold of myself.

'Lou?' The cajoling tone was gone, back to brusque and curt.

'All right,' I whispered, hanging up the receiver.

I went immediately, before thoughts and fears could overwhelm me. I left the file at reception; I was in and out without seeing Marco or Andrew, back to the car before the memories of Jenson Coast and its proximity to the hills and the scenes of that night could overpower me.

But I didn't go home. I took Marco's advice about checking out the yacht race, and for an hour I sat and watched the boats. It was safe here, a place I'd never been with Jessica, or Ben, or Marco. I let the peace that only usually came at the cottage wash over me on the warm breeze. When Robbie grew restless, I treated him to a smile.

'Shall we go back to the hotel, see Daddy?'

He clapped his hands, beamed at me, and as I watched the other children playing on the beach, I felt guilty at what I had kept him from.

'All right, we'll see if we can keep this going,' I said, more to myself than to my son. 'Let's go.'

I came across Andrew before I saw Marco. I paused at the doorway to his office, looking at him with narrowed eyes.

I wondered what he thought of the fact that Jessica never came back here. As far as I was aware, he hadn't seen her since her wedding day. She didn't come to France and he didn't go to England. Did he ever think of me? Did he wonder why I stayed away? Did he ask Marco, and if so, what excuses did he come up with?

How cut-off we had all become, I thought. How fractured compared to what we once were. None of us really talked; we all skirted around each other, ignoring the elephant in the room.

Andrew hung up the phone, leaning heavily on his desk. Though he turned towards me, he didn't seem to see me. Holding Robbie's hand, I walked into his office.

'Hi, Andrew,' I said, cautiously, since he seemed a million miles away.

He stared down at Robbie, didn't answer me.

'Andrew,' I began, with a nervous trill in my voice. 'Are you—'

He pushed himself upright, the cords on his neck and his arms straining with the effort, before giving up and slumping back in his seat. The chair was on wheels and it rolled away from him. He staggered, clawed at the neck of his shirt, then his fingers closed into a fist and he thumped at his left arm.

'Andrew!' I shouted, dropping Robbie's hand and hurrying around the desk to steady him.

He leaned to one side, and under the sudden weight, I tipped backwards. We crashed to the floor, with Andrew landing painfully on top of me.

'Andrew,' I sobbed as I rolled him off me and kneeled over him. Looking back over my shoulder, I screamed for help, then watched in horror as his lips peeled back in an awful grimace.

'It was a lie. I phoned… It's all been a lie!' It took every ounce of his strength to hiss those words and they made no sense at all.

I heard feet thumping down the corridor and Clive, one of the barmen, raced into the room. He took one look at Andrew, paled, and lurched over to the telephone.

With help on the way, I turned back to Andrew and took his hand. He wrenched it out of my grasp, grabbed my hair and pulled me close to him.

'The counsel… counsel… Louise, you must…'

'Shh, Andrew, don't try to talk,' I soothed, extracting my hair and leaning back out of reach. 'An ambulance is on its way.'

He fell silent then, and I looked away from him and focused on Clive, listening intently as he spoke urgently into the telephone.

I looked away because I knew that Andrew was gone.

–

We came together again, Marco, Ben and I. Two of the group were missing now. But Andrew was dead and Jessica would have to return to France. I shivered. She would come back, but Patrick would be with her.

Everything and everyone was okay when I stayed in the compound that had become my home. Not perfect, but safe. Functioning. Why had I left? Why had I tried to pretend I could live a normal life?

We sat in a closed-off section of the bar, Robbie on my lap, Marco and Ben talking quietly, a sense of shock and disbelief shrouding the room.

'Somebody needs to call Jessica,' said Marco, raising his voice a little to include me in his statement.

My heart jumped at the thought of speaking to her, finally, after all this time, before it sank again. Not like this, not with this news.

With a sideways look at Ben and me, Marco threw back his brandy. 'I'll do it,' he said, and picked up the phone.

It soon became clear that he was speaking to Patrick. The conversation didn't last long, and I found myself chewing on my lip, imagining the scene across the sea in England.

'Andrew was saying something about a lie,' I reported to Marco after he hung up. We opened a fresh bottle of brandy. 'What could he have meant?'

'What exactly did he say?'

I tried hard to remember, but it was difficult. That moment, those brief minutes when Andrew was dying, was a nightmare vision I couldn't escape, another haunting image to add to the one that already smothered me.

I shook my head helplessly. It was Andrew's strained face, the pallor of his skin, the sweat on his brow that I remembered, not the words that he had spoken so fervently.

Marco caught hold of my hand, rubbed his thumb up and down my wrist, encouraging, comforting. Out of keeping with how he normally was with me.

'He said that something had been a lie.' I concentrated, staring into the amber liquid. My eyes swam, and I blinked. 'And also something about a counsellor.' I looked over at Marco. 'He wasn't having counselling, was he?'

Marco shook his head vehemently and I smiled, embarrassed. Of course Andrew wasn't having therapy. He wouldn't; he was of the generation that would sink their worries into a bottle, or a chat with a close friend. Me, though, that was a different story. Perhaps I should have sought therapy. Too late now; my therapy was the cottage, a place I never should have tried to disengage from. It was Cannes I should have distanced myself from, not my home, regardless of what Marco said.

–

It was three days before the coroner completed his postmortem, declaring that Andrew's death had been caused by massive heart failure and releasing his body so funeral preparations could be made.

Back in my safe cottage now, the three of us together again, we pulled our chairs in a close semicircle, drinks poised, me distracted as I watched Robbie playing, blissfully unaware of the horrors that adulthood could bring.

'Place is looking nice,' said Ben, the same words he always said on his sporadic visits to us.

I watched him with interest. He had always been the outsider, with a life that I often came close to envying. Though he was a firm friend – mostly of Marco, though he always tried to include me – he came and went as he pleased, jetting off to far-flung locations with all the fervour of a boy scout. His life was far removed from ours; without responsibility, he chased excitement, adventure and danger that he went willingly into, head first. When he wasn't in France, Marco and I followed him on the screen, and in the years I had known him, his fame had escalated.

He kept a clean sheet; there was never any dirt to dish on him and I wondered about his private life. Was he a ladies' man? Did he still think of Alexis and Jessica, or were they just notches on the bedpost to him? I didn't think so, because though he could get any girl he clapped eyes on, there was something about him: humility, a truly humble nature. He really was a genuinely nice guy. There were moments over the years when I wondered if he still saw Jessica, but he was a closed book. If he did keep in contact with her, he concealed it very, very well. I would never ask him. Up until now, none of us had spoken about her. She was like someone who had died. She was simply a memory. A ghost.

As if hearing my thoughts, Marco said her name: 'Jessica isn't coming to the funeral.'

In the hushed silence that followed his announcement, my breathing suddenly sounded very loud.

'What?' I asked, leaning forward.

Marco avoided my stare. 'I spoke with Patrick this morning. He didn't go into much detail, but reading between the lines, I got the impression that Jessica is struggling to accept the news of her father's death.'

I was the quiet one. Unflappable. Organised. But at this, for the first time since Marco had known me, I lost my temper.

'Well, fucking hell!' I exploded, slamming my hand down on the arm of the chair. 'We're all fucking struggling with it, but this is what happens, people die, their loved ones gather to remember them, we all come together to give and get comfort. This isn't on. She hasn't even come to visit him since she went to England. No...' I shook my head, my lips pressed together in a firm line. 'No, I won't accept this.'

Ben looked at me strangely. 'I don't think she *can* come.'

'What do you mean?' I asked.

He blinked at me, looked away, retreated into himself. 'Ben?' I said.

'What about Patrick, is he coming?' He changed the subject.

'Ben, what did you mean?' I pressed.

Marco ignored me. 'I don't think Patrick's coming either. I think he's going to have to look after Jessica.' He looked at each of us in turn, his eyes resting on me a little longer than Ben.

–

Andrew's funeral wasn't marred by the absence of his only child. We put on a show fit for a king, and though Marco worried that some people still recalled Andrew's connection with the murder of Alexis Dubois, the community on the whole did us proud.

After it was over, I retreated back to the cottage, happy to stay there, unwilling to try to return to the real world again. It wasn't safe out there. Here, I was protected.

I looked at Marco, watching him as he made drinks for us. I wondered what would happen to Andrew's half of the hotel. Would Marco get it? Or would it go to Jessica?

I shivered at the thought of Patrick turning up again, throwing his weight around, ordering Marco to do this and that. I didn't want to ask outright, didn't want to jinx it, didn't want to voice my fears in case they happened.

Instead, I said, 'I don't think we'll hear anything of Jessica again, not now.'

He shrugged. Relieved, no doubt.

But I was wrong.

Three days after the funeral, Marco found me in the garden behind the cottage. With a rare display of anger, he slapped a magazine down in front of me. His mouth was puckered, his cheeks were flushed, and I snatched up the magazine, desperate to find the source of his fury.

'What is this?' I didn't need an answer. As I stared at the page, I could clearly see that it was a photo of Jessica, dressed to the nines in a black evening dress, a glass of champagne clutched in one hand, the other held in Patrick's tight grip. She was grinning up at him with a smile so wide and filled with happiness that I blanched. I scanned the accompanying article. 'The annual gala for the members of the Law Association of the UK and Europe,' I intoned. My gaze went back to Jessica. She looked stunning – a little too thin, I thought, but that was more envy than concern. Most of all, she looked happy. 'When was this taken?'

'Two nights ago, in London,' replied Marco.

I gaped at him, then stared back at the picture until it went blurry and the magazine shook in my hands. 'Impossible,' I whispered.

He pointed to the opening paragraph of the article. The date, 4 October, screamed out at me.

'You said she was having a breakdown. You said… Patrick said…' I stopped and looked sharply up at him. 'Where did you get this?'

'Andrew subscribes to it. I'm opening his post so I can sort everything out for the business.'

I nodded and stood up slowly. I walked back to the house, Marco behind me, and when I reached the kitchen, I pushed the pedal on the recycling bin and dropped the magazine in. Jessica's smiling face beamed up at me from among the used tins and empty wine bottles. I closed the lid on it.

'I never really knew her at all, did I?'

Marco didn't answer; instead he trailed a finger down my bare arm as he passed me. It was a silent comforting gesture. I needed more of those gestures. I needed Marco to act like that more often.

Then maybe I wouldn't think of her at all.

But the photo in the magazine played on my mind. Even though I'd put it in the bin, even though I'd looked down at it, obscured by bottles and cans so I couldn't see her grinning face any more, I saw it still when I closed my eyes.

Later, when my husband and son were sleeping, I pulled the magazine out and wiped it down with kitchen roll. Then I looked again, looked harder. Looked at the face I'd once loved more than my own.

Those eyes… those eyes.

—

Marco watched as I packed a small bag early the next morning. He didn't say anything. I turned around to see Robbie standing in the doorway. My heart lurched as I looked at my little boy, his dark hair, his liquid brown eyes, his quiet demeanour identical to that of his father's.

'Robbie, darling, can you get Mummy's passport from the kitchen?' I asked, blowing him a kiss.

He wandered off and I turned to Marco. 'I've got to go,' I said, in reply to his unasked question. 'I've got to make sure she's okay.'

'That *photo*,' he spat the word, 'shows that she's more than okay.'

'She was our friend once, she's Andrew's daughter.'

'Do me a favour,' Marco said, suddenly, urgently.

I stopped packing. He rarely asked me for anything. 'Of course, what?'

'Just don't bring her back here.'

With that, he left the room, ruffling Robbie's hair as he passed him. I sank down onto the bed, still clutching underwear to pack in my bag. I looked at it, at the swaths of silk and lace in my hands. I crumpled the soft material and clenched my fists. I didn't wear stuff like this, I hadn't worn it since that summer. I wore comfortable cotton, form-shaping, stomach-holding mummy garments. Why was I packing lingerie like this?

I thought of Marco's warning not to bring Jessica back here. Had he seen me with the fancy underwear? Had he realised that I didn't wear it for him but I was contemplating wearing it for... who, her?

With a shudder, I pushed the silk and the lace back in the drawer, replaced it with boy shorts and sensible pants.

I plucked my passport out of Robbie's hands, kneeled down and pulled him in close.

'Mummy will be back soon,' I promised.

They waved me off, my two boys. As I pulled away, I waved frantically at them, watching in the rear-view mirror until they were tiny dots.

When they'd faded from my vision altogether, I pulled off the road into a petrol station. The fuel tank was full, but I bought two packs of cigarettes, even though I'd not smoked since I found out I was pregnant with Robbie.

Already the bad habits were coming back, I noticed, as I unwrapped the plastic wrapper greedily and pulled a Marlboro from the pack with my teeth. They helped me, though, calmed my nerves, which became shredded as I drove, shuddering and shaking all the way to Calais.

On the boat, I wandered from deck to deck, sipping hot black coffee and smoking hard. And as the white cliffs came into view, her face faded from my vision to be replaced by *his*.

The fear came back, tenfold. The memory of us dancing at Jessica's wedding, his hand holding mine so tightly I thought the bones were breaking. Glancing over at Marco sharing a joke in the corner with Andrew, knowing that my husband didn't feel the danger like I did, knowing he'd never believe that Patrick could present such a threat. The silent breath in the telephone call I'd attempted, the ice pick delivered anonymously in the post.

As I rolled the car off the ferry and touched down in England for the first time since I was a teenager, I was enveloped by a wave of paranoia. I got as far as Folkestone before turning rapidly off the road into a lay-by. I pulled out the second packet of cigarettes, smoked them one after another, lighting the next one with the butt of the previous.

I thought of how it would be when I turned up on Jessica's doorstep, how it might be Patrick that opened the door. How he would look at me with those cold, hard eyes. How I would be able to read his mind, his unspoken words.

Don't you remember my warning, Louise? Don't you remember how I told you to keep your little family safe? How it was all in your hands?

I'd left my family back in France, alone. Marco, so relaxed, thinking we were untouchable. I'd left them wide open to a surprise attack. My son, who had never known danger or heartache.

I imagined the three of us, Jessica, Patrick and me, sitting in their cottage. Patrick would glare hatefully at me, accusingly, silently telling me that I'd disobeyed his orders by coming to see Jessica. He would excuse himself to make a telephone call, speak quietly but firmly to a contact in France, give them our address, tell them where Robbie went to nursery…

Before my imagination could run away with me any further, I started the car, lit up my last cigarette and drove back to the ferry terminal at Dover.

Back on the deck, that I'd been on only hours earlier, I watched the white cliffs again. This time they grew smaller, and with each mile the boat put between me and Patrick King, I breathed a little easier.

Finally, when I couldn't see the coast of England any more, I moved to the front of the ship, eager for my first glimpse of France, anxious to get back to my cottage.

'Sorry, Jessica,' I whispered.

But the wind took the words from my lips and whipped them away, so nobody heard my apology.

Chapter 32

Jessica's Diary
October 2015

I stayed in that car until Patrick went to work an hour later. Silently he removed me from the passenger seat and led me up to the house, where he deposited me just inside the door. In some part of my mind I marvelled at how easily he moved me around, like I weighed no more than a carrier bag or a briefcase. Wordlessly, he left.

I stayed for a long time in the hall, letting the central heating defrost me, until my legs felt sturdy enough to carry me up the stairs. There I searched in Patrick's bedside drawer for the sleeping tablets he had been prescribed a while ago. I had none of my stash of pills left and I needed something other than alcohol to knock me out.

Finding nothing, I moved to the cupboard that held the horrors and pulled open the door. The grating noise that it made was like water torture, and I clenched my teeth and shook my head to rid myself of the echo. I pulled a chair across, went through Patrick's things one by one, desperate now for a pill – anything would do, just a prescription painkiller or two. I ignored the shotgun and went higher up the shelves until I couldn't reach to see any more, slapping my hand around sightlessly. The uppermost shelves were empty, devoid of anything, and I was about to retreat and concentrate my search for medication in the kitchen when my hand happened upon something that wasn't wood. It was flat, and I stretched onto my tiptoes to draw it closer. Wrapping my fingers around the mysterious object, I pulled it off the shelf to study it.

It was a passport.

I opened it up, flipped through to the back page and stared down at the photograph.

It was my photograph.

It was my passport.

I held my breath as a strange movie reel played in my mind: Patrick telling me upon our return to England that my passport had to be handed in to the authorities because I was still under suspicion for Alexis Dubois' murder; Patrick explaining to my father why I couldn't go back to France. And finally, Patrick telling me only days ago that there was no way to get around the authorities so I could attend my father's funeral.

Lies. All of them filthy, stinking lies.

I let out the breath I had been holding and it emerged as a scream. At the same time my legs dissolved from underneath me. I crashed down, banging my jaw on the chair back, and toppled off to land on the floor. I stretched out, starfish-like, and howled as I threw the passport with all of my might.

I didn't shed any tears – I was as dry as a disused well – but I screamed so loudly and for so long I thought it might kill me.

I slept or I passed out, I'm not sure which, and woke up hours later, my body cold from lying on the wooden floor in the thin black dress, my chin throbbing where I had hit it on the chair. I willed my black hole to come back to me. I needed to sink back into nothingness, into the void I'd visited so much over the last few years. It was a good place, because there were no feelings there.

But the black hole wouldn't materialise and eventually my eyes came into focus. Through the toppled chair legs I saw a patch of dark red – my passport, which had landed in the corner when I threw it – and like a snake, I crawled on my stomach towards it.

I didn't pick it up. I collapsed, my arms and legs splayed out, and studied it from ground level.

The lies. The awful, wicked, terrible lies he'd told me. All for… what? To keep me by his side? Had he known all along that my heart was never with him, that I longed for Ben, for freedom, for France and all the lands beyond?

A painful fist bunched in my stomach, vomit rose in my gut and I opened my mouth. But all that came out was another scream.

Later, much later, a strange sensation came over me, starting in my toes and tingling all the way up my body. When it reached my fingertips, I stretched them out, flexing and clenching them at the knuckles. I identified the feeling and the sudden knowledge caused me to smile.

It was desire. I'd not felt it for so long. Even when Ben came, I was mechanical with him, so deeply dead was I. But now, now the feeling was returning. And my entire body burned with it.

I was coming back to life.

Chapter 33

Jessica

'You were frightened of Patrick. He threatened you when you were pregnant.'

My words to Louise were blunt, emotionless, just the way I felt. The truth was coming out now, all of it. I allowed myself a small smile at the thought of her telling me how she had lived her life since I left. Not the high-roller, not the popular one. A recluse, contained within the walls of her home, just like me. But while her threat had been the memory of that night, mine had been very real. *My threat had shared my home.* It was strange how the carnage of that evening had left its mark on her, stunted her life. It had left a mark on me too, the one I tried to conceal by brushing my hair across it. But that was the only evidence. I wondered if I too would have been so traumatised by Alexis's death if I hadn't been shunted straight into another nightmare. I didn't think so, that wasn't my style. But Louise had always been softer than me.

She shrugged, played with a piece of loose thread on her sleeve before abandoning it. I leaned forward, watched her through narrowed eyes.

'I hated you for not helping me,' I said, averting my gaze to stare out of the window. 'All of you. I hated you for leaving me here, with *him*.'

'What did you do, Jessica?' she asked again. 'When you found out your passport hadn't been taken away, what did you do to him?'

I looked out across the fields, replaying my finest moments over the last five years. I still recalled the feeling of coming back to life, of finally having a goal to aim for. And it was no longer a fight for my freedom, it was simply justice.

'It's best served cold, that's what they say, isn't it?' I said, my eye caught by the tiny robin that flashed in and out of the hedgerow bordering my home. 'Revenge, I mean. That's why it's taken so long, so many years.'

I thought back to the CCTV that Hart had watched, of all the times when Patrick had been here in the house, buried in his work or sleeping upstairs. All those times I had silently stripped to my underwear, quietly opened the door and flung myself out onto the path as though I'd been pushed there. I would kneel and keen, wrap my arms around myself, nodding towards the door as though someone was standing there, shouting admonishments at me. I would crawl to the door, lift an arm and throw myself back into the house. To an outsider it looked like I was being dragged by my persecutor.

I had watched the tapes myself, when Patrick was away. I deserved an Oscar for my acting ability.

'Hart was appalled at how my husband mistreated me,' I told Louise, describing the CCTV scenes to her.

'But didn't Patrick check the tapes himself?' Louise asked, looking around the kitchen as though she too were caught on camera.

275

She wasn't, of course. I had switched them off. We had no need for them any more, neither Patrick nor I.

'Religiously and to the point of obsession,' I confirmed. 'But not the tapes I made. I switched the hard drives, didn't I? Because I got clever.'

'And Ben's visits. Did you switch the hard drives whenever he was here?'

'We both knew where to step. We simply used the camera blind spots, and I checked them thoroughly before Patrick came home and watched them himself.'

I could see Louise's mind whirring now and it was a genuine smile that lit up my face as the kettle clicked off and I made our coffees. I took mine black and added a healthy slug of skimmed milk to hers, whipped it until it frothed up. Pale and creamy, just how she liked it.

'That's why you weren't concerned when the police took Patrick's laptop, because it *wasn't* Patrick's laptop, was it?' she asked, shaking her head in disbelief.

'You catch on quick,' I remarked as I put her coffee down none too gently in front of her. 'I could have done with your help the last few years. Maybe you could have knocked up some more photographic evidence.' I glared, and she looked down into her steaming mug, wrapping her hands around it and shifting uncomfortably on her seat. 'How did Patrick end up with your fake photographs, Louise?'

'*He* had them?' She stood up, knocking the table, and I reached out to steady her mug.

'You didn't know?' I asked, moving the coffee back towards her.

She picked it up and took a scalding sip. 'I suspected. My apartment was broken into and those photos were the only ones that were stolen.' She slammed the mug down, slopping the brown liquid. I watched it track down the side and pool onto the table. 'You're right. He threatened me, at *your wedding*, he threatened my unborn baby, he told me to stay away from you.' She was properly furious now, and I regarded her steadily.

'He broke into your apartment, he threatened you and your family and still you let me leave with him.' Hatred left a taste in my mouth more bitter than the coffee. I licked my lips. 'Nice, really nice, what a great friend you were to me.'

She sat down, abashed. 'I thought you were happy, I thought you wanted to be with him,' she pouted.

'ENOUGH!' I roared, slamming my own mug into the sink. It cracked, and I watched the black liquid pool around the plughole.

Louise stared, frightened now, and I breathed deeply. *Don't lose it, not yet.* I turned to face her with a tremulous smile. 'Sorry, it's been hard. Drink that, then we'll open some wine.' I smiled winningly, letting her see the old me, the real me that she used to know.

Placated but still wary, she picked up her mug and sipped, her eyes constantly on me, ever watchful.

'So, it really is all over?' she asked. 'You don't have to stay here now that Patrick's... gone. You can do whatever you like, go wherever you want.'

I couldn't help but throw her a look of disgust. I tried to rearrange my features, but it was still there, on my face, in my words, in my tone.

'Where would I go? To my father? Oh no, he's dead. To you? Oh no, you've got your own family now.'

'Maybe to Ben? He's still here, he still cares.' She drained her coffee, pinched at the corners of her mouth with her fingers to wipe away any residue.

'Ah, Ben. I had an interesting chat with him just the other day. About secrets.' I paused, looked her dead in the eye. 'Secrets and lies.'

She scratched at her fingers, the skin in between them. I saw the redness there, knew it was a sign of her angst, her nerves. Some things you just can't change or hide.

'What do you mean?' she asked quietly.

I leaned forward until I could smell the coffee on her breath. 'Ben gave you a note to pass to me, an invitation to join him in Italy.' I paused, sank back into my chair. 'What happened to that note, Louise?'

It was my *pièce de résistance*. The most important factor in all this. Yet one I had been unaware of until recently.

She scratched harder, white streaks now on the red of her flesh. 'Uh…'

'You didn't give it to me, did you?'

Screwing up her face, she shook her head. 'I'm so sorry,' she whispered.

I knew it, Ben had told me, but hearing it, hearing her apology, sent wave after wave of fresh rage through me. My head spun and I wrapped my arms around myself as the anger pulsed.

'Don't you see?' My words came out jagged and harsh. 'Don't you understand that if I'd gone to Italy with Ben, none of this would have happened? I wouldn't have gone to that stupid party, Patrick wouldn't have dragged me here, I wouldn't have had to do what I did. I'd have had a life.' On the last word, my voice cracked.

'But it's over now!' she cried. 'It's not too late. You can be with Ben, he loves you.' A strange smile – of desperation? – stretched across her face. 'You can finally be with him.'

I snorted a laugh. 'Of course I can't.'

'Why not?'

Her genuine look of confusion made me want to smack her. 'Ben thinks my passport was taken away from me. I can't explain to him that it never was, can I?' I replied, with more patience than I felt.

Louise made a little noise in the back of her throat and frowned. She seemed to be having trouble following my words, 'Why not?' she asked again.

I threw my hands up in a gesture of hopelessness. 'Because he's not stupid. He'll jump to the conclusion as to why Patrick is suddenly out of the picture, just like you did.'

She placed both hands palms down on the table and stared at her lap. 'But I know the truth.' She stopped, her words ever so slightly slurred. 'Why tell me and not Ben?'

'You *think* you know the truth, Louise,' I corrected, holding up a finger. 'You think you know everything, you always did.'

'But you could explain to Ben... He loves you,' she whispered. 'Why don't you tell him?' Urgent now, imploring, perhaps sensing something was coming, like the police officer before her? Hart had begged and cajoled before the length of wood with the rusted nails had stopped her words.

'Because Ben is a good person. Inside him beats the biggest heart of any man in the world. He couldn't live with suspecting I hurt Patrick. He'd cave in, he'd go to the police eventually.'

She seemed to digest this before looking back to me. 'But you trust me not to tell anyone?' Her words were quiet, her expression expectant and hopeful. Yes, just like the police officer before her. Snatching, grasping at some-thing, anything to hold onto.

I tipped my head back and laughed. Louise chuckled too, but her mirth was tinged with uncertainty. She grew very quiet all of a sudden.

I moved over to kneel in front of her, and took her hand in mine.

We stayed like that for a long time, neither of us speaking. I thought of all the other times we had held hands.

I squeezed her fingers to let her know there were no hard feelings. Her hand flapped uselessly against my palm, clammy with sweat. 'I don't trust you,' I said. 'I simply know you'll never get the chance to tell anyone else what you think I did to Patrick.'

I let go of her hand and it flopped to dangle at her side. I looked into her eyes, saw the horror that had been captured and frozen in the moment of realisation. I put my face up close to hers, heard the shallow wheeze of her breath and felt it as it tickled my ear.

I left her there, slumped helpless in the chair as I collected her mug and washed it under the tap. I poured the milk that I'd laced with liquid GHB and succinylcholine down the sink, chased it with a hefty dose of bleach and ran a damp cloth over the tabletop.

Then I sat down opposite Louise and looked at my former best friend. Loyal and trustworthy, she would once have done anything for me, until the time came when she wouldn't. How did I feel now, now that I'd gone so far with my revenge?

'Just remember, Louise, this is all your fault. If you hadn't betrayed me, if you'd passed Ben's note to me, none of this would have happened. You thought I'd stay here quietly, like the good little wife I was expected to be. But I showed you, didn't I? I showed you all.' I pushed my chair back and put my feet up on the table. Exhaled, smiled, because this was something I'd not been able to do for so long. Just relaxing, in my own home.

Not that it would be my home for much longer. Just a few more things to take care of first. Speaking of which…

I looked over at Louise. She wasn't gone; she was simply paralysed in every part of her body except her mind, her sight and her hearing. She was aware, yet unable to react. Succinylcholine was my most recent discovery. Chattily, I told her all about it as I made my last-minute preparations. I informed her how it was used as one of the three injections in an execution, the others being a sedative to put the prisoner to sleep and potassium chloride to stop the heart. My drug cocktails were my best work during the last few years, the research that I'd put in worthy of a science degree, in my opinion. I would have to finish her off by hand, just as I had with Nina. Just as I had with Patrick…

I smiled ruefully as I remembered Sally and how close she had come to being in the position that Louise was in now, meeting the same end her own son had endured, for I had blamed her too. After all, she had raised Patrick, hadn't she? But she had got a last-minute reprieve, a stay of execution, as I realised that she was just as much a victim of Patrick as I had been.

I snorted a laugh, recalling snatching her coffee mug away before she could drink it, and no doubt earning her undying love with the alcohol I'd given her instead, which she had so obviously needed. I still wasn't entirely convinced that I'd made the right choice on that score.

I stood up, a little bit heavy in my limbs, which was annoying as I was nearly at the end now and I should be buoyant. I should be like the deer of so many years ago:

shot and hit by Patrick, but escaping with its life, with just flesh wounds to show from the encounter.

It wasn't over yet with Louise; there were still things I had to tell her, to show her. She had to understand that I felt betrayed by her, and she had to understand the chain of events that had been put into place when she had cast me aside.

But I had other things to do while she got used to her new body form and I couldn't stand her watching me as I worked. I picked up a tea towel and placed it neatly over her head and face.

That was much better and my mood changed immediately, like a switch being flicked. As I began to work on the last stage of my plan, I whistled a cheery tune.

Chapter 34

Louise

Now

I found myself on the floor of a bathroom and recognised it as Jessica's en suite.

I tried to push myself up into a kneeling position, but my arm wouldn't move. I looked at it. What was going on? Had Jessica and I been on a massive bender like the good old days and I'd passed out here? Had I lain awkwardly on my arm and it had gone to sleep? I jerked it: nothing.

And then, piece by piece, I remembered. Jessica leading me to believe she had killed Patrick. Jessica blaming me for the mess her life had become. Jessica drugging me so I would never tell anyone what I suspected.

Jessica was killing me.

Slowly.

I remembered making coffee for Ben, Jessica and myself a couple of days ago. Her shouted instruction that they would take theirs black. Then they'd run off together, leaving me with three steaming cups. I hadn't drunk mine; instead, as I watched them leave the house, I'd pulled out the bottle of wine and sipped from it, ashamed at how hard I was trying, heartbroken that she wanted Ben and not me.

What would have happened if I'd drunk my coffee that day? What would have happened if I'd made some for the police officers who came calling? Would Jessica and Ben have returned to three corpses? Hadn't she thought of that? Did she even care? Or had she added the poison to the coffee just today? Was today the day she had snapped?

That was the thought that stayed with me. Jessica had lost her mind, and because of it, she had no limits.

I screamed, but nothing came out. I couldn't even whimper. I couldn't even cry.

I lay on the floor and with all my might tried to move something, anything; any part of my body, no matter how small, would be enough.

But nothing moved.

I wasn't even sure if I was blinking.

For a long time I wasn't even sure if I was breathing. Maybe I was already dead.

But I was thinking, and now that I saw the marks on my wrist, the memory came flooding back. I would have shuddered if I could have as I recalled her fashioning a pulley system, then putting on a pair of gardening gloves and positioning herself at the top of the stairs, the ropes that bound me dragging me upwards.

Where was she now? How long had I been like this? How long before this shit she had fed me in my coffee wore off? *Would* it wear off, or would I just go to sleep, forever?

Suddenly I didn't want to see my useless arm in front of me any more. But I couldn't even close my eyes. If she came back to finish me off, I would have no choice but to watch her.

And then, my ears seemed to fizz and pop, and I felt, rather than heard, the vibration of someone approaching.

Silently, I begged a God I didn't even believe in to let it be someone else: the police, Ben, anyone but Jessica.

But as a pair of scuffed trainers came into view, I knew it was her.

She sat down, arranged herself into a cross-legged position and leaned against the wall as she studied me.

'I didn't want to have to do this,' she said, calmly and quietly. 'I never in a million years thought I'd have to do this to you, Louise.'

You don't have to! You can let me go, let this wear off and let me walk out of here! I screamed at her mentally, tried to portray my desperation in my eyes, but I knew I'd failed.

'Where were you when I needed you? That summer, you were full of opinions about Patrick. You hated him, you looked out for me, you tried to save me with your stupid faked photos – and then, when I really needed you, you just gave up. You left me, you let him bring me here and you never even bothered to call.' She stood up so all I could see were her feet. 'You didn't even phone me to tell me my father had died.'

But he threatened me! I wanted to scream at her. *And I thought you wanted to be with him!* My thoughts were useless, she couldn't hear them. Besides, I'd already said them to her earlier, and my words had made about as much difference as my thoughts. Precisely zero.

Her right leg went out of sight for a split second and then it came hurtling back towards me. The toe of her shoe smashed into my mouth. My head moved, but I felt nothing.

Please let me pass out, I begged inside my head. But I stayed unmercifully conscious, if this state could be described as such.

She stayed standing, breathing jagged and loud. On the floor in front of me, blood dripped from my face, collecting to form a little pool under my cheek.

I concentrated on my feet, tried to wiggle my toes.

Nothing.

Time had no meaning now; it could have been minutes or hours that passed before she moved again. She spun on her heel, her left foot brushing my face as she walked past me out of the room. When I could hear the sound of her breathing no more, I set my attention on my feet again. Was that something I could feel in my left toe, kind of like a pins-and-needles sensation? I gave it my all, silently praying, concentrating so hard that it took me a moment to realise I could hear something else. Scratching and scraping, metal upon metal. Finally a screwdriver dropped into view from above me, landing inches from my face.

She was back.

She kneeled down this time, and I watched in terror as her hands came towards me. She grabbed me, I wasn't sure where, I couldn't feel, but suddenly the world tilted and I was now looking up at the ceiling. She stood up and moved over my body, looking down at me.

If I hadn't have known that it was Jessica doing this to me, I'd never have recognised her. It was someone else in her body, it was the physical form of the girl I'd loved and laughed with, but it wasn't the beautiful diva princess I knew. This Jessica was demonic, possessed and quite, quite mad.

She sank downwards to sit atop my hips and took my chin in her hand.

'Louise, I'm going to have to put you away now, because I need to leave shortly.'

She stroked my face, and when she withdrew her hand, out of the corner of my eye I saw blood on her fingers. The startling claret against the paleness of her skin jolted me, a reminder of just how much danger I was in. I wiggled my toe again; definitely felt pins and needles. But it wasn't enough. I couldn't defend myself against a maniac with just my toe.

Come on, wake up, wake up, I instructed my body. But it wouldn't listen to me.

She put her fingers on my chin again and pushed my head to the left so my cheek was flat on the floor. I stared forward, unable at first to make out what I was looking at.

It came gradually, the knowledge that it was a hole, a kind of crawl space, a big blank area where the side of the bath panel should be.

But the space wasn't empty.

There was a body in it.

Every fibre of me screamed except my mouth. The body was coming closer, and mentally I struggled, but still it approached: a pale, blurred shape that morphed into a white face with red cheeks.

No, not red cheeks. A bloodstained face, a misshapen head, with hair that had once been blonde but was now stained dark.

Hart.

Oh God, she'd killed Hart too.

The world tipped again, and suddenly it was clear that Hart wasn't coming towards me, Jessica was pushing me towards *her*, into the crawl space, into a makeshift coffin in which I would certainly die, lying next to a woman who was quite clearly already dead.

'So you'll be my fifth victim,' she said in a conversational manner as she pushed and heaved me into the hole.

'I do hope you'll be my last, because I don't actually enjoy this, you know. I never set out to kill five fucking people, and that first one, it wasn't even my fault.'

She stopped pushing and sat back on her heels, and though I couldn't see her, I imagined her wiping at her forehead, taking a brief breather from the manual labour.

'And I'll tell you something else,' she said, her voice low and husky. 'Each and every dead body is down to you. Because if I'd never met you, none of this would have happened. What do you think of that, then? Well?'

I couldn't answer, she knew that, but while her attention was aimed at directing stupid, insane questions at me, I concentrated on my feet again. I thought I gasped, though it must only have been in my mind, but I was sure I had moved. I tried again, and this time I felt my big toe against the top of my left shoe.

In slow motion, her words filtered through me. I would be her fifth victim? There was Hart, Patrick and me, which was three...

I tried to make eye contact with her, and though my gaze was dead, and the hurt and the pain and the confusion weren't there for her to see, surely she could feel them, surely she could sense them?

She paused, seemed to rethink, before giving me a final shove. I skittered over the bathroom tiles, and though I couldn't feel it, I knew I'd come to a stop against Hart's shoulder. My head slumped so I was looking out into the bathroom, and Jessica's face came into view.

'You don't believe me, do you? Or have you just never thought about it before? You were too concerned about yourself, too worried about your family, your precious baby, your fortune. Taking my place, taking my father.'

She spat each word at me, her last sentence through gritted teeth. Andrew. She thought I'd stolen her father, to have for a dad of my own. Yet enclosed in my cottage, I'd barely seen him.

Suddenly my vision was blurry. I wondered if I were crying, but remembered that I couldn't. The wet on my face was from Jessica's spit.

She put her face very close to mine and spoke in my ear:

'I'll make you see. I'll tell you everything, and then you'll understand exactly how this is all your fault.'

She pulled back and smiled.

And then she began to talk.

Chapter 35

Jessica

Then

'This is fucking freaky,' said Louise as we got out of the car. 'Where *is* everyone?'

It *was* weird, not only the street being in darkness, but all the houses that lined the grass verges too. Simultaneously we closed the car doors and moved to the back. I waited while Louise rooted around in the boot, muttering to herself, and inside me irritation simmered.

'I'll meet you in the house,' I said, but I didn't think she heard me.

On the porch, I glanced behind me before yanking at the streamers and leaving them trailing on the grass beside the front door.

Inside, it was dark and deserted. I sat for a while on a chair, then got up, restless, trailing my hand over the moulded antique banister. I was in half a mind to leave, to go home to Jenson Coast and meet up with Louise later, when I heard a rustling noise coming from across the hallway.

There was a glow of light, and quietly I moved through the archway into the lounge.

Her face was lit up by the eerie glow of her phone as she stabbed at the buttons. A floorboard creaked, and she looked up and frowned.

Alexis Dubois.

'*Qui es-tu?*' she asked, her voice plummy and shrill, nothing like the breathy tone with which she'd spoken to Ben that day in the car.

I blinked at her dumbly, looked her up and down.

'*Êtes-vous l'ingénieur?*' Belatedly, she held up the phone towards me, using the light to assess me.

Am I the engineer? I laughed out loud and turned around. I was definitely going home, I didn't even know why I'd come in the first place. Then she spoke again, this time in English.

'You, what are you doing here?' Her tone was clipped and sharp, accusing almost, though of what I didn't know.

'Don't worry,' I shot back. 'I'm leaving.'

She came towards me, her phone held high, and stopped a foot away. 'What are you looking for in my house? Sneaking around like a common thief in the middle of a power cut!'

With her free hand, she grabbed my upper arm. She was surprisingly strong.

'Get off me, Alexis,' I hissed, pulling away.

She turned towards the door. 'Thief!' she shrieked as she strode away, though I don't know who she was shouting to; there was clearly nobody else here.

'I'm not a thief.' I heard my words, my tone; wounded when it should have been angry.

And as though I had needed permission from my inner self, suddenly I *was* angry. Not simply at her branding me a thief, but the way she had looked right through me in the car that day as though I didn't exist; the way she had threatened my father's business over her stupid druggy territory. The way she thought she was better than me, when my father had everything hers did, possibly more.

Oh, Alexis, you think you're so much better than everyone else, but you're nothing but a drugged-up brat. I caught a glimpse of the two of us in the large mirror that hung over the fireplace, and shame burned inside. We were the same. Status, money, social standing... it all meant nothing when you'd sunk as low as we had. Shiny gold exterior, that was what we were, scratched away like tin foil. Ruined by the fortunes of our parents.

I pulled my eyes away from the mirror. I didn't want to see any more. I didn't want to be here any more. I lowered my eyes, but as I moved to leave, she turned away with her phone, leaving me in darkness. I walked heavily into something, something that toppled and landed on the stone fireplace with a clatter. My ankle twisted, sending me down onto my knees. She had almost vanished through the door, but I saw the bobbing light of her phone as she turned back.

She said something, I fought against the heat in my head to translate the words. *Lesbienne voleur.* Lesbian thief. *Fucking Louise, why did she have to fawn all over me in front of everyone?* I felt the shame, the embarrassment as Alexis laughed, one hand over her mouth, her eyes shining.

'It is why Ben left you, why he came crawling back to me, yes?' she said, switching to English again, still smiling maddeningly. 'You were no good for him, because you like the other women, no?'

'He didn't crawl back to you, he... he didn't!'
Did he?

She turned to go, a sneer on her beautiful face. I shook in the darkness, wanting to put her straight, wanting her to know that what Ben and I had had was nothing like the short, sharp fuck he'd got out of her.

Awkwardly, I tried to stand up, sending whatever I'd crashed into before spinning across the floor. The noise was loud in the quiet house. I peered closer, identifying it as the coal scuttle that I had upended and kicked across the floor. Alexis turned, looked over her shoulder, paused in the middle of stalking out as she surveyed the previously pristine carpet, now dark with coal dust. I waited for the explosion, but she hesitated, seemed to decide it wasn't worth it and spun around to sashay on her way.

Still on the floor, I reached out and clamped my fingers tight around her ankle. The world turned to slow motion. In the sudden glow of her phone light, I saw her foot twist painfully to the side, out of the six-inch heel she wore. Even falling, she was graceful, spiralling down, her hands up in a macabre pirouette. The scattered fireplace implements lay all around me. How easy it was to grope for one in the semi-darkness. How simple it was to raise it above my head. How natural it felt to bring it down as hard as I could manage.

A strange exhalation broke the silence. I peered at her, saw nothing except the whites of her eyes. Then all was quiet.

I stumbled over, pulled her up, felt the sticky mess at the back of her head, saw that the claws of the poker were still locked into her skull.

A scream pierced the silence. It took a frighteningly long moment before I realised it was me.

I pulled the claws out of her head, gagged as blood dripped onto the floor. It came towards me, that crimson sea, mixing in with the black coal dust, growing and spreading. I knew then that Alexis was dead, and nothing was going to revive her.

I don't know how long I crouched, frozen in time, wishing, praying to rewind, just go back five minutes so I could walk out, or fifteen minutes so I never would have come into the house at all. Time had no meaning until the slow realisation pierced my dulled brain that the room wasn't as dark any more, and I turned so that my back was to Alexis's inert form. One by one, lights began to come on along the road and in the houses.

The electricity was back on.

I looked at the poker, still matted with her hair and stained brown with her blood. I looked at myself holding it. The thoughts rushed at me now. The prints that would be on it, invisible to my eye but there all the same.

A thump at a door – somewhere in the house, in response to my scream, or outside? I didn't know. I glanced at the French doors, quickly looked away as a shadow lumbered towards the glass on the other side.

There was no plan. There was only time to react.

I closed my eyes, screamed as I aimed the poker at my own head, and screamed again as it made contact.

And then, light-headed, bleeding myself now, I lay down beside Alexis.

Chapter 36

Louise

I lay back in my makeshift coffin and waited to die. After all, what else could I do?

I said a silent goodbye to those I had left behind in France. My son, my baby that I had created, that I had raised, who I loved more than I had ever realised. And my parents, who I still never invited to come and see me. Who I never bothered to keep in contact with, even though they'd reached out to me when Robbie was born. I thought regretfully of Marco. I thought of all those times when he had laid his hands on me with a gentle touch, all the times I bemoaned the fact that he didn't do it more often, when I never did it to him at all. We could have worked. Dying, I finally admitted it. If I could have got over my obsession, we could have worked.

After a while, I realised two things at the same time: I could smell the foul stench coming off the battered and broken body of Hart, and I could move all my toes.

The effect of this was electric. I clenched my toes back and forth, willing the numbness to carry on dissipating and the feeling to start spreading. It felt like days, but it wasn't much later that I found I was able to rock my lower body to and fro in the limited space. I churned and squirmed each time my left side hit Hart's corpse, and then again when I went the other way and hit the stiff leather of my bag.

My bag!

I tried to remember if I had taken my phone out when I arrived at the cottage. What if it was downstairs in the kitchen? Or still in the hands-free cradle in my car?

The wait for the feeling to come back to my arms was agonising, and eventually I drew my legs up and nudged at my bag with my knees, but it was pitch-black under the bath and I had no choice but to remain useless until I could move my hands.

Finally, with claw-like fingers, I lifted my right arm and dipped into my bag. Absurdly, I sang an old Beach Boys song to calm myself as I dug around the interior, cringing at the slurred words that emerged hesitantly from between my cracked and parched lips. And then my claws closed around something hard, and oh so carefully, I manoeuvred it out and cradled it in both hands as I brought it close to my face.

It was my phone.

I choked out a sob, but bit my lip to stop it. I couldn't lose control, not yet; it wasn't over yet. There would be plenty of time for that when the bath panel had been removed and I wasn't confined in this awful space with a festering dead police officer.

I turned on my right side, laid the phone carefully face up and stabbed at the menu until I reached Ben's number.

Answer, answer, answer, answer… I prayed, lowering my face to wipe a mixture of blood and sweat out of my eyes with my sleeve.

'Louise?'

His voice came through the speaker and I let out a sigh.

The words tumbled out of me, a quick-fire explanation and a plea for help, but as my speech emerged in a garbled mess, I realised that the drugs hadn't completely worn off.

I did weep then, knowing he couldn't have understood a word I said. I knew he would think I was pissed and being stupid, that he'd probably hang up and continue on his way back to France or wherever the hell he was headed next. My temporary strength, which had been fuelled by adrenaline, vanished, and I rested my head on the floor and sobbed. I heard his voice, tinny and distant now, and when the call disconnected and I was once more in darkness, I stopped crying and closed my eyes.

–

I drifted away, not to sleep, but to some other world that was between death and consciousness.

And then, later, I heard my name.

It was Ben's voice.

Oh, thank God, I thought, as the adrenaline coursed through my body again, and I rocked and yelled and shrieked and kicked my feet. Even when I heard him on the other side of the panel, scratching away with something to release me, I carried on flinging my arms and feet out and screaming at the top of my lungs.

Then there was light, and strong arms underneath mine, and I was still kicking, my feet landing blows on poor dead Hart as I was pulled out.

I lay on my back on the bathroom floor, Ben's face hovering above me, and I felt the cool of the tiles beneath me, and I breathed in the fresh air, and yet still I screamed.

Ben slapped me eventually, then, contrite, he fetched a washcloth from the basin and attempted to wipe the blood from my face where Jessica had kicked me. His hands slowed as he stared into the hole he had dragged me from.

I turned to look, and a juddering sob caught in my throat. Finally I was able to see the mess that Jessica had made of the policewoman. 'She... Jessica...' My stomach churned, my skin flushed, and I crawled over the floor to vomit into the toilet. I missed. It splashed onto the tiles to mingle with the blood that covered the floor.

More blood.

Always there was more to be shed.

Behind me, I heard Ben move towards the bath. I threw up again, aiming more carefully into the bowl now, then watched as he pulled Nina Hart gently out to lie on the floor. His long fingers moved around her neck, her wrist, though we both knew it was a useless exercise.

My stomach hardened and I grabbed Ben's arm, my fingers stronger now. Snatching the washcloth that he still held limply in his hand, I flung it over my shoulder.

'She's gone,' I slurred, gesturing to Hart. 'But Jessica can't get away with this. And I know exactly where that bitch is heading for.'

–

As though I weighed barely anything, Ben half carried me through the haunted rooms of this terrible home filled with bitter secrets. He kept glancing over at me as we raced in his car up the track, onto the high street, down the dual carriageway before eventually joining the A12.

'She... she did this?' he asked, suspicious, wary. 'To you, and to the policewoman?'

I nodded, my mouth pinched tightly. 'And Alexis.' My tears betrayed me. All this time we had believed in her innocence, and all this time she'd actually been guilty. 'It all led to this. Patrick, the policewoman.' I looked at him sideways. 'Me.'

He stared ahead, dazed, stunned, his knuckles white as he gripped the steering wheel.

'We have to catch her,' he muttered. 'If she… if she were to find out…' A noticeable shudder ran through him, and he passed a hand over his ashen face.

The car sped up as he pressed even harder on the accelerator, grim determination on his face now. Beside us, the trees streaked past in a blur.

'Ben. *Ben.*' I touched his wrist. 'Slow down. What do you mean?'

He shook his head. 'It doesn't matter. Just… We just need to get to her. Get the police to her in time.'

With my hand still on his arm, I squeezed gently; then, when he didn't slow down, more firmly. 'Ben,' I said.

The words burst from his mouth as though his own wicked secret couldn't be contained any longer. 'I told the police where she was! I made the call to them, back in Begato. I… I betrayed her. And now, all this. My God, if she ever found out what I did…'

His words came out in a rush, spilling through his perfect lips in a torrent, as though the secret he'd kept all these years had just been waiting to be released.

'You! *You* were the one who reported where she was?' I let my hand fall from his, shocked at his confession, even more shocked that after tonight there were still secrets, still lies, still more revelations that could surprise me.

I remembered that day so clearly. It was imprinted on my mind, in my heart, the vision of her beautiful face in the red dirt, Ben sloping away, running before the authorities came. What had he said to me? *I can't be part of this. I have to think of my reputation. I need to leave.*

I fell back in my seat.

He was right: Jessica could never find out that he was the one who had turned her in.

'Ben, we really let her down, didn't we?' When I could speak again, my words were sorrowful. 'You, me, her father, all of us… we let her down so badly.'

This time he grabbed my arm, his fingers closing painfully around my wrist.

'Don't tell Marco, please, Lou.'

I had thought that after this, when this night was done, the secrets and lies would be finished as well. I had been naïve, as always.

I pulled my arm out of Ben's grip and looked away from him, out of the window, at the landscape that still blurred. He had at least slowed the car. The unformed trees that passed us by were now obscured by fresh tears that fell from my eyes.

A sound, half sob, half laugh, emerged from me. All this time I'd thought that Ben was the only innocent one out of all of us. How wrong I'd been. I smothered my cries with my sleeve. I felt Ben's hand again, his fingers groping for mine. I twisted out of his grasp once more. 'Just drive,' I managed.

We sped towards Dover, joined en route by four police cars and a random ambulance as I spoke to the police and attempted to tell them the whole story. My voice still didn't work correctly, and I barked out a frustrated 'For fuck's sake!'

Ben took over the call then, and I watched him as he told them everything the woman he'd loved for so long had done. Jessica was partially right: he had been a good man. Him, Marco, me, we were all good people once. Our mistakes and pitfalls had been born of a desire to look out for ourselves. Somewhere along the way, human decency had turned into something else. Something greedy and wicked.

In a line we raced down the motorway, the police cars that flanked us with their flashing blue lights allowing us to travel well over the speed limit. As we travelled, my finger hovered over Marco's number in my phone. Finally I clicked it off. I couldn't even begin to explain to him what had happened tonight, finding out the truth of what had happened eight years ago and everything in between.

The police followed us to the ferry terminal, and we convened outside, where I told the whole story again. With our cooperation, they made hasty plans for Ben to approach Jessica first. The paramedic tried to patch me up, but I batted her hand away.

For a brief time, I was me again. I was Louise Wilshire, battling to survive, living on her wits, not Louise Cooper, privileged wife and mother, who hid herself in her cottage in the middle of the French countryside.

It was my last assignment, getting on that ferry and hunting her down. After it was done, I'd go back to France, happy to be alive. Happy to spend the rest of my life making up for what I'd done to Marco by chasing her, thinking of her all these years. If he would still have me.

But first, we had to find her.

–

They located Jessica's position on the internal CCTV, and as Ben and I climbed the stairs to the deck, I glanced at him.

We said nothing, a heavy silence settling between us. There was nothing more to say, and so we pushed upwards, emerging to stand side by side in the cold sea air.

She was watching the cliffs as the ferry drew further away.

She looked tiny. She looked young, innocent.

All I could hear was the sound of my own breathing. I moved so I stood behind Ben, and as I watched him, I saw how taut and tense he was.

Without thinking, I reached for his hand.

Chapter 37

Jessica

Now

I followed him up to the bedroom with a fresh cup of coffee and attempted to chat to him about his day. He was surprised, with good reason; after all, that wasn't how we lived, or how I behaved.

He sat down on the side of the bed, loosening his tie as I took a seat in the chair opposite him. He was regarding me with a frown that was on the verge of becoming a scowl.

I wondered why he had bound me to him with those invisible shackles. It wasn't as though he was happy. Neither of us was.

But he wouldn't cut me loose. He would never set me free.

I made a point of looking out of the window to the fields beyond, desperate to appear nonchalant and casual, not to arouse suspicion with my behaviour and sudden interest in him.

I glanced back at him as he sipped at his coffee, his eyes still on me; then, realising I had actually bothered to go to the trouble of grinding his favourite beans and making it with just the right amount of skimmed milk, he gulped it greedily down.

I turned my chair around then and sat looking out over the countryside. In the distance I heard a train announce its arrival as it passed the crossing. Two kinds of trains ran on this line: passenger trains and freight trains. I couldn't see them, but I knew which was which. The passenger trains, usually only one carriage, glided almost soundlessly on the track; the freight trains, towing their snake of metal, grated and grinded as they passed.

I heard the horn, heard the whisper as the train moved smoothly along the rails, and almost at the same time, a ship's horn blasted three times, long, low and loud. It was the Madrid Maersk, *inching its way into the port. I recalled the local free magazine's recent article boasting about the imminent arrival into Felixstowe of northern Europe's biggest container ship. Hundreds of locals would be flocking to the viewing point to set eyes on this little piece of history. The time had come, the ship had arrived. And Patrick's ship was about to sail.*

'Hmm.'

At the strange sound he made, deep in his throat, I twisted my head around to look at him.

A deep indentation appeared in the bridge of his nose as he frowned. The empty cup was on the bedside table. Patrick was still sitting on the side of the bed, but both hands were now planted on the bedspread behind him. His arms shook with the effort of keeping himself upright. A vein stood out on his forehead, as though he was concentrating very hard on something.

I turned in my chair, drew my knees up to my chest and wrapped my arms around my legs. I held my breath and watched him. After a moment, the strength in his hands left him and his upper body fell backwards.

Still I didn't move, still I kept my eyes on his chest, which rose and fell in a steady, even rhythm. Finally I cast a last glance out of the window before getting up and moving over to the bed. I looked down at his form. His feet were flat on the floor, his arms lay limp at his sides and his head was tilted back, resting against the mattress, his eyes wide and staring.

'Patrick?' I called his name, injected panic into my voice, just in case the drugs hadn't worked and any minute now he sat up and said he was just joking.

Not that he would. Patrick didn't joke, ever.

I repeated his name over and over, a staccato beat of a drum – 'Patrick-Patrick-Patrick-Patrick-Patrick.'

When he didn't respond, I pushed at his shoulders, his arms, his stomach, his legs, my touch growing firmer with each body part that I poked, until I reached the tender flesh on the underside of his arm. Through his shirtsleeve I pinched his skin, digging my nails in so hard that crescent moons appeared red through the fabric.

He didn't even blink.

I allowed a triumphant yell to escape as I clambered up to kneel beside him on the bed.

Then I began to talk, telling him every single reason why I hated him, and that all those reasons added up to why I was killing him.

I wished he could respond. I wished I could see the fear that I knew he must be feeling.

'You nearly killed me,' I whispered in his ear. 'You took me away from everyone I loved and you lied to me when you said I couldn't go home.' I paused, swallowed down a sob. 'You made me miss my father's funeral when I could have gone. I hate you for that…' I tailed off, my breathing coming hard and fast like a racehorse.

No, I couldn't think or talk about that too much, or I would get his shotgun and blast his fucking face off. That would never do. This had to look self-inflicted.

I skipped off the bed and into the bathroom, bringing back my box of secrets, which I laid carefully on the bed. I drew them out one by one, like party favours, and held them up in front of his eyes.

'These are my birth control pills,' I said, conversationally. 'I've been taking them since we moved here, because I'd rather kill myself than give birth to your child. If I'd got pregnant, I

would have killed the baby too. This is the mobile phone I use to keep in contact with Ben, because he's been coming here for years when you're away.' I smiled, showing all my teeth. 'He sleeps where you're lying now, he fucks me right here in this bed.' Triumphantly, I whipped out my passport. 'And this, you utter, utter bastard, is what you hid from me.' I raised my right arm, slapped his face with the passport again and again, finally using my left arm to physically stop the assault.

I couldn't chance leaving any marks on his skin. Through the fabric of his grey shirt, I rubbed at the dents that my nails had made. In contrast to my assault of only moments earlier, my touch was tender.

A tear ran slowly down his face, tracking its way down the side of his nose before changing direction and running underneath his ear.

That tear stopped me cold. I remembered that he shouldn't be able to cry, not with the drugs I'd pumped into him, and the thought that he might sit up and overpower me at any second brought me back in control of myself with the force of a sledgehammer.

I nipped his nostrils together with my fingers and covered his mouth with my other hand.

Another tear leaked from his other eye.

I looked away from him, out of the window, over the fields.

I kept his airways closed off a lot longer than was needed, just to make sure.

—

I would tell the police later, when they spoke to me, that he looked peaceful. But he didn't. His eyes were filled with horror and fear, frozen, a macabre photo that I would carry in my mind for the rest of my life. I loved that picture that I conjured up. It made me happy.

Afterwards, I tidied up. I bleached the coffee cup in the basin of the en suite and visited every single room in the house to make sure I hadn't left anything that could point to me. Everything I left untouched was what I wanted the police to find.

I got the laptop out from my hiding place underneath the bath and stared at it lovingly. Over a period of months I had visited sites that first made me want to vomit. Later, once I'd become accustomed, they'd sickly fascinated me. I had cleared my search history many times, knowing that the police could and would burrow deeper into the bowels and brains of the machine and find it anyway. Even though I'd always worn gloves when I used the laptop, I cleaned it thoroughly, and then I brought it to the bed and pressed Patrick's fingers to each of the keys before taking it downstairs to his study and placing it inside a desk drawer along with the external hard drive upon which I had acted out my finest CCTV moments. I took his actual laptop out of his briefcase and hid it underneath the floorboards, behind the bath.

And then, my work finally done, I inhaled, exhaled, in and out, feeling like I was breathing for the first time.

–

I stood on the deck and remembered Patrick's final hours. I hadn't written that down; I didn't need to. My diary, my scribbled notebook that I'd 'accidentally' dropped in the police station, had done the job it had been planned for. If only it could have ended there. If only Constable Hart had used the correct bathroom.

If only, if only…

It didn't matter now. The bodies under the bath would be enough to end me once they were found. But when that time came, when the door to my cottage was opened and the panel removed from the bath, I would be long gone.

I watched the white cliffs fade into the distance. I wouldn't see them again, but I didn't mind. I never wanted to return to England. Or France, for that matter. This ferry was taking me to Dunkirk, and from there I could make my way through Belgium and Germany, or up to the Netherlands, or even further east through Poland and Russia. Maybe I'd keep going until I happened upon China or Japan. I'd never seen much of Asia and I fancied trying out the lifestyle I had heard so much about. Perhaps I would find one of those islands like in Alex Garland's novel *The Beach*, minus all the drug lords and subsequent murders.

No more death. Not at my hands, anyway.

Of course there would be one more reported, when this ferry emptied and I left on foot, when they found my abandoned car and then, later, scraps of my clothing that I would leave strategically placed so it looked like they had been caught on the rail, and my backpack that would eventually wash up on the shore. And then I could move freely, with a new identity and without having to look over my shoulder.

My thoughts settled on Ben for a moment. I knew that from here on he would become like my father in my mind, someone I had loved so much that I would only be able to think about him in small segments.

There was no going back. I could only move forward, and I had to do it without him.

I pushed myself off the rail, chilled suddenly, and was about to go and sit down inside when I heard a voice in the darkness.

I turned, took a step, came to a halt as though I'd walked into an invisible wall.

Ben.

Had my loving thoughts conjured him up? Was I dreaming? I banged my fist against the metal railing and felt pain shoot through my hand. Not a dream, then.

'What are you doing here?' I whispered the words, but the wind whipped them away.

More than anything, I wanted to run into his arms. I wanted to tell him everything and still have him love me.

'Jess,' he mouthed at me.

A smile quivered on my lips at his pet name for me. He was the only one who used it. Hope sprang in my heart, for surely he wouldn't call me that if he were angry with me? He didn't know what I had done, it was just a huge coincidence that he was on this ship. We could finally be together, start a new life. I could make something up about why I was here. I was a good actress. I was a good liar.

I took another step towards him, grinning. At last, I was totally and utterly happy.

I stopped.

On the otherwise abandoned deck, a figure stepped out of the shadows behind Ben. She appeared smaller than I remembered, diminished somehow, and she was holding his hand, pulling him close to her.

I narrowed my eyes and gripped the railing again, moving backwards now, not forwards. A dream? Was all this a dream? That strange sensation again, that this wasn't really happening. I brought my hand up to my face, scratched my nails along my jaw. But my face stung, and on my fingertips I felt moisture. I glanced at my hand. I'd drawn blood.

My thoughts of hope and happiness trailed away, dashed by the look on Ben's face.

It wasn't anger – I could have dealt with that. He was hurt. I knew then that he had gone to the cottage, and somehow, probably because of the dented bath panel that I had kicked in anger, discovered Louise. And Hart.

I heard a guttural, animal sound. It came from me.

'I saw your ferry ticket in the kitchen.' Louise's voice rang out into the night. She was still slurring, and I saw now that she was clinging to Ben's hand for physical support. The effects of the drugs hadn't totally worn off yet; she was still unsteady on her feet.

My ferry ticket. I thought back, remembered I had left it in plain sight on the side next to the Indian takeaway menu.

Damn.

I had grown sloppy. It was leaving out my box of secrets that had led to me having to kill Hart, and now I'd made this stupid mistake?

I glanced at Ben, but he wouldn't look me in the eye. Instead his gaze settled on something behind me: the cliffs, perhaps, as they grew ever further away.

'I need to tell you I'm sorry—' He stopped before he could finish his sentence, choked. His fist went to his mouth, and now it looked like Louise was the one holding him up. She shushed him, and I saw him wince as her fingers curled around his arm. Not a comforting gesture. A warning. What did Ben have to be sorry for?

Louise moved forward to stand in front of him, blocking my view of the face I would always love. In that moment, I hated her all over again.

She spoke. Her words were whipped away by the wind, but I knew what she'd asked. *Who else did you kill?*

Five victims, I had told her. Louise would have been my fifth, and I knew she couldn't figure out who the missing one was.

The power, what remained of it, shifted to me for a brief moment as I thought of Francesca, the convict who had hitched a ride, uninvited, with Marco and me. It had almost hurt, the trusting way she had let me lead her out of the public toilet to the edge of the quarry. She had thought I was going to let her stay with me, but that was never an option. I wouldn't speak now, wouldn't give Louise the satisfaction. She would never know that Francesca had been the second of what was supposed to have been five.

Through the portholes behind my former friend and my lover, I saw movement, crew members coming up the stairs towards the deck. I'd been dead for a long time and only recently had I begun to fight. I'd clawed my way out of my dark hole, and I wasn't ready to be locked up again.

Now I had another decision to make, and there was no time for planning. It was to be another spur-of-the-moment choice. Just like the night I had clubbed myself on the head with the poker so it didn't look like I had killed Alexis. Like a fast-flowing river, I was suddenly charged with excitement and a need to carry on living. And with no more thoughts, no further planning, I twisted my body and clambered up the railing as though it was a ladder.

I heard a shout behind me, footsteps that broke into a run, and I spread my arms wide, crouched, and jumped into the crashing waves that slapped against the side of the ferry.

The sea was midnight black, there was no moon that I could see, and I surrendered to the ocean.

Maybe it would drag me down, and my final resting place would be its watery depths.

Perhaps I would wash up on a shore somewhere, battered but alive.

Time would tell.

Chapter 38

Louise

I don't sleep much these days. Six months after the fateful night that began in a Suffolk village and ended a few nautical miles off the coast of Dover, I'm still waiting for her. I don't rely on the trees and bushes to form the boundary around my cottage any more. I had Marco arrange to construct high walls and electric gates, alarms and CCTV.

When I do sleep, I have nightmares. I am on the beach with Jenson Coast towering behind me, the sun is setting and out of the azure sea, Jessica appears. She staggers up the sand towards me, covered in ocean debris, her body pale and her face bloated.

When I wake from these dreams, I go downstairs and watch out of the window. I see my own reflection in the glass. My hair, which I've stopped lightening. I've let it grow back to how it once was, before I knew her, before my obsession began. It is time to be me. It is time to let her go.

In these moments, I reassure myself that if Jessica were to wash up on a shore, it wouldn't be here in France; it would most likely be somewhere along the Kent coast. I still watch, though. I still wait for her. I think she still waits for me, somewhere. I think I'd know if she'd died in the water that night. I think – and this is the warped part – that a little bit of me would have died along with her.

When she jumped, I turned around to let the police pass me in the narrow doorway. She saw them flooding towards her, and there were so many of them that for that moment, that vital second, she was out of my sight.

I think that is what haunts me the most: that I didn't witness her jump overboard. I missed it, and I believe that is what keeps me awake.

I tried to explain it to Marco not long ago.

'If I had been looking at her, I might have caught something in her expression. If I'd had eye contact, I might have got something from her.'

'Such as what, sweetheart?' Puzzled, he rubbed at my arm.

I reminded myself to take his hand and hold it, part of a promise I'd made to myself when I was underneath her bathtub. *Touch him more. Show him you care. Make this work.*

'I might have got a message from her, an understanding maybe, that if she survived, she wasn't going to come after me.' Even as I spoke the words to the person who was now closest to me, I hated how weak I sounded. But it was a very real fear.

'Oh, doll,' Marco whispered as he pulled me close. 'Nobody is coming after you, I promise you that.'

I pulled free of him then, wandered back over to the window where I kept my constant vigil. I knew he was just saying what he was supposed to, but it annoyed me. He couldn't promise me that she wouldn't come looking for me; he didn't know that. Look at how long she had plotted and planned Patrick's death, and the murders she had committed seemingly without a shred of remorse. She had lived an eight-year lie. What would be next – a ten-year lie, a twenty-year lie that came back to haunt me? For if I'd discovered anything about my former friend, it was that she was hell-bent on revenge. If she was still out there...

Sometimes the nightmare blends into an easy, light dream. I see her the way she was: fun, crazy, exciting, intoxicating. In those moments, in my sleep, I am still aware of what she did, of how she tried to kill me. But in a way that is as twisted as our relationship and my obsession, I find myself still wanting to see her again.

I miss her.

Perhaps one day she'll turn up and we will be reunited.

Time will tell.

If you loved *The Eight-Year Lie* and want to be the first to know when J. M. Hewitt's next gripping novel is out, then sign up to her mailing list now at www.jmhewitt.net

Acknowledgements

As always, I'm so grateful to have so much support. Firstly, I send so much love and so many thanks to my parents, Janet and Keith Hewitt, and to all of my family.

And to Marley, my unconditional friend and constant writing companion.

My wonderful agent, Laetitia Rutherford of Watson, Little, for constant support and championing my books. My editor, Louise Cullen, thank you for your support and enthusiasm. Leodora Darlington, for loving *The Eight-Year Lie* and also copy editor Jane Selley, who did a tremendously thorough job as always – you are all hugely appreciated.

A special mention to fellow crime fiction author Ruth Dugdall. It seems like such a long time ago I was working on *The Eight-Year Lie* and we had our little writing group going on. Your visions, ideas and comments were valuable, as is your friendship and support. Also a shout-out to Noelle Holten: your enthusiasm is fabulous, your friendship is priceless.

The crime fiction community. The writers, bloggers, publishers, and book clubs, everything you do is appreciated.

Finally, a huge thanks to you, the reader, and as always, as long as you keep on enjoying my books, I'll keep on writing them.